TO THE DEVIL - A DIVA!

a&b

TO THE DEVIL - A DIVA!

PAUL MAGRS

This edition first published in Great Britain in 2004 by
Allison & Busby Limited
Bon Marche Centre
241-251 Ferndale Road
London SW9 8BJ
http://www.allisonandbusby.com

A catalogue record for this book is available from
the British Library.

10 9 8 7 6 5 4 3 2 1

ISBN 0 7490 8380 8

Printed and bound in Wales by
Creative Print and Design

Paul Magrs is the author of six highly acclaimed novels, *Modern Love*, *Marked for Life*, *Does it Show?* *Could it be Magic*, *All The Rage* and *Aisles*. He is also the author of two books for children.

PART ONE

SALLY

Tea was the thing that calmed us down. They knew it would have that effect. It would shock us with its sweetness and heat and there'd be no more tears. Crying embarrassed them. It made more trouble for them. They didn't want that. The grown-ups in charge had enough to think about. We had to bolt the tears back and bite our lips. That was the proper thing to do. We couldn't upset our parents. Didn't they have enough to think about? Weren't they letting us go?

It was strong, hot tea in tin mugs that set your milk teeth on edge. Our fingers were chilled and it felt like they would blister. But it calmed us down as we queued.

These huge urns set out on tables, right on the platform as we waited for the trains. The paper table cloths were whipping up and rattling and trying to take off and all these volunteers in their heavy coats and gloves were watching on, helping out. Looking concerned in the steam from the trains and the urns. Whooshing noises, screeches, wailing and the stamping of feet. The volunteers were those big old-fashioned women with the huge bosoms wrapped tight under their coats and scarves. Heavy-set matronly women, like you don't see anymore. Murmuring to each other: full of competence and concern.

Bless their little hearts, they kept saying. They're going

on a big adventure. They're going to have to be very brave. Well, everyone was crying by now. Everyone togged up against the wind and the cold. It was bitter. It was meant to be spring, but I'd never felt so cold in all my life. Chapped to bits by the knifing wind that came through the dark station. Our platform was up on a height, away from the main concourse. We'd been pushed to one side. Up in the eaves, it felt like, up in the rafters like the train that was coming for us would be sailing through the air. All the clouds that morning were a soft purple grey, as if just laundered. We'd be sailing into them, into those clean spaces. And our mouths would be bitter with tannin. With the taste of the iron arches and nuts and bolts that made up the station. The dirty taste of engines and oil and pigeons.

Katy's hand was squirming into mine, her frozen, mucky fingers clenching on. She was determined not to leave go. My mother noticed and she approved. She was glad I had someone to look after. To make me feel responsible. 'She's your little sister, now,' Mam bent and told me, whispering. I flushed. Because she wasn't. She weren't no blood of mine.

Mam had her headscarf on. The fabric was fraying at the edges. That used to be a silky, glamorous thing she wore. Something she wore for best. Mam was my blood, she was my only blood. This Katy wasn't. Really, she had nothing to do with me. I could feel her fingers warming up in my grip. I could feel the dirt of her fingers on my skin now.

We had little boxes tied around our necks, all our stuff in cases. Labels on us, reminding us who we belonged to. Ready to go and everyone bawling their eyes out. It's pitiful to think of. But they gave us this tea, so hot and strong it stung your lips and scalded all the insides of your throat. We drank it down dutifully. It seemed like a very grown-up kind of drink to us. We drank it down boiling hot, like it was medicine. And we pretended it was calming us down.

It was some ungodly hour. Mam said this. 'Ungodly' was her word that day and it stayed in my head as we trudged through the streets of our town. It wasn't even light when we set off from ours and made our way into the centre. At first it was like an adventure, striking out with all our precious things in these cases and boxes with labels. The night before Mam had made it into a game for us: unpacking and repacking all the things I would need and checking off the list. She saw that I had everything I needed. We'd begged and borrowed a few things. We imagined it was like going to some posh school, where all the nobs go. I'd need a hockey stick and a straw boater. All that.

That last night seemed a long time ago now. At the end of that game, with my case packed again, and time for bed, it seemed like I'd never have to wake up and actually set off anywhere. I'd just fall asleep in my own bed and it wouldn't be the last time I'd see it. I wouldn't have to leave my mam alone after all. It was all of it a game and I could stay with her.

But then the morning came anyway and it was still dark. We set off. We walked across town, carrying the things that they said I would need. My mam was brisk and deter-mined, her headscarf clamped on tight and her hair still in curlers. We took Katy with us.

'That poor little thing,' Mam said. 'I don't suppose her mother's going to stir herself. Her or her gentleman caller. We'll have to take charge of her, Sally. She'll have to come with us.'

Sure enough, there was Katy on our doorstep that morn-ing. Crack of dawn and she looked like she'd been awake for days. Filthy. She was always filthy. They were a dirty family, everyone said, and Mam told me we weren't to draw attention to it. Her mother knew no better and we were all to take a hand in bringing up Katy. Otherwise she'd be dragging herself up. And anything could happen to the poor mite. It was up to the rest of us to look out for her.

Well, I was nine. She was nine. Mam thought we should

be best pals. I couldn't stick the sight of her back then. I thought she made herself like an angel when there were parents about. When it were kids alone, that was a different story. Katy always knew how to get what she wanted.

There she was. She had bits of cardboard sticking out of her clumpy old shoes, where the soles had gone. Her knees were black like unwashed potatoes, and so were her socks. Her hair hadn't been cleaned in days and I knew what Mam would be thinking: there's allsorts crawling in that. Katy had this thick, black Irish hair. I'd been jealous of her hair since we started school. Mine was fluffy and pale. I felt like a baby duck next to her. And she didn't even wash it! That made me seethe. Her bright lilac eyes, too. They were a gift. That morning they were clotted and stuck with dirty tears and sleepdust. Usually they were big and round, taking everything in. Mam said she had an old head on her shoulders. Then she'd look at me like I didn't. Like I was still the baby. But now she was telling me I had to watch out for Katy. She was the baby now.

Mam tucked Katy firmly under her wing. Dragged her in our house, even though she must have been thinking that girl will have ringworm, nits, the lot. Katy always liked having a look at our house. She liked all our things. Never said much, just gazed around at Mam's little palace, as she called it.

Mam gave her breakfast, just as we were having ours. She found a crust or two to spare for Katy. Her heart, she said, bled for that child. Her mother wanted stringing up. And I had to think of Katy as my sister. And I'd always wanted one of them, hadn't I?

Well, no. I hadn't. And now it looked like I was being given one. One who was all sweetie-pie in front of my mam and then, when we were alone, scowled at me, and tried to kick my legs so they were as scabby as hers. She'd taken the last spoonful of sugar Mam had in the house. Sat there, sucking the spoon like she'd never known the taste before. Her purple eyes twinkling with pleasure. Kicking me under the table, mind. And I just knew my mam's heart was going out to the girl.

Mam kissed us both goodbye on that platform when the train was there and we went surging forward. The official people had their clipboards, shouting out and ticking us off. Mam had her arms round the two of us, pressing our heads together and she was all choked up. She felt so bony and I was thinking, she'll have more to eat with just herself in the house. She wasn't going to start crying, though. I never actually saw Mam cry, though I'd heard her, through the walls of our house. She was careful not to, in front of me. That morning was when she came closest.

And then we were gone. It only took a matter of seconds. We were on the train and there was a bit of waving out of the window. Mam came to stand right by where we were sat together and she rubbed at the dirty brown window with her mitt to see us better. Getting dirt on her sheepskin, but she wanted us to see. She wanted to make sure I remembered her face. We didn't know how long we'd be apart. And when I thought of Mam after that, it was that face in the window I saw: in the smear of clean she'd wiped on the window. Mam's long face and her wide-spaced eyes. That wisp of brown hair on her brow. She had a long-drawn face - like a camel, she'd always been told. A sad face, all down-turned. I thought it made her dignified and solemn. No one outside ever really saw her smiling. She was trying to smile through the window, trying hard to grin at the two of us. Then, before we knew it, there was whistles going and the train moving under us with a violent lurch, and we were pulling out, over the viaducts. We slid across the rooftops of the middle of Manchester and they were blue and green in the early sunlight. The whole place looked peaceful and barely woken up. And Mam was gone. All those waving us off were gone, standing on that platform and it was like they wouldn't move again until it was time for us to come back. They would stand there in their heavy clothes, with their arms

11

still raised, waving us off. They'd be there until everything was over and the train shunted us back to meet them. We couldn't imagine them turning away, walking back through the cavernous station, turning back to home, without us.

'My mam won't know I'm gone,' Katy said. Her voice was very deep and lilting with her mother's accent. 'She'll get up and run around the houses. She won't know.'

I looked at her. We were sitting with two other girls and one had blonde hair in pigtails, the other was bright ginger. They weren't talking to us. The ginger one was fat and her face was bright red with crying. She was off again, getting disgusted looks from her pigtailed friend.

'She had her fella in last night,' Katy went on. 'It was one of them nights. She won't get up all day. She's never happy when he's been round.'

I didn't want to get pulled into the kind of stuff Katy talked about, but I was fascinated. There was something mysterious about that house of hers, where these fellas came and went. We didn't have that many people coming through our front door. Katy's house - mucky as it was - seemed much more part of the wide world than ours. I asked, 'Why does she have them in if they make her cry?'

Katy looked at me like I was daft. I was used to that. One of the reasons I hated her was that she gave me looks like that, made me feel I knew nothing. And I was the one who was meant to be her big sister. It was too much of a pretend for me. I wanted to know what she knew. But I wasn't going to ask her outright.

'They're my uncles,' she said, at last. She was looking out of the window. We were going by chimneys and the edges of town. You could see out on the backs of terraces, taller than ours. You could see all their dark windows, almost see into their rooms. 'That's what uncles are like. They come round and make you cry. But they bring ciggies and eggs and chocolate, sometimes.'

'What does your mam do with them?' I knew the two

other little girls were listening. The fat ginger one had stopped sniffling and she was holding her breath. They came from a few streets up from us. They thought they were better because they had bay windows in their fronts.

'She says they play cards,' Katy said. 'And she tells them their fortunes.'

The blonde girl snorted at this. 'Your mother's a whore, Katy MacBride. She takes their ciggies and chocolate and then she lets them touch her. Everyone knows that.'

I saw Katy's eyes flash violet. Her whole body tensed up and it was like she was made out of steel. I thought she was going to round on that girl and smack her one. I'd seen her do it before in the schoolyard, and round the backs. I'd seen her just about rip some girl's face off for calling her mammy. That blonde girl looked frightened for a second and she knew she'd gone too far. But then Katy relaxed. All that tension went out of her. She sagged back into her seat and she was just a little girl again, too small for her age. She said, 'You know fuck all. You're only a whore if you have lots of men come up to play cards. If you have one on the go for a while it doesn't count. I only have one uncle at a time. My mammy's not dirty.'

The blonde girl rolled her eyes at her ginger friend, but she didn't dare say anything else.

We were quiet for a long time after that. We were all looking out of the windows. I'd never been out of Manchester before and I wanted to see the houses and factories fall away and I wanted to see all the green and the hills when they started up and we moved, rumbling and rolling, further north. I wanted to see all that, to distract me, because my stomach felt hollow and folded over. I was sick with worry for myself and where I'd end up, and I felt sick with bitter tea for the sake of my mam. She'd be back in our house by now, and she'd be briskly wiping down the breakfast table. Flapping the tablecloth out in the backyard. She'd be in the quiet house and emptying the last of the cold tea away, scooping out the dead leaves to dry, to use

13

again.

Katy was looking at the landscape as well. But she was managing to look interested, like a seasoned traveller. She'd been to Ireland with her mother. She had a family over there and they'd gone last summer on a ferry. She had lots to say about travelling and what her family over there was like. How they lived in a big house and how they had stables and she went on a horse. And there was a grandad with tickly moustaches and how they had singing and dancing. How glad the whole lot of them had been to welcome back her mammy and the baby and forgive her. They'd been welcomed with presents and drink and it was like they were home. Katy had told me this story again and again. She was used to going off to places and getting a good welcome. I knew she didn't feel the same as me, sitting on that train. Still, some of the spite of the usual Katy had gone out of her. On that train journey she only kicked my ankles a couple of times. Maybe she felt a bit bad after all.

A tall woman in a blue woollen suit came past with another clipboard. Didn't talk to us. She read our labels and marked something down. Katy shouted out, asking when we were getting there and when we were getting fed. Mam always said that girl had hollow legs. 'The Irish are always hungry,' she said. 'That's in their bones, passed down.'

The woman in the blue suit was stern and she didn't answer.

***

Soon there were gentle hills and long stretches of mossy green. It was all the colours of nature, I suppose, and we weren't used to that. Us kids were a bit subdued in our carriages. It wasn't just the shock of moving away, it was the sight of those greens and browns and the occasional glimpse of the sea: flat and dull and copper one moment, then silver and blazing in the sun.

14

The skies were wider and this amazing blue. I wanted to drink them all in. I'm sure my memory's made everything more lurid, the way that memory is apt to do. And I know we were only heading for the Lake District, and that isn't really the Alps or anywhere. But those hills were stretching up higher than we could crane our necks. We peered up through our mucky windows and we couldn't see how deep down we were. Our train was scraping and screeching through narrow clefts of valleys, and scarves of mist were streaming past.

I was still toggled up against the dawn in Manchester. As we ploughed into the morning and the sunlight came filtering through the shifting foliage I was lathered and uncomfortable with sweat. The backs of my knees were soaked.

'It's like going into the jungle,' I said, without thinking. I was staring up into the overhanging trees, flinching as the branches reached out to scrape our window.

Katy was smirking, half-shrouded, half-brilliant in the sun. 'They have jungle creatures in the Lakes.'

'Do they?'

She nodded firmly. 'Especially in Kendal. Wild animals like monkeys and snakes and them big fucking tigers.'

***

And then we met the Figgises. I don't even know how to start explaining them. It's like they were always there, just waiting to meet us and make us part of their lives. They were waiting patiently for Katy and me, biding their time on the tiny platform in Kendal. Waiting with all the other, more ordinary people.

It was quite a scene at that station when we arrived. As the train pulled in there was a kerfuffle in all the carriages, as the tired and overwhelmed kids came back to life and remembered that they were supposed to be noisy and uncontrollable. Everyone was pressing themselves against the windows and looking at the people waiting for us. The strangers who had said they would take us in.

That skinny woman with the clipboard went hurrying up and down, telling everyone to quieten down. If we didn't watch out we'd get no one. None of those strangers would take nasty, boisterous children, would they?

Katy looked unimpressed with the whole lot of them out there. She sat back with a sigh on the bristly velveteen and made it plain she wasn't in any rush to get outside. She fixed me with a stare, dead in the eye.

'We're sticking together, me and you,' she said.

I was parched and a bit tearful. 'Yes,' I said. 'We'll stick together.' Like we'd made a pact. Like we had become Tonto and the Lone Ranger.

'Jesus,' she said. 'Look at them two out there. I bet we get stuck with them.'

The Figgises stuck out like sore thumbs in that crowd. The other, normal looking people were dressed up in their best coats and hats and they were hugging their new children. Others were milling and there was a breathless excitement about it all: they all seemed happy to be paired up like this. Cheerful city children and their replacement parents. I thought for a second some awful trick had been played on us, because everyone seemed to know everyone else. Katy and me didn't know anyone. But we had noticed the Figgises, shoved to one side, looking a bit weird. And, with a sick dread, I realised Katy was right. That troll-like man in the green serge suit with the thick white beard. His pale, flossy-haired tiny companion. They were our destiny. They had turned up to collect the two of us.

We were among the last to be sorted out. The stern clipboard woman shoved us forward like we were meeting the mayor and mayoress.

'This is Mr Figgis and his sister, Isla,' the woman said.

Then the old man's hand was grasping mine and it was like holding a handful of cold pork sausages. His handshake was very gentle. His fingers were shaking as he touched mine. I turned and saw that Katy was giving the

16

old people a very superior look. Amazing that she could pull that off, standing there with her hair messed up and a dirty blouse on. But the couple looked cowed at the sight of her pinched face. They seemed scared of the two of us and the woman in charge of us was alert to that.

'I am sure they will give you no problems,' she said. She wanted us off her hands pronto. 'They hail from one of the poorer areas, but often those are the better behaved children.' When she said 'poorer areas' she only mouthed the words.

'I'm sure they will be fine,' said Mr Figgis's sister. We all jumped at the sound of her voice. It was extremely high-pitched and whispering. With the sun in all her fine-spun hair, and her standing no higher than my shoulders, it was like we were being adopted by a fairy. 'Thank you so much, Mrs Beech.'

The clipboard lady nodded solemnly and moved away. She gave the two of us a warning glance first. Then we looked at our new parents again. We were at their mercy. Mr Figgis was clutching a packet of printed papers. It was like they had bought us at an agricultural fair.

'I suggest we get them home, Michael,' Isla Figgis fluted. 'Get them settled in. They look a bit mithered.'

Mr Figgis grunted, took a hold of both our cases for us, and led the way out of the station. As we walked the short way into the town I realised that both Katy and I were hanging our heads. I wanted to be happier. I wanted to be a better choice for them. I didn't want to be a disappointment to either them, or to my mam, who I knew would be worrying at home. And then I was thinking: I don't need them. I don't need new people. Who do they think they are? And they're odd as well. We've got the oddest ones of the lot.

As we walked onto the high street and saw it was gloomy and everything was slate blue, overcast, dull, I turned and caught Katy's eye. She mouthed something at me. I couldn't tell what it was.

'I said, we've got a right pair here,' she hissed.

We were walking behind the Figgises. They were bustling down their familiar street, nodding at people they knew. No one else seemed to think they were strange-looking at all. They'd explained they lived in a house right down at the end. I couldn't wait to get there. I was blushing and scalding over with shame. But the Figgises took their own sweet time, ambling along past the shops. They were quite at home here, in this tiny town. And now we had to be as well. I realised that Katy was holding my hand again.

***

You had to go through a wooden gate and up a dark, narrow alley to get to their door. The house was a tall, thin one on the main street, but it was hidden away and you'd never know anyone lived there. We slipped up that ginnel and it smelled mouldy and wet. But when Isla Figgis let us into their house we found it warm and pleasant and full of orange and yellow light. We walked straight into their dining room from the alley and the room was dominated by a round table covered with a hairy green cloth. The little woman urged us to unwrap our winter things and to sit ourselves down. The old man started fussing with the log fire.

'It's very nice,' I said politely. I didn't want them to think we had no manners: Katy was glowering at everything.

In the middle of the table there was an arrangement of pale church candles, melting into each other. There was also some very strange-looking pottery figures. Lumpy, misshapen people made by hand. I didn't like the look of them and tried not to stare.

'This,' said Mr Figgis, 'is your home now, for the duration of the hostilities.' He got up from the fireplace and rubbed tree bark off his fat fingers, all down the front of his suit. 'Now, I know you two will be fretting about your parents in the city, but we have to get through this as best we can. We're a little family of our own now, the four of us, and we have to make do.' Then he beamed at us and we saw that his mouth was crowded with lots of very square teeth. His voice was as deep as his sister's was high. 'You're very welcome here.'

We smiled shyly. Even Katy. But we must have looked half-starved, because Isla fluttered into action, muttering to herself. She seemed to float around that small dining room, darting hither and thither. 'A special treat for our famished new guests,' was all I could make out from what she was saying. Mr Figgis dashed to help her in the small kitchen alcove.

Katy and I looked at each other. They were going to feed us. What if we didn't like the kind of food they ate here? What did people like the Figgises eat?

The tiny Isla Figgis came back through with a large clay fruit bowl that she had to hold in both hands. She set it down on the tablecloth with a great show of ceremony. She smiled at the looks on both our faces.

'We've been storing these up,' she said, 'just for today.'

The bowl was full of chocolate bars. In every shape and size, in bright, multi-coloured wrappers. The likes of which we had never seen. Mr Figgis was fussing around in the tall bookshelf in the corner. He was reaching behind the stacks of paper-covered books and producing fistfuls more of the things. He tossed them into the bowl. Bar after bar. They were like magic.

'Dig in, girls,' Isla Figgis cried. 'It won't be everyday we can eat like this! Make the most of it while it lasts!' Then she selected a bar for herself and unwrapped it greedily, her silver eyes shining.

*⁎⁎

The chocolate (which the four of us demolished completely that first dinner time together) was the first of the strange things, besides the appearance of the Figgises themselves, that we came across in Kendal. We got used to the ways of this curious brother and sister very quickly. I suppose that's how kids are: how they have to be. They adapt. It's not like I didn't think about Mam, or talk about her, in those first few weeks, but there was so much to get used to and to absorb in this new place. And there was Katy to look after.

The Figgises had a sort of double life. Outside they looked a bit weird as they trundled about the town together, but people respected them. All the men raised their hats to Isla, and Michael was greeted properly, as if he was someone quite important. Neither lingered to chat with people: they were in some private bubble of their own.

Home in that narrow house, things were different. The Figgises grew livelier, wilder in their private world. Without, all was scrimped and saved for, hushed and careful and everything for the war effort. Within their walls, there was a lightness and a gaiety. They liked to find cause to celebrate. Their house was in a different world to the one in which a war was going on and bombs fell on houses and people were being locked up and tortured. It was as if they were trying to live in a different time.

Isla Figgis played her musical saw in the evenings. She did so that first night we were there. For that occasion, she put on a very old-fashioned white and silver evening frock and took up a chair by the fire, the gleaming saw wedged between her little knees. Well, we just about fell about laughing at the sight of that. Then she started to play, drawing a long, quivering bow across the savage teeth of the instrument. This thin, unearthly music filled the dining room. And we fell quiet. We sat enraptured, just like Michael Figgis did, watching his sister, though he must have heard her play many times before.

Brother and sister were devoted to each other. There was a bond between them of the like I'd never seen. They drew the two of us strangers into their warmth and there we felt secure, almost immediately. Only once or twice we'd wake from the drowsy spell their love put us under, and start to think it a bit out of order. A little unhealthy, perhaps. We'd start to look with outside eyes, at this thing that had grown in their private world. It was unconditional love, was what they had. And that they lavished upon the two of us waifs. They had chosen us and we got the full brunt of their attention and care. In those first weeks, even Katy started to relax and relent in their unwavering love. She let Isla Figgis clean her things, even wash her hair as Katy sat in their bath at the top of the house. She came down to dinner that night with her black hair shining like I'd never seen it. She'd even let Isla tie a blue ribbon in it. I admit I laughed at the sight of that: Katy being the properly-behaved little girl. Katy trying to make herself pretty. She wrenched that ribbon out and stomped back up to our room. She pulled that girl's dress over her head and put some of her old rags from home back on. She sat on her bed and wouldn't talk to me. Michael Figgis had to go up and talk to her, coaxingly, carefully, damping her resentment down. I wished I hadn't laughed at her. I knew I had to be careful with Katy: I knew how touchy she was. But I was relaxing, too, in the Figgis's household. I was letting my own guard drop.

'They're filling out, Michael.' That was one of Isla's favourite phrases that spring. 'They're getting some colour in their cheeks. And look!' She would clamp her little fingers around my arm, or Katy's and pinch to show how much flesh we'd gained. 'Look how much plumper they are!'

This gave us the willies. The way the two of them cooed over how much healthier we were. How we'd filled out. In our bedroom at the top of the house, Katy and I would whisper to each other across the dark space between the beds.

'They're feeding us up because they want to eat us,' said Katy. She loved to say this. She knew I would shriek and hide my head under the heavy counterpane. 'They're stoking up the fire and they're going to shove us in that fucking pot. You watch out.'

We'd laugh ourselves daft over stories like that. We'd only say these things when we were alone in the room they had given us. It was our own world within the Figgises' world.

Though we laughed, there was still something a bit sinister about the way the two old people examined the bloom in our cheeks. The way they congratulated themselves on the care they were investing in us.

One night, Katy said, 'They go on daft with us because they can't have kiddies of their own. That's what I reckon.'

I scoffed at her. 'Of course they can't. They're brother and sister.'

'So they can't,' said Katy. She left a little gap. 'And they're too old as well.'

Something in her words made me feel a bit funny. For a few days after that I watched the Figgises closely. I never had a brother or a real sister, so I didn't know what was normal. I watched them as they cooked our meals together, as we went around the shops on the high street. I watched Isla's devoted face, listening to Michael as he read to us in the evenings. She would hug the two of us girls to her tiny form and we would gobble up every word that the bluff old man read aloud. Ghost stories mostly. Very strange ones indeed, which he read from the paper-covered volumes he took down from his shelves. Those books were the only things in the house we weren't allowed to touch. Only Michael himself could take them down, and he would share fragments of them with us all: his deep voice trembling through that ragged beard. Aunt Isla's thin fingers clutching our newly-plump arms at all the scary parts.

In the end we couldn't help congratulating ourselves on our good luck. We saw that the Figgises were soft touches. We had landed on our feet. They were so keen to please us, to look after us and give us everything we needed. We knew this wasn't the case with other children who'd arrived on our train. Once or twice we saw the girls who'd sat in our carriage with us. The girl with the blonde pigtails and the fat ginger girl. They were in the butcher's with their new mother, a pinched-face woman who was causing a ruckus over the counter, claiming she was being diddled again. The two girls looked like they'd lost all their spirit. Their hair had been hacked right short and they both wore these awful woollen caps on their heads. They glared at us morosely as we stood behind them in the queue, either side of Isla. Katy and I looked at each other and thanked our lucky stars. We felt proud of our tiny, fairylike adopted mother in that moment.

You'd hear such stories about what work the other kids were put to. People exploited them, used them like servants. We really were at the mercy of whoever we went to. The most that Katy and I ever had to do was work Michael's allotment with him. He was growing vegetables for his war-work and we went early in the mornings with his barrow. We'd spend the mornings turning over the earth and tugging out these frozen cabbages and beets. It was this work, as much as anything, that put the colour in our cheeks. We'd have a break and sit outside his dilapidated shed, drinking tea from his flask. Nettle tea, which Isla stewed up on her great big pot on the hob. The result was dark green and tarry and, gradually, the two of us got to like it. We never quite got to like the beetroot soup our new parents loved. It was worth waiting for those days when they would produce those magical chocolate bars, suddenly, out of the blue. That happened sporadically, all unannounced, and our guardians gobbled up the chocolate with the same relish we did.

Another of mine and Katy's tasks was collecting up the nettles from the woods just outside of town for Isla's specially-brewed tea. We would go soon after it was light on those spring mornings and we took a basket and thick, heavy gloves, to protect our hands from stings. These occasions were another time that we had free from the Figgises.

We were growing to love the two of them, but they could still be overpowering sometimes. I think the Figgises realised this, and so sent us out on these errands.

We were coming back one day when we saw those girls again. It was on a little lane and the two of them looked just as pale and miserable as they had in the butcher's. Their hair was growing back, and it stood out in nasty tufts on their heads: one ginger, one pale yellow. We said hello and they sneered at us.

Samantha, the blonde one was called. 'What've you got in your basket then? Are you eating weeds in your house? Dandelions to make you piss in your bed?'

Katy stopped in her tracks and, because she was carrying the other handle of the basket, I could feel her start to tense up. 'Don't talk to them,' I told her. 'They're just baldies.'

'It's nettles we've got,' Katy snapped back. 'And we're gonna stew them up into a magic potion. And it'll do worse than make your hair fall out.'

This retort was a bigger success than either of us had expected. The fat ginger lass looked alarmed. She grabbed hold of her friend's arm. Samantha shook her off. 'Aye, I bet it will, as well.'

'What's that meant to mean?' I knew Katy was really bridling for a fight. She'd been denied any outlet for her anger for weeks. The Figgises were just too good to be angry at. Katy was spoiling for a row by now. She dropped her side of the basket and was clenching her fists.

'I just said that brewing up potions and spells is just the thing round your house. With them two.'

'You what?' Katy thundered. I was secretly pleased she could get so worked up on the Figgises' behalf.

'Our new mammy has told us all about them two,' Samantha said. She rolled her eyes. 'All about them. She says you two are in the right place. In their midden. In all their muck.'

That was when I found my own voice. 'Their house is

24

immaculate! You don't know anything!'

'Yeah,' Katy jeered. 'At least they didn't have to cut off our hair. At least we weren't infested.'

Samantha lunged at Katy then and, the next thing we knew there was a fight on. It didn't last long, because me and the ginger girl were there, momentarily allied, in pulling the two of them apart. The blonde girl had tight hold of Katy's long hair. She was really scragging her. Katy had nothing to get a grip on, but she was lashing out with those deadly feet of hers. That little lane rang out with our shrieks.

Then suddenly it was over and we were all panting, glaring at each other. All of us were shocked at the violence that had broken out. Our nettles were strewn all over the rutted road.

'She told us! It's true! Our new mammy said!' Samantha started shrieking.

'What are you talking about?'

'That dwarf woman lets the devil suck her titties of a night! And that old man puts his thing in her bum! Everyone in town knows all about it! They've seen it! My mammy's seen it happen! All of it's true!'

Katy was frozen. The language coming out of that girl had brought her to a standstill.

Then the two of them were running away. Their voices came floating back, mocking and scared.

'You two are in the right place! You're in an evil midden! That's where you live!'

They were gone. Katy and I looked at each other and then at all our nettles lying everywhere. All our morning's work. We didn't know what to say.

***

We were left feeling very odd. And resentful, too. We hated those two girls. Who were they to go shouting things out about our newfound adopted parents? We could shout back and we could drown out the gobshites. But something about what they had said stuck with us. We couldn't stop thinking about it, or going over it at night when we whispered across the space between our beds. We were at that point where your imagination goes a bit funny. We were ripe for that. And the two of us kept seeing, in our minds' eyes - lurid and childlike as they were - that picture of Michael Figgis putting his thing up Isla's bum. And then Isla with a devil suckling at her breast. That was the kind of picture that stayed with you, that no amount of chocolate bars (just where did they get them from?) in their sunny dining room could dispel.

We knew what devils were like. We knew what they looked like and all about them. Short, oily-skinned and lizardy things. Grinning imps and gimps of the perverse. We picked this up from the nightly readings that Uncle Michael treated us to. When we sat by candlelight with Isla and she clutched our hands in fright: that was the kind of stuff he read aloud in his husky voice. All about the demons, the good and bad ones, that lurked out there, beyond the strong protective charm of the homestead. He gave us their strange-sounding names in old-fashioned languages and made us repeat them like prayers. And we did so, in time with Isla's high, smooth voice, because we didn't want to upset them both. We knew we were guests in their tall skinny house and so we'd better do what they said. We learned the names and habits of made-up beasts and monsters and we intoned them back in all innocence.

Michael told us that these imps and gimps roamed the dark countryside, and all the hills and dales, and they were looking for souls such as ours. Stainless, the two of us, and apt for the taking. They could nip in like a wolf into the sheepfold. We were lucky to have the Figgises to warn us. To shoo the bad devils away. And we nodded, and agreed, and again we counted up our lucky stars.

'They're just crackers,' is what Katy said, hissing across our dark bedroom. 'Harmless and crackers.' With her Irish connections, Katy knew all about superstitions. She thought the Figgises simple country people.

26

'Do they ever come to town, these demons?' she asked Uncle Michael one night, interrupting his tale-telling. He looked startled, silhouetted by the fire, this bulky old dog of a man. He had one of his treasured books open on his lap. His face creased as he stared at us, and I wanted to nudge Katy for breaking into his flow. But then he smiled gently, and looked glad that she was taking an interest.

'Oh, they do,' he said. 'Of course they do. Cities are full of corruption and blasted hope. The people there came from the countryside and they went to work in those evil factories and mills and lived in those tiny, dirty houses. And when despair sets in, that's when the demons seize their chance. The demons love all that muck and disaster. The narrowness of those lives. Where you've been living is full of that kind of evil. And just think about what is going on there now, in those great big powerful cities of the world. The bombs falling on them; the lights switched off; the wailing sirens in the night and whole houses collapsing in flames. It's the very image of hell, girls. Of course there are demons in your cities.'

He had to stop then. Shushed by Isla, who had started up in concern: her silver eyes flashing. Because I had burst into tears. Before I knew it I was sobbing and heaving: great jagged wails came gasping out of me and I threw myself into our tiny aunt's arms. I was shouting something about my mam, my poor mam, left behind in that wicked city. And the bombs falling on her and I could see our whole street doused in fire like hell itself and I knew that she was dead.

'You've scared the child, Michael,' Isla said levelly. My face was buried in her neck, I was almost suffocated in her yards of crinkly hair. She gripped me hard and sounded furious with her brother, though she didn't move from her dining room chair. Beside us, Katy was quite still. Fascinated and probably disgusted, too, with this show of emotion from me.

'They need telling, Isla,' was all Michael Figgis said.

'They need warning. You know that. The young have to toughen up. They have a lot to face in the future.'

His words hung over us. A ghastly benediction. Katy said later, much later, that it was as if Michael Figgis had known exactly what the future held for all of us. That he had read all about it in those strange old books of his and he'd absorbed it, horrified, line by line. As for now, though, he just got up, as I tried to regain my breath and composure in Isla's tiny grip, and he pulled on his old coat and plucked up his walking stick. I heard Katy's quick, indrawn gasp. She thought he was about to beat us. But he flung open the door into the alley and muttered that he was off to walk the fells. It was nearly midnight. But it was spring and the moon was bright on the hillsides.

'You mustn't mind him, my pets,' Aunt Isla told us both. 'He has his set ways. He believes in what he believes in and he always has. We both do. All he says and does is because he loves us all very much and we are under his care. He wants the best for us.'

'But he really thinks demons and stuff are real. And the devil.' This was Katy. Calmer than me. Answering back. Wanting to know more.

'So does your great Roman church,' said Aunt Isla. She talked to Katy almost like she was a grown-up, I noticed. In the Figgises' eyes, it was me who was the child. They looked at Katy more keenly, more appraisingly, as if they both recognised something there. I didn't know what. I was surprised they didn't think her cheeky.

'There's no Bible up there,' Katy said, nodding at the shelves that were crammed with all of Uncle Michael's precious things. 'There's no good book.'

'No,' said Isla flatly. 'There isn't.'

Then she shooed us off to bed and, exhausted, I must have slept straight away, because I never heard Uncle Michael come back from his walk.

***

I got the occasional letter from home. The postal service was shaky, of course, but I longed for those days when there would be a crumpled envelope on the hairy green tablecloth. Mam's writing, large but unsure, spelling out my name and my new address. It struck me she was writing the name of a house that she had never seen. She didn't know the rooms that I lived in now, and that upset me, even as I hurriedly, excitedly, ripped open her letters.

Her tone of writing to me was rather polite, quite formal, really. It was the tone of someone unused to writing, I suppose. I was coming on in leaps and bounds with my education under the Figgises' roof and I'm ashamed to say that I read Mam's letters and I frowned at the phrasing, the spelling, the grammar. That was me at nearly ten. Within a few years I'd look back on those letters and see, underneath all the awkwardness of the language, the writing that went big and then small as if in relation to her confidence in spelling out these lines, and I would see the love there. The determination to remind me where I came from and who my mam was. Bless her.

I was glad she was still alive. That the bombs falling on Manchester hadn't taken her away. That she was still living a quiet, single life in the house that now seemed to me like somewhere I knew from a dream. She listed the streets that had been ruined and the homes that were now just rubble. All the ones with bay windows were gone. That was where our arch-enemies lived. The ones who thought they were better than us. Those girls were homeless now. They'd have to live in the gutter. When I showed this letter to Katy she laughed like a drain.

Nothing ever came from Katy's mam. We'd hear that my mam had gone round to see her, but she never got much sense out of Mrs MacBride. She was sitting up in her bed and the sheets weren't clean. The room smelled of gin and she had some mangy old cat sitting there with her, and the cat had sores all around its neck. Mam thought Katy's mam was losing her way. You didn't even see gentlemen going round there these days. Katy listened to the news but she kept her lip buttoned. Never made any comment at all.

'Well my darling I must go now and get on with things,' was how Mam always rounded off her letters. 'I hope that you are being good and well-behaved for Mr and Mrs Figgis and that you are not showing your old mam up. You stick in with your lessons and learn all your three rs like I never did. You have got to get away from living in places like weve alway had to live in Sally. You arnt to be Sally from the back ally like in the song now arent you love (ha ha). Well enough from me now with everlasting love your mother.'

'Your mam sounds a bit daft in these letters,' Katy sneered. I'd walked in on her in our room one day. She had them all out on my bed and she'd been reading them, holding them up close to her face. I was really cross. She'd been in the special box where I kept them, all tied up. I'd written 'private' on the box and Katy had waited till I was busy - out on the mangle in the back yard - before diving and going through all my business. My arms were aching and the front of my dress was soaked with sudsy water and I just saw red. I flew at her and next thing we knew we were rolling about on the bare boards of the attic room. Screeching and spitting and yanking at each other's hair.

'You fucking little bitch!' Katy kept shouting, right into my face as she wrenched my hair. 'They're only letters! They're just letters!'

It was the first time I'd ever fought back. I'd shocked her and I'd shocked myself. She'd bitten her tongue and, when she shouted, she was spitting blood all over my face and panting hot, frightened breaths at me. Soon we were covered in fluff off the floor and each other's blood and sweat. We tired each other out scrapping and no one came running to see what the noise was. Eventually we lay apart, winded and still, trying to breathe.

I said, 'My mam isn't daft.'

Katy didn't answer. She rolled over and spat blood on

the floor. She looked at me murderously from under her fringe.

'She's been good to you, Katy. And she goes round to see your mam. Keeps an eye out for her.'

Katy grunted. 'People shouldn't bother.'

'You shouldn't have gone through my things,' I said.

'I'll go through what I want.'

Then she stood up, smoothed down her dress, and was gone.

***

Katy must have felt like she could say what she wanted about my mam and what she had written to me because we were both improving so much in our own schoolwork. Before we'd left Manchester I'd only been okay with my letters and my numbers and Katy could hardly hold a pencil. We'd been in a class of nearly fifty in our old school and so we hadn't had much encouragement. That was just how it was. But here in Kendal, under the care of the Figgises, everything had changed. We were tutored at home by Isla herself, at the dining room table. We both had these exercise books with smooth creamy pages and thin blue lines drawn in. They looked like they came from the last war, but they were fresh, untouched inside. We wrote with proper pens, dipping them in a bottle of red ink.

That's what I remember most about those peaceful afternoons, learning our letters. The clink and dab of metal nibs in the bottle of ink. The crackle of the fire and that heady scent of woodsmoke. Isla being all teacherly and the sternest we ever saw her: she would hover at our shoulders and check what we were writing.

She was a brilliant teacher. Though we were sure we were learning about things they never taught at proper school. This was more exciting stuff. We copied out her recipes for her. We made lists of names and bits of things in what I think was Latin or really old English. And then our tiny aunt would heft down some of Uncle Michael's old

31

books (With him not there! The idea thrilled us both) and she would make us copy out passages that left us baffled. Our favourite was a bestiary, which Isla said meant a book of beasts. We had to write down descriptions of these creatures and instructions on how to tame them, or to kill them or to banish them safely to another land. What I liked doing best was copying out the drawings of them in bloody red ink. I was painstaking. My beasts were the best. Much better than Katy's, who had no patience.

One day Katy asked Isla (we were both drawing a basilisk: some awful serpent thing with goggling eyes): 'Where did you learn to be a teacher, Aunt Isla? Where did you go to school?'

I looked up then from my own work to study our aunt. The nib dripped red blots on my page, but I didn't notice that until I looked down again. For the moment I was transfixed - we were both transfixed - by the dreamy look in Isla's eyes.

'North of here,' she said softly. 'Not too far. It was an old school, not there anymore. A special place. Our parents wanted Michael and me to have the very best education.'

'A posh school!' Katy laughed. 'Like where all the nobs go?'

'Not posh,' Isla smiled, fluffing out her hair. 'No money was paid. But not everyone could go. Just certain people's children. It was a sort of secret, really.'

'Why?'

'Because it was a bit out of the ordinary and people mightn't have approved,' she said. Katy and I exchanged a quick glance.

'Did you have to live there, or did you come home each night?'

'Oh,' smiled Isla. 'We both lived there all the years of our childhood. From five till we were sixteen.'

We were shocked. 'And you never saw your mam or dad?'

'They came sometimes. The school would have a lovely

open day twice a year. At the solstices. We would have a fête and a special celebration. It was wonderful.'

We sat quietly, listening to the fire, staring at her.

'There was acres of fields to play in. We lived in this huge big house. There were no set times or classes. We ran wild, really. Completely wild, and that was the idea, that we would learn most by doing exactly what we wanted. There was a big iron sign at the entrance, at the bottom of the drive, and that's what it said in these huge letters, hammered out of iron: 'Do What Thou Wilt Be The Whole of the Law.' Aunt Isla looked at us both. 'That's a line from William Blake.'

We knew who William Blake was, by now.

'All schools should be like that,' said Katy. 'Doing what you want.'

'People are scared of that,' nodded Isla. 'They think children should be controlled and told what to think. Michael says that destroys their natural talent, all their natural desires. It makes everybody the same and the passion goes out of them.'

We never really understood. How could we?

'Michael says that, while we have the care of you two, we must think of it as a blessing, since we have no children of our own. We should teach you the ways we would have brought up our own. We have been lent you. And we have to do right by you.'

'You have been very good to us,' I said automatically.

Aunt Isla suddenly looked very sad. Suddenly very much older. We were used to her being light, dancing about the place. 'You will have to go home soon enough. We will lose you. You'll be back in that city.'

We went quiet at that. Any mention of home made us shiver hot and cold. Michael had slipped into the room behind us. For a big man he could really creep about.

'So we have to make the best of the time,' he said. 'Train you up to live a proper life and teach you the ways while you're still here. This is a rare chance you've got, girls.'

I looked from him to Isla, to Katy and back again. There was something very strange in the air. It was just like we were waiting for bombs to fall and we sat there suspended. Exactly like in Mam's letters, when she said you can hear that evil whistling from a long way away. And it gets closer and you pray it won't hit. But she also said that it was worse if you heard nothing at all. That's when the bombshell hit you out of the blue. That's when you bought it and your number was up.

Well, that dining room was silent just then. It was as if an obscure offer had been made. Michael's eyes were wide and his mouth stayed open, a thread of saliva stretched between his lips. Aunt Isla was apprehensive - as, I realised suddenly, she often was in her brother's presence. But Katy was looking very sure of herself, both arms resting on the table across her exercise book, her shoulders squared and resolute.

'I want to learn,' she said, nodding firmly. 'I want to learn about it all.'

The Figgises nodded and smiled back at her, Michael first and then - perhaps more tentatively - Aunt Isla.

***

Of course I was having all sorts of dreams and waking up with the screaming ab-dabs. Hard enough just being away from home, hard enough thinking of Mam in the city, but all this funny stuff going on as well: it played on my mind. Those creatures we drew out of the old bestiary went lumbering and romping through my dreams. It was the basilisk clumping down the cobbles of our street. It was his fiery breath that did for our house. Wheeling and screeching through the smoky dark air came the demons: their leathery hides and vicious wings picked out by the searchlights over Salford.

I'd wake up screaming and, more often than not, Katy would be there to administer her brusque care for me. She whispered fiercely and reminded me where we were. We were safe. We were in the Figgises' house. I wasn't so sure anymore. I felt there was something in the atmosphere of that place that was seeping and silting into my brain. They were grinding something up, chopping it fine, and sprinkling it into our late night hot milk, our breakfast powdered egg, that bloody beetroot soup of theirs. Bit by bit they were taking us over: the Figgises and whatever worked through them.

'They'll take us off to hell,' I found myself saying, all breathless and tousled, to Katy one night.

She laughed at me.

Sometimes when I woke and the dark attic room was spinning around - and then it settled and I realised I'd just been ejected from my latest lurid dream - she wasn't there. Her bedclothes had been cast to the floor. The imprint of her body was there on the sheet and the mattress, the shape of her head on the pillow. But no Katy. This happened once or twice every week, I soon realised.

I once stepped outside of the room to see where she had gone. The painted boards were freezing on the soles of my feet. I stood out on the landing and there was nothing to see and nothing to hear but the ticking and clicking of the old house's bones. No sign of Katy. But in the morning, there she'd be again, large and bold as life. Jumping out of bed, dashing across to the jug and the bowl to wash the cobwebs out of her eyes. She'd become cleaner and she'd become more confident. There was a new life in her, a new eagerness. Better behaviour, too.

I'd lie there and watch her, the candlewick bedspread pulled modestly up to my chin. She'd have been sleeping starkers and that surprised me. She stood with her back to me, scrubbing at her skin with cold water. She was bright pink, flushed with life and blood. Her hair had this marvellous sheen to it. She was growing. When she turned to look at me you could see her breasts were coming. She had no modesty.

Something else I saw, when she went skipping out of

35

bed like that, full of the joys of spring. Her feet were dirty, and all up her shins. She was black with mud from outside.

'What were you doing outside?' I asked her, more than once. 'Why were you out there in the middle of the night?'

She laughed again. 'You don't want to know, Sally,' she said. 'You said you didn't. So you'll never know, will you?'

And that was an end to it. I thought all of this was just part of the mysteries. The usual kinds of mysteries that seem to be everywhere when you're growing up. One day she hopped out of bed and she had blood on her fingers, and some on her chin. I didn't say anything. I shrieked. I thought she'd started her monthlies. But why on her fingers? Her mouth?

Katy just washed herself. Didn't tell me anything. She cleaned herself meticulously, like a cat, every particle of herself scrubbed clean in the morning. She had suddenly become very proud of who she was. Who she was in the process of turning into.

And I suppose I was feeling very left out.

***

I knew the city was a wicked place really, but I was still longing to get back. One day, some day soon I would be sent back to Manchester, to Salford, and to my mam. The Figgises would have to release me from their warm, fierce protection and I'd never have to swallow down any more of their curious potions.

Perhaps that bloom of health and clean-living that was so clearly and rosily apparent there in my face - perhaps it would wither and die. I would be a pale slum child all over again. I'd have bad bones, skinny legs, lank hair, the lot. Just as I'd had before. Just like everyone else we knew at home. But at least I would be at home.

The place had taken on mythical proportions for me. I read Mam's sporadic letters like they were fairytales and I dreamed about our back lanes and about helping Mam and the fire wardens, putting out flames in the watches of the night. I'd have my own tin hat and a gas mask. I'd be with people of my own sort.

Here in Kendal I was made to know I was different. Not in any bad way, it was just clear to all of us that I was cut from different cloth. Isla Figgis and Michael and Katy would talk about things and I'd hear their voices raised before I walked into the room. They'd lower their voices or change the subject when I came in. I didn't really feel left out, but I had the vague sense that I had failed some sort of test. And that they were being kind to me. Like I was going to miss the boat. When the day of reckoning came, they would be forced to bid me a fond and regretful goodbye. I've had a similar feeling, in the years since, from certain hardline Christians. People who, though not setting out to convert you, let you know that they are putting you into their prayers. That's how it was with the Figgises and Katy in those last days of the war.

Since she's the reason for all this spilling out of my past - she's the excuse, the alibi for all of this - I ought to say a bit about how Katy had changed through that time.

It was clear that she was in utter possession of herself. The way she talked, the way she carried her whole body, there was a confidence there. A quiet self-regard. She had gone from being nothing: being the poorest kid on our street, whose mam was beyond help and who smelled of days-old wee, into being what was to all intents and purposes a young woman. All proud and, if not stuck up, someone who knew her own worth. She had turned slim and curvy and her hair had grown glossy and long. All the Irish had come out in her and she was dynamite, even in the clothes Isla stitched out of remnants and hand-me-downs. Heads turned on the High Street when Katy went by. They all knew her.

I, meanwhile, had gone dumpy. All puffy-faced and short of breath. I had eyes like two currants stuck in a soft white barm. I cursed my luck and hated myself for not being a bonny kid anymore. Mam would never recognise me. I'd turned into a hefty girl who came from the countryside. All those eggs and fresh, rich cream. And the chocolate bars with which the Figgises tried to buy our love.

Not that they needed to bother bribing Katy. She adored the two of them without question as time went on. She was their adopted daughter and she let them kiss and pet her and she looked ever so smug about it. She, who'd always bridled and hissed like a feral cat when anyone had tried to make a fuss of her. Now she'd settle and look primped and pleased at their attentions.

Then came the day they took us both to one of their solstitial celebrations.

It was what they had instead of Christmas, just a few days before, in the middle of the night in the woods and Katy was their chosen winter queen. She was a natural choice and she revelled in all the preparations, as they fitted her in a white dress; silk spun as fine as Isla's frizzy hair. Neither of us had seen such a garment before. Katy stood on a wooden chair in the front room as Isla pinned up her hem, and I knew what she was thinking. It all went back to the nativities our school used to put on, back when we were little kids. Katy had never been chosen. She had glared in utter contempt at the Marys and Josephs and angels of all those years. Even at the shepherds in their tea towel turbans. I'd always been picked for a shepherd, taking my role very seriously.

Now Katy was the star. For this celebration she was Mary, the Angel Gabriel and Jesus all rolled into one. Isla made her a little coronet woven out of mistletoe and holly. It prickled a bit, you could tell, but Katy looked ever so festive.

***

When I looked at Katy in those days I had some awful thoughts. I was jealous. Of course I was. It was my age back then, the age of both of us: when everything whizzes around in your blood and it stirs you up and you wonder if you'll ever be worthy of love.

What I remember is tingling and fizzing all over, just under my skin. As if great things were going on beneath the surface and no one could tell. They just saw Sally, covered in puppy fat, covered in shame. Even I only half knew what was going on inside of me. I felt special and like no one else and only I knew about it. Of course I was going to look enviously at Katy, whose every gesture and word were credited as unique and amazing. They thought she was marvellous and I started to resent that. Why was she worth so much love?

They lavished love upon her.

I told myself it was because she'd been neglected as a child. She'd only just dragged herself up. I was still obeying the words of my mam, and keeping an eye out for the young MacBride girl. Making sure that Katy was all right. So I watched as Isla sewed Katy into that silky white dress in that run-up to Christmas. I watched her place that tiara of briars and holly and plump mistletoe berries on her head and wreath her hair through it so that it tangled and fell in these wild, ravished locks. They had her up on that chair like a goddess and Katy basked in their attention. The fire was crackling. Outside the snow was bashing against the windows and the wind was singing through the gaps in the badly-fitted panes. And we were going out that night, to celebrate, in all that weather.

I was sitting in my duffel coat with the hood up. I was in a pair of Michael's old wellies with the tops rolled down and newspaper stuffed around my feet. I watched the Figgises gasping and oohing over Katy and I decided that I was going to lose all respect for them. They were silly old people. They were freaks, just like Katy had said, right at the start.

Isla was broiling up some foul-smelling wine in their tiny kitchen and she came hefting in the smoking pot. She ladled it into china cups for us. Heavy wine, mulled in strange spices. They cajoled me into taking some and I couldn't refuse. It would keep out the cold. The fumes were heady and acrid. At the first sip I could feel them curling and twining around inside me. It was the weirdest sensation. After half a cup of Isla's solstice wine I felt almost removed from myself. I was a few paces behind, peering out from deep within this plump girl's eyes, observing the others in my adopted family getting tipsy and excitable. Aunt Isla fetched out her musical saw and gave us a quick tune. Michael danced a little jig in front of the fire. I'd never seen him do anything like that before. He looked too jolly to be himself. He was giddy and sweating, hopping about on one foot, then the other, so that the old floorboards rattled and rumbled. Then he bade Katy dance with him. She twirled very carefully and proudly in her new winter dress.

Then it was near midnight and time to go out. They had been passing the time, quelling their excitement. We had to leave. It would be the last time I was ever in their house. Though, of course, I didn't know that then.

***

I was surprised because it was the butcher's van we were going in. I'd known the Figgises had friends in the town, special friends who shared their beliefs, who greeted them and nodded with respect at them in the street. Sometimes these neighbours and townspeople came to sit in the front room and they'd make a night of it round ours. Michael would take down some of his heavy, musty books and read to them, just as he would read to us. They would listen just as we listened, rapt at his growling voice, half-understanding what he said. I had never seen the butcher at these gatherings and, even if I had, I'd still be surprised that he'd offer the use of his van, of which he was very proud.

It was really cold in the back. They let Katy sit up front in the cab with the butcher, on account of her pristine frock. The rest of us, meanwhile, were shoved standing up in the back. It was dirty and it smelled funny. A heavy oily smell like blood and poo all mixed in.

Other people were joining us. They shuffled up out of the dark and the whirling snow on the High Street. They were greeting each other, and us, in low, gruff tones. They were going on like they were just getting on a bus. But it was midnight. It was the longest night of the year and there was a blizzard in the offing.

Isla pulled me close to her as the butcher's van filled up. We were pressed against the walls and when I touched them they felt slick. 'It isn't far,' she whispered to me. 'We won't have to stand for long.' Even in the murky light her silver hair still glimmered and shone. That was the last adopted mother-like thing she ever said to me.

The wine was making everything dreamlike. I decided I would pretend that's just what it was.

Some of these faces I recognised. Most of them I didn't. None of them talked to me, even the ones that had been to our house. I was quite unimportant. As the van choked and wheezed into life and we were all flung together and jolted and rattled along, I was squeezing my eyes tight shut. I wasn't really there.

But I was. And Katy was up in the front of the lorry, preening herself. I had one of those weird sensations, where it's as if you're looking back on yourself. Like what you're living is the memory of what you did. That makes you feel safer.

That rattling journey was endless. There weren't any windows in the back, so after a while I didn't know where we were headed to. It must have been further out of Kendal than I'd been in ages. I had been stuck there, in a small radius, for what seemed like most of my life. I had a little fantasy that the van would go so far it would take me back to Manchester. The doors would open eventually and show us the streets I remembered. I'd drift out and wander back up to our front door. Maybe they really were taking me home.

Wherever it was, it was uphill for a long time. We were clinging to the insides of the van, onto each other. It was

41

like the metal was ripping the nails off my fingers. It was knocking me sick. Aunt Isla tried to gather me up, to bundle me and steady me, but of course she was too small.

At last we came to the woods.

***

When the doors opened it was eerily bright. The snow had stopped falling and the moon was full over the network of stark black branches above our heads. No one spoke. That was the oddest thing. They hung around as if they were waiting for someone to tell them what to do. It was just like being cattle led off that truck. I kept my eyes down and wouldn't look at them. I kept my hood up as well.

They all turned to watch Katy getting out of the cab in her dress. Again, that special treatment for her. More oohing and aahing. She did look special, though, even I knew that. I still hated her. That look on her face. Those stupid twigs and berries in her hair. The way she took in how all the Kendal midnight people stared at her. She took it as her due.

She always has known how special she is.

Then I had a nasty thought.

I thought, maybe they're going to sacrifice her. Perhaps that's what it was all about. She doesn't know it, the daft mare, she's afloat and excited on all their flattery and what they're planning on doing is ripping out her throat and her belly and pulling out all her insides and eating them. That was surely the kind of people they were, with their old books and their talk of demons and spirits. Could she not see? They might be falling over themselves to pay homage to her now, but soon enough they'd be dancing around her bloody and ruined remains.

See? Kids can be vicious with what they think.

It was Michael Figgis, of course, who took the lead and who started walking into the woods, between the thick and wide-spaced trees, crunching through the snow, through that old and frozen light.

42

It had to be sacrifice. The way they were caring for her. The way Michael took her little hand and drew her into the forest. I was remembering what those two daft girls had said, ages ago, when we had that fight, the day we were getting nettles for tea. They'd said about the stuff they reckoned the Figgises got up to. Horrible things. I hadn't thought about it much. They were just silly girls. They had kept right out of our way since then, though we'd seen them in the street. They looked away when they saw us. Now that Katy had come into her own, she'd stride right by them, defying them to stare.

I wished I was with them now. Somewhere normal. Away from this lot, up in the hills, quiet in the forest.

**

We came to a clearing at last. For a while we had seemed like some strange and unfortunate folk who had been turfed out of their homes and set to walking through the night. Looking for a new place, like we'd been walking forever in fear, never looking back and never going back to human civilisation. This was just our lives now, trudging through heavy snow, with the frost-rimed branches slashing at our faces.

Of course I know now that, just at that time, there were people all over Europe doing just the same as us. They carried a few things from home, some clothes, a bit of plate, their babies on their backs. They had been turned out for real and they didn't dare look back. But we had chosen this. The Kendal people were doing this because they wanted to.

In the clearing they busied themselves unpacking the bags and hampers some had been lugging through the woods. A midnight feast. With that old pale eye of the moon peering down at us. Soon there were delicious smells, warm smells insinuating themselves on the frigid air. The butcher had done us proud. I could taste sausages, game pie, rabbit in rich gravy and jelly. We really were to have a feast. And a knees-up, it turned out. From seem-

43

ingly out of nowhere, Aunt Isla whipped out that musical saw of hers. I saw others tuning up battered violins. Someone had some jungle drums, which he started pounding into resonant, primitive life. Another was tootling away merrily on a kind of flute thing. People began to sway and then Michael was cajoling them into building a great fire in the centre of the clearing.

Then I knew what I'd suspected was going to come true. Katy's goose was cooked. Silly little cow: stood there feeding her face with sausages. She didn't have a clue what was coming to her.

'Hey,' I jabbed her, as the first tongues of flame went writhing through the pyramid of branches and old crates. 'Aren't you scared?'

She looked at me in scorn. The music around us was harsh and like nothing I'd ever heard before. They were making a symphony from the weird notes Isla drew from her musical saw. Great bubbles of discordant noise rose up from the players, up above our heads and out into the clearing: clashing and blending in curious harmonies.

'Why should I be scared?' she laughed. 'This is all on account of me.'

I scowled at her. I wanted to slap her, but I knew she'd thump me back. Curvaceous she might be nowadays, but she was still strong and wiry underneath. She hadn't lost that.

There were bright bursts of light, fanning out across the glade as other vehicles arrived for the celebrations. It was hard to take in the details, but other faces were joining the crowd. The noise grew quite fierce. These newcomers were more talkative and excited. There was a profusion of different accents, some I didn't recognise. Their breath came out in smoky gasps and soon we were jostling for space.

They came by to look at Katy in her winter queen frock.

'Get some more of this down you,' she told me, passing a tin mug of that spicy wine.

I sipped it, wanting to hold my nose as I did so. I said to

her, 'You know what all of this is about, don't you? You know what they do?'

She admitted she was vague about some of the details. But she had the gist. It was only a bit of harmless fun, really.

I shook my head at her, cold in all that crowd. I thought of her going out at night and coming back with mucky feet and scratches on her skin. She'd seen more of this stuff than I had. It wasn't up to me to protect her. She'd gone too far for that.

She laughed at me. 'What do I care if a few funny old fellas want to worship me and fiddle on with me? It's a good laugh. They think I'm Chosen. That's all.'

I shuddered at the tone in her voice.

She was greeting some of those strangers then, as if she was a friend of theirs. Greeting them over my shoulder, like she was at a cocktail party. I moved away.

Poor Katy. She was always centre of attraction after that. That was the real beginning for her, I suppose. Silly cow. And yet ... Yet I suppose she really did know exactly what she was letting herself in for. That's the funny thing.

I moved away and went unnoticed in the press of the crowd. I shuffled through acrid billows of churning smoke and waves of hot and cold air, battening me back. The fire had leapt up from the frozen branches with unnatural quickness. Around it, the revellers were singing along with that awful music. They were eating meat that wasn't on the ration. I watched their teeth squeezing down into crispy flesh and juices running freely down their chins.

I kept my head down, making for the edge of the group. I wanted fresh air. I wanted quiet again. I didn't want to see what was going to happen to Katy. I knew that much.

I leaned against the gnarled bulk of an old tree and watched the lot of them from afar. From here you could hear the real life of the forest. The owls shrieking in alarm; the creatures in the undergrowth stirring at all this alien hullaballoo. I breathed deeply, hating the lingering taste of

45

that tainted wine.

That was when I turned and saw the big posh car parked there between the trees. It was as strange as if a ship had docked there: a stately galleon stilled in the frosty air. I suppose it was a Rolls Royce or something, all silver. For one thing, it wasn't at all like the motley assortment of lorries and butcher's vans and whatnot everyone else had turned up in. This car stood out a mile and I was drawn right to it. To me it seemed like real magic, just appearing there. The real thing, with its windows all black and wound up against the cold. It was immaculate. Like something from another world.

Without a sound the window on the driver's side rolled down. It seemed to me that whoever was inside wanted to speak to me. I felt like they had been watching me, plodging and crunching in my wellies, away from the gabbling, rabble-rousing crowd. Whoever owned the car had noted that I was the odd one out - the wallflower - and they wanted to see that I was all right. That's what I thought, trusting thing that I was. My insides went all watery at that thought.

I'd watched the films. I knew what those stories were about. When a big car stopped by like a silver ghost and a hand came out of the window and crooked a finger at you, that meant someone had spotted your talent. They'd take you to Hollywood and put your name in lights and you would do anything for them.

So when I stepped up to that car I was full of mixed feelings, but I was sure that someone had seen my true quality shining out through the duffel coat and all my puddingy flesh.

In a way that was true.

Someone special had, in fact, noticed me. Perhaps the most influential person I'd ever meet, in all my life. As I rested my fingers on the silver skin of that car, and felt their tips start to freeze and stick, it was just like I was touching greatness.

There was a beautiful man sat inside. And beside him, a beautiful woman. They were rich and grand and they were both wearing lavish fur coats. I had never seen people like them before. They smiled at me, together.

Now how do I explain Fox and Magda Soames?

I think back on these very early adventures of mine and they all seem to be about searching for new parents. I ended up in one set of laps after another. As did Katy. But I never wanted new parents. I just wanted Mam. I was quite happy when it was just me and Mam. But then great world events intervened and I couldn't have Mam and I was sent to the Figgises instead. And now, it seemed, as I opened up their car as I was told and clambered onto their back seat, I had Mr and Mrs Soames.

Straight away I knew they were taking me in. They were rescuing me in the Silver Ghost. I didn't belong with the midnight people and so I was being led away again. Because I didn't understand - or I understood all too well - what was going on in those woods.

I was just a little girl. Them two took one look at me and they understood. She's just a little girl. She's out of her depth in the dark and dancing woods. We need to pick her up and take her away.

They were good, well-bred people. Cultivated. They didn't like what the Figgises did much either. But they were involved.

We slid out of those woods, down off those hills, away from the Lake District. It was like flying, the car was that grand. I think I fell asleep in the warm, scented air.

Do you know, I've not been able to go back to the Lake District. Never. It takes up this whole space in my memory and in my mind. I can see the crags and the rough grass and the valleys. And I can see the Figgises and Katy but they're only faraway specks. In my head I can see it as from above, in the dark of a winter night and I can see the shape of its lakes in moonlight. Splashes and blobs of mercury. And there's a stealthy, silver car leaving the place behind, bombing down the empty roads, towards Manchester.

I was rescued that night by the most glamorous pair I've ever known. The gallant novelist and his lady wife. They had the kind of authority that no one could face up to: they didn't care about the war or Hitler or witches or the evacuation board. They could see I needed taking back to Mam.

I was rescued. Like a little girl should be.

'What about Katy?' I asked them, eyes wide as we hurtled south.

'You'll see her again,' Fox Soames told me. 'One day. But she's in a story of her own now. It isn't the same as yours.'

I lay back on the upholstery of the back seat. Over the furry shoulders of the Soamses' his-and-hers plush coats, I watched the night through the windscreen, rushing up to us. And I thought about what my mam would say.

PART TWO

BACK IN MANC

ONE

The first Lance knew of it was that morning, from the Daily Mirror. Well, from the milkman really, who'd yanked the paper out of his box and had already turned to the full story on pages four and five. He was scanning the columns with some interest on the front doorstep of Lance's flat. Lance noted that he still managed to hold a pint of full cream in one hand as he read. That's dexterity.

'I don't take full fat these days, Dennis, thank you very much,' Lance snapped. The milkman looked at him, blinking.

The daylight was all a bit much up here. It was turning the rooftops and the turrets of the city centre the colours of salmon, butter and just-done toast. Lance had tottered direct from the shaded recesses of his boudoir. He'd only just cast his face mask aside. Now he was confronted with the full glare of the city's rooftops. He clutched his dressing gown tight, making a moue of displeasure as his milkman passed him the bottle of milk. He looked like he was about to start rabbiting on about whatever had snagged his interest in the paper. But first he was reading to the end of page five. Lance sighed.

Already smells of breakfast from the cafe bars five

storeys below were wafting up to Lance's terrace. There was still the tang of last night's booze - fizzy lager and alcopops - drifting over from the rooftop bar that adjoined his little garden. Only a short hop and a jump from Lance's Tuscan paradise to the aluminium garden furniture and heat lamps of that bar - Slag! - next door. Well, this was what you got for living at the top of an urban village. Hordes of them drifting by at night, outside the bars, along the canal, craning their necks to catch a glimpse of him - the star in their midst - up in his swanky pad.

Oh, he was living the metropolitan life. He'd waited long enough for success and money, and now he'd take it whichever way it came. Sometimes you had to pay to live in the heart of life - and not just through the nose. Lance's price also involved over-familiarity. It was the bane of Lance's kind of celebrity. If you were on telly like he was - especially like he was - all of them owned a little piece of you. This milkman, for instance, was getting far too cocky just lately.

Lance leaned against his doorway and made a show of toying idly with the decorative pebbles of his Zen meditation garden with one bare foot. He hugged the offending bottle of full fat milk to his hairless chest (brrrr) and said at last: 'Come on then. Tell me. What's so fascinating?'

The milkman's face came out of the paper. He grinned. A louche grin. The bastard even doffed his cap in serio-comic deference. And so he frigging should, thought Lance.

'Have you heard about this?' the milkman said. He had a jaunty local accent and his white coat was pristine. He looked like he'd been dressed by the wardrobe department to be the very image of a milkman. 'You must know this already. It can't be news to you.'

'What?' Lance snapped. He knew he was making himself unsympathetic, even this early in the morning. But he was on his own turf. He was nearly forty and at the height of his personal success. Kind of. And if he couldn't be stroppy here and now, this morning, on his own front doorstep, then when could he be? Most of his life he had to spend being polite. Obsequious, even. Don't piss off the fan-base. You have to appease the public. He yanked the paper out of the milkman's hands and looked at it.

'Oh.'

On the front page there was a picture that filled most of the available space. It was of his most loathed enemy in all the world. With her bazoomas out.

'Like mangoes, aren't they?' his milkman pointed out helpfully.

'You mean melons,' Lance sighed, and flicked to pages four and five.

And that's when he found out: Karla Sorenson, veteran queen of the lesbian vampire exploitation flick, to join cast of ailing porno soap in bid to up ratings. Full story with mucky pics.

'Oh, fucking hell,' Lance hissed.

His milkman Dennis grinned again. His lips were very thin, the hair under his milkman's cap as he removed it showed up blonde and cropped down to the skin. 'You asking me in then, Lance?'

And Lance - rather bad-naturedly - let him surge into the cool dark balm of his exquisite rooftop pad.

***

'This is awful news, just awful...'

The milkman perched himself on a tall stool at the breakfast bar and watched his host clatter about, from juice squeezer to coffee machine. Lance was clashing cupboards shut and switching on a lime green portable telly with unnecessary force. The Daily Mirror was strewn over the kitchen counter. Karla Sorenson was showing her perfect bosoms to the world.

She must be sixty if she's a day, thought the milkman.

'Fuck, fuck, fuck,' Lance kept muttering as the coffee started to burble and the people on the daytime settee went

51

chuntering on.

Dennis the milkman smiled to himself, watching the whole drama unfold. Hey, this was good. A hissy fit at half ten in the morning. Dennis felt privy to something not many people in this life got to see. But this was in the nature of his job. And what a fantastic job. His steely grey eyes flicked casually around Lance's kitchen walls - noting the posters, the playbills, all the glorious trappings. A framed signed photo of Lance standing with Barbara Windsor at what looked like a garden party at Buckingham Palace. A piccie of Lance, head-bowed, meeting the Queen Mother backstage at the Royal Variety. This was real stardom. When you're a milkman, Dennis was thinking, that's how you see the real stuff. Stuff like this: everything that lies behind the bland facades of these rooftop pads.

He decided to rally his pal. 'Oh, come on, Lance. It's not all bad. You've said yourself that the show's going down the pan. No one's watching anymore. Maybe she'll help it come back to life...'

Lance was obviously taking it hard. Pride, Dennis thought. Lance was the star of the show. Now they were bringing in a lesbian vampire as a crutch. That must sting.

Lance turned on him snarling. 'Who asked you? You're the milkman, for fuck's sake. What do you know?'

Dennis gave a leisurely shrug. 'I know what I like on the telly. And as a punter, as a member of your audience, what I say is more important than what you do. And your show's been looking a bit lacklustre just lately. Yeah, it was shocking when it first started ... but it's not moved on really, has it? Maybe Karla Sorenson's just what it needs to perk it up. I'll start watching again when she comes on...' He pulled the paper round to look at her publicity shots again. 'I wouldn't mind getting a closer look at those bazoomas...'

Lance cursed and turned to the coffee pot. It was brimming now, bubbling away, and even it was looking smug to Lance this morning. So Dennis has stopped watching the show, has he? Oh, there was no hope left. 'You don't know anything about it.'

'About what?'

Lance jabbed his finger. 'About that woman. About what she's done. What she is responsible for ...'

Dennis's eyes widened. 'You know her?'

Lance tutted. 'I'm a celebrity. Of course I know her. I know everyone.'

Dennis nodded. Of course. Actually, now he looked more closely, Lance did seem as if he'd had an actual shock that went beyond professional pride and irk. He looked really horrified at this news about Ms Sorenson joining the cast of his show. Dennis had just thought it a laugh, but Lance was somehow taking it personally.

'I'm sorry then, Lance...'

'Mr Randall, to you.'

'I'm sorry for upsetting you,' said Dennis glumly. 'I never realised it was the kind of news that needed breaking gently. I'd have thought you'd be interested and pleased...'

Lance looked at him closely, alert for satire of any kind. But the milkman was hanging his head as he sat on that stool: the picture of contrition.

'Well,' said Lance. 'Never mind.' He turned, slightly abashed, to his portable telly, and turned up the sound. The folk on the sofa were saying that later in the show they'd be going over cervical smears.

Lance busied himself making coffee in his hand-thrown bowls. Special treat for Dennis. He'd trust him not to chip it. Full fat milk, though. What had he been thinking of? That'd put the kybosh on Lance's dietary regime. And he had volume two of his thigh and bum video to shoot in the next month.

He sighed, glugged in the gold top, and turned to hand the milkman his fresh, foamy coffee.

Dennis was still looking down at himself. Still abject and ashamed, Lance thought at first. Perched there on his

Alessi stool. Well, good. So he should be. Trouble-making gobshite. He bloody ought to hang his head.

But, no. Dennis was stroking the lobster-red head of his cock, standing out of his milkman's trousers at the length of a baby's arm. Lance set down the coffee with some difficulty.

'Oh, for heaven's sake, Dennis...'

The milkman looked up from his doings with a lopsided grin.

'Look,' Lance hissed. 'I've said before. I'm not really a porno star. And I'm not even really queer. Whatever you see on the telly...'

Now Dennis was manipulating himself to a quite remarkable degree. Such dexterity. Wrists strengthened, presumably, from hefting weighty bottles, two, three, four, five at a time. The end of his cock was glowing stickily red in Lance's immaculate kitchen. It looked like a creature in its own right, clamped to the milkman's midriff and exerting this fascination over the pair of them. Dennis's hand went up and down sharply, pacifying it somewhat brusquely.

Lance's mouth was dry.

'Oh, fuck it,' he said and dropped to his knees on the slate blue tiles. He had to shuffle forward a bit and set his palms on the milkman's knees to steady himself.

'You know you want to,' said Dennis, after a few hectic moments. He said this rather politely. 'Suck it, you bitch. You dirty sod. You know you want to suck it good.'

Lance could hardly believe his ears - trapped, as they were, under both of the milkman's hot palms. He arched his neck and struggled and took him gradually, all the way down his throat.

This was becoming a rather regular occurrence.

TWO

'I know. I know all about you. I know what you really are.'

The words were still ringing in Karla Sorenson's delectable ears. Just before they came out of the commercial break and into the interview segment, her plump and matronly hostess on the Brunch Show had looked her dead in the eye. Plain as the daylight through the plate glass studio windows she'd said: 'I know what you really are.' And poor Karla, sitting ready on the orange settee in one of her black lace ensembles, had to go through the whole cervical smear phone-in gathering up her composure and trying not to wonder what the batty hostess had meant by that.

Karla yanked up the sleeves of her fishnet batwing cardigan and plunged into presenting her public face, exactly as she knew she had to. No one could accuse Karla Sorenson of being unprofessional. She was a star and had been one since 1958. She'd been in the public eye since she was 21 and no clipped little snippy comment from a daytime TV trollop was going to put her off her stroke. Not now that she was about to become huge again.

Immediately after the phone in (a partial success. Wasn't really Karla's bag, medical advice) they had cut to a segment about making furniture for cats. Then it was another break. Then it was a countdown to the coffee time interview and Karla would have to field questions from the matronly presenter, Brenda, and her pillock of a husband.

The floor manager was a girl with purple hair who was quite in awe of her ('I adored you in 'Get Inside Me, Satan!' she whispered, showing Karla to her position). Karla was feeling rather hustled this morning. But these were the trappings of success. She remembered. Being successful meant feeling harried all the time. She was just out of practice.

Just before they went back on air she managed to ask Brenda, the presenter: 'What were you talking about earlier?' She gave Brenda the benefit of the doubt and put on her trademark seductive murmur.

Brenda was dishwater-blonde and sneering. She clutched her script and acted evasive. 'Don't you think the phone-in went well? I think we've saved some lives this morning.'

'Bugger that,' Karla said. 'That's not what I'm here for. My agent never said anything about a rubbishy phone-in. I meant, what did you mean before, when you were whispering to me?'

Oh - Brenda's mascara. Thick like engine oil. The presenter was batting her eyelashes, all a-tremble. It was like a never-you-mind kind of gesture and the floor manager was counting them down to going to out live. Just as the pillocky husband came bustling up in his River Island suit, scanning a clipboard and running a hand over his hairspray-sticky hair.

'Jesus - you're a big bugger!' he laughed in Karla's face. 'Look at the size of you! You're huge! No, no, don't get up. Don't mind me. I'm always honest like that. It's just my style. The viewers love it. And it's a shock, really ... I'm a great fan of yours. I have been since I was a kid and you were in all those horror movies ... But, God. You've really piled it on, haven't you, love?'

Karla narrowed her lilac eyes.

'Welcome back. We're both here with our very special guest, Karla Sorenson. Who you might have already noticed this morning, splashed liberally over the gutter press. Now, that hasn't happened in twenty years or more. She's here to tell us why she's about to come out of retirement. Karla, good morning...'

'Good morning.'

'Now tell us, what's it all about? I mean, it's a bit cheap, isn't it?' Brenda smiled sweetly.

'Yes,' said the pillocky husband. 'Why don't you explain to us why you're coming out of obscurity again.'

Karla sat back on the tangerine sofa and took her time. 'It's all very simple. As you know, I'd semi-officially retired from acting...'

The pillock grinned. 'All your parts dried up, eh?'

She ignored him. 'Then just last week my agent Flissy rang me out of the blue and announced there was a peach of a part in the offing. It had my name all over it.' She smiled at camera two and paused.

The two hosts looked at her expectantly.

'It's on a very famous show, isn't it?' said Brenda.

'Indeed,' Karla said. 'The five-times-a-week late night soap, Menswear.'

'The controversial late night soap, Menswear.'

The pillock added, 'The one that's had droves of viewers switching off in disgust...'

'Pah,' Karla waved her hand and made her jade and amethyst rings glitter under the studio lights. Without even thinking about it, she was letting her eastern European accent grow thicker. 'I have always been involved in very controversial work. It is just in my nature, as an artist...' Then she seemed to grow self-conscious under the pillocky husband's gaze and she drew her batwing cardigan over her breasts.

'Indeed,' he said, as if prompted. 'I remember all your saucy movies. I'm sure our viewers do, too. Especially our male viewers. We get a lot of unemployed men watching us, don't we, Brenda? You were a big part of my adolescence, Karla. I used to sneak in the pictures to see you, even when I was too young.' He chuckled at this.

'Really,' said Karla.

'You've been a colossal inspiration to growing boys, through the past - God knows how many - decades.'

Karla frowned.

Brenda had to burst in. 'So tell us ... will the part you'll be playing in Menswear be a similar role? To the frosty lesbian vampire queen we know and love so well?'

'I don't know,' Karla said. 'They have not shown me a script yet. All I know is that my character is called - surprise surprise - Karla, and that I turn up as the new manageress of the department store in Menswear. They intend

57

to expand into ladieswear and haute couture and that obviously causes friction.'

The pillock slapped his knees. 'I bet it will! Well, I'm sure we'll all be tuning in for that. Even if it has gone right downhill.'

Brenda was primping her lipstick with one lilac fingernail. 'The show's been in some trouble, hasn't it? The ratings have been falling off. You're coming in to spice things back up really, aren't you?'

Now Karla was on familiar ground. 'I always spice things up.'

'It's hardly as if Menswear needs any spicing,' the pillock said. 'It's drawn more complaints - hasn't it? - than any TV show in history.'

Karla shrugged. 'I like to be where the action is.'

Brenda smiled. She was noting the floor manager doing the wind-up gesture behind camera one. 'Well, we know that's true.'

'One more question,' the pillock butted in. 'It's a racy show. Will you be doing full frontal?'

'I beg your...'

'We know you're not averse to splashing your bosoms over the papers, but will you go the whole hog?'

'I don't really see...' Karla looked to Brenda for help.

'It's a valid question,' shrugged Brenda.

'It's a raunchy show,' the pillock said. 'Just how raunchy do they want you to be?'

'I've had no discussions yet...'

'Breasts? Fully nude? Full-on sex?'

'I--' Karla gaped at the pillock.

'Beaver?'

'Karla Sorenson,' said Brenda, 'thank you very much for joining us on the sofa for coffee this Brunchtime.'

Karla sagged back. 'That's quite all right.'

Then the pillock seemed fired by further inspiration. 'Wait a minute. Menswear - that's Lance Randall's show, isn't it?'

His wife was glaring at him. 'You know it is. Lance has been on here talking about it. Why?' She slapped his knee affectionately. They knew the viewers loved that. A hairs-breadth from a spat.

'Lance Randall is the son of the late, great Sammi Randall, isn't he?' said the pillocky husband. 'And she was your co-star, wasn't she, Karla?'

'Ha!' said Brenda. 'See? He said he was a real fan.'

'Hm,' said Karla. 'A fan indeed. And yes, Mr Randall's late lamented mother was my co-star in 'Carnival of Flesh' and numerous other movies. She was very well known to me.'

'I'll say she was!' mugged the pillock. 'That 'Carnival of Flesh' was like my whole education in ... in...'

'Yes?' asked Karla, and batted her eyelashes.

'Well, everything,' he finished lamely.

His wife punched his knee again. He was quite deflated.

'I'm sure it will be very nice for you,' Brenda said. 'And a vast, huge success. It will be lovely to see you working again.'

'Thank you,' said Karla. 'I'm sure I will be fantastic.'

'Let's go to that break now. Late, but who's perfect?'

***

Karla caught up with Brenda again in reception.

'What did you mean, you know what I really am?'

Brenda snatched her elbow away and her face was white with fury.

'Get your filthy frigging hands off me,' she hissed. Her eyes were blazing. 'Don't touch me - you succubus ... you incubus...'

'You what?'

'You fucking ... devil woman!'

THREE

Having got rid of Dennis the milkman at last, Lance went into his spare bedroom and worked off some of his tension chucking empty wine bottles four storeys down into the alley below. He did this quite a lot. No one had complained yet about an alleyway full of broken glass. It was an alley that went between the back doors of pubs and clubs, the village taxi firm and a kebab shop. Maybe they thought it was normal. This morning, though, all the crashing and tinkling wasn't doing much for his pent-up tension.

He shuddered as he lobbed his last Montepulciano D'Abruzzo into the crevasse and tried to reign himself in.

Fucking Karla Sorenson. She'd ruin his life all over again. That's what she was: a destroyer. The kind of person you never wanted to come across. Let alone twice in one lifetime.

And Lance had been on such a cushy number with Menswear. He knew it. His life these past three years had been going just fine. Better than fine. Terrific. Terrific for the first time in years and years of disappointment and mediocrity. Of course it was inevitable that some evil frigging bitch from hell would have to swoop down and bollocks it all up for him.

He hadn't seen her for years. He hadn't seen her since he was fourteen. Still he hated her with a passion that disturbed him. It was a broiling hatred that had lurked under his gym-toned muscle all these years, biding its time till a morning like this when it could erupt again afresh, like eczema. It was making him shake as he stood by the open window in his dressing gown. It was incredible. He put a hand to his cropped, dark hair and found he'd come out in a fine, cool lather of sweat.

Shower. Then phone his agent. Then phone the producer. There was an order to this. A proper way of doing things. Of course they couldn't have gone over his head. He was the star. They couldn't be treating him like this. It was a publicity gimmick, a stunt. It was all a fake. It just wasn't possible they were doing high-profile casting and then going ahead and publicizing it and not telling him about it. It was ridiculous. He just had to play it calm. Calm down.

Lance went to light two scented candles under the 1963 studio portrait of his mother. She was in chiffon. Looking every inch the star, her head tilted just so. Listening intently, eyes wide with anticipation. Lovely dangling earrings, hair all beehived up and white-blonde. Sammi Randall at her greatest. Sammi radiating stardom and calm, calm, calm.

Lance meditated fiercely for a few moments, as he usually did at this point in his daily routine. Truly believing that his mother had her ears cocked and was picking up his faint, fervid prayers. Today he was a little louder and even more impassioned. He needed - more than ever - that benign and glittering spirit of his mother to descend upon him today.

Oh, Mum, Mum, help me now, he whispered, coming out of his trance with his heart beating hard. Don't let that bitch curse me. Don't let her get me like she got you...

***

Lance went to shower off traces of Dennis the milkman. His bathroom was all smooth granite, hardly any features in it to draw the eye. Very calming. Oh, frig ... why does she have to come back into my life now? Do people have no sense, no tact?

No, he decided. On the whole, they don't.

He towelled himself vigorously and dressed hastily in jeans and a zippy top. Dressing down. It was a slack day. He could afford a stylish negligence.

Straight on that mobile. His new phone that looked like some kind of stupid Ladyshave; lavender blue and lighting up fluorescent green. That pissed him off, too, the ugliness of his new mobile.

First - a text message from his feckless agent: 'Drling -

apologies - u can hate me for not breaking it 2u first - I'm in Japan - XXX.'

When he tried, no one in her office would take his call. The producer next. Adrian, that slick little gobshite. The man behind this casting fiasco.

'He's not taking calls, Lance,' the secretary said. 'I'm sorry. Not even from the likes of you.'

'The likes of me?'

'The likes of you. I'm sorry.'

'You just tell him he's got some explaining to do.' Lance found himself speaking through gritted teeth. 'Tell him to ring me.'

'Will do, dear.'

That secretary was far too cavalier for Lance's liking. He clicked her off.

Who next?

He was stymied and cross all over again. Standing barefoot on the stripped pine of his living room.

He had to get out of his flat. Suddenly the whole apartment seemed claustrophobic.

He yanked his trainers on and thundered out onto his terrace, down his private fire escape and into Slag! bar next door. He realised he'd brought the scrunched-up Daily Mirror with him.

The upstairs bar was just about empty and looking, in the morning light, even more like an airport departures lounge. There were wide Bridget Riley-type canvases that swirled vertiginously on every side.

Lance hurried to the copper-plated bar. No public here. He ordered a gin and tonic. The bar staff knew his habits. It was that skinny lad Colin serving on, in a black t-shirt, 'Slag!' in silver letters between his nipples. His hair was tweaked up in red spikes.

'Nice hairdo,' Lance growled.

Colin grinned. 'Thanks!'

'Ok, don't get carried away. Have you seen this fucking travesty?' He spread the paper out on the beaten copper of the bar top.

'Oh,' said Colin, pouring tonic on ice, making it glisten and crack. 'I have, as a matter of fact. My gran gets the Sun, but it's the same story in there.'

'You still living with your gran?'

Colin nodded. He pushed the chunky drink into Lance's waiting hand. 'Until I get some sugar daddy whisking me away, yep. Up in the tower block with me old gran. She's a barmaid, too. All her life. Says there's nowt wrong with it.'

'Nice,' said Lance.

Colin peered at the headline about Karla Sorenson and turned to pages four and five. 'Isn't it good news, though? She's what I call a real, old-time star.'

'Is she?' said Lance bitterly. 'I wouldn't.'

'Oh, but she's been around years, hasn't she? She's as old as my gran, I think. And look at her! Still a goer! Still a slagbag!' Colin was hugging himself with pleasure.

'And that's good, is it?'

'Oh, yes,' said the barboy, clutching the tall pumps thoughtfully. 'I'm not like the rest of them you see in here. With them, you're dead if you're over 25. It's all the cult of youth. No, I can see why you'd want to live longer ... to live as long as her and still be out there, being sexy.' He smiled shyly at Lance. 'Or your age, even. You've lasted pretty well, Mr Randall.'

Lance looked at him and smiled stiffly. 'Well, that's as maybe...'

'I finish at one,' said Colin.

'Pardon?'

'My shift. I'm free all afternoon.'

'So?'

'I don't know. Just in case. If you feel like showing me round your apartment. I've had a spy through the window from the terrace bar. It looks very nice.'

Lance shook his head disbelievingly. 'I'm afraid I'm very busy this afternoon, Colin. And besides...'

The barboy laughed. 'And besides, you're not queer.'

'That's right.'

'I was only after having a look round your studio pad, you know.'

'Yeah, right,' Lance laughed, and necked the last of his gin. 'And next thing you knew, we would be up to all sorts of impromptu naughtiness. Just like it is on TV.'

'Well, wouldn't it be like that?'

Lance put his glass down. 'No. I'm not gay.'

'Yeah. Right.'

'Anyway. There's bigger things at stake this afternoon, than a little tumble in the hay with an overkeen barman...'

'Suit yourself.'

'I do,' Lance grinned.

'What's got you so worked up, anyway? Scared that Karla Sorenson's gonna take the limelight off you?'

Lance grew suddenly grim. 'No,' he said. 'I'm scared she's going to kill me and suck out all my blood.'

FOUR

'I can't tell you what a pleasure this is, Ms Sorenson...'

He was saying it again. The old fool. She watched the back of his head as he drove. He had great tufts of white hair coming out of his ears. His head was all bald, blushing with pleasure and pride. All right, all right, she wanted to tell him. Just drive. Get me where you've been paid to get me and shut your mouth. She'd had quite enough chat for one day.

Still, it didn't take much to nod graciously and acknowledge the chauffeur's pride. God knew, Karla hadn't had that much adoration lately. She sat back on the dove grey leather and smiled to herself. Gazing at the M6 going by. Heading north. Her new home.

'You'll be buying a big house up here, then, Ms Sorenson?' asked the chauffeur. 'If you're going to be on the telly five times a week I suppose you'll have to move to the north...'

'I suppose so, Rupert,' she said loftily. 'To be honest, I haven't had much chance to think.'

Her life had changed direction so quickly. Plans were underway. They wanted her up in Manchester this afternoon. To start work Monday morning. They were putting her in the TV company's own hotel. They'd given her Rupert, this talkative, excitable driver. Really, none of it had properly hit Karla yet. From accepting the part, to the papers coming out this morning, to parking her bum on the Brunchtime sofa this morning. It was only then, as that poisonous Brenda and her twat of a husband started nattering on that it had all come home to Karla.

She was going home. Back to the north. Back to Manchester. She was going to be a star again. Flooding the late night TV screens, purring her lines, being a personification of voluptuousness itself and probably flashing her knockers.

The good old days had come back again.

But coming back to the north. She hadn't even been on

a visit, in all this time. She wondered if she was ready to face it. All this time. She was a different person now, surely. She could face it. She could do it.

And, as the miles went by and the landscape shifted and changed and she could see hills in the distance beyond fields through her tinted windows, she felt the weight of the south falling away. She felt the north coming back into her. She was ready to see those faces again, and ready to hear those voices again. They would love her. They were her people and they'd take her to their bosom again.

'Hey, it's a mucky old show you're going to be in though,' laughed her driver, Rupert. 'You've seen it, haven't you? It's a right scream.'

'I've caught it once or twice,' she smiled tightly.

'I won't let my kids see it, of course. But me and the wife tune in now and then. It's amazing, isn't it, what they can get away with these days...'

'Yes,' said Karla. 'Things have moved on.'

'Well, what I say is this,' said Rupert, warming to his theme. 'There's nowt wrong with a bit of titillation. Everyone likes that. A bit of slap and tickle, a bit of suggestion. Well, like those old films you used to be in, Ms Sorenson. A bit of messing on. Nothing too explicit. Nothing too graphic. Like you vampire ladies copping a bit of a feel of each other. Well, that's quite respectable now.'

'Hm,' she said, watching the traffic. It was spitting on to rain. Manchester, here I come.

'I hope you'll bring some respectability to that show. That Menswear. A bit of old-fashioned decorum and class.'

'Oh,' she said. 'I'm sure I will.'

''Cause some of it's been bloody filthy. That old woman they've got on there. She's a disgrace. And that younger bloke. That whatsisname. The big fairy. Well, that's not nice. The way he goes on.'

This perked Karla's interest. 'Lance Randall, you mean?'

'Aye, that's the woofter's name. Fancies himself star of the show. Cock of the walk. Well, I reckon you'll show him a thing or two. Knock him off his big poncey perch...' Her driver chuckled and rummaged a finger in one of his hairy ears.

'I certainly intend to.' Then she grew charitable. 'But give the lad his dues, Rupert. He was the first man, after all, to get away with a full-blown erection on a late night terrestrial soap.'

'Bloody disgusting. Who wants to look at his nasty business?'

Karla shrugged. 'Plenty of people.'

'Well, people have obviously got bored with it. Otherwise they wouldn't be getting you in, would they, to rescue it?'

Karla smiled indulgently. Oh, she was looking forward to this.

Her mobile trilled. Number withheld. She knew who it would be, though.

'Daughter...'

'Yes?'

'You are doing very well...'

The voice was sepulchral. Vile. She gave an involuntary shiver each time it spoke into her ear. But still it thrilled her.

'Thank you, Master. You saw my interview this morning?'

'The brothers are not accustomed to tuning in to Brunchtime...'

'But you saw it?'

'We did indeed. You acquitted yourself well. And your topless pictures in the papers this morning were a nice touch. We have been watching on with great pleasure. And great anticipation. Things are proceeding nicely, daughter...'

Karla felt herself glowing. Just the sound of his voice could turn her insides to soup. 'But Master ... what are my instructions now? My agent Flissy told me about the job and got me onto the TV this morning, and the company is putting me in the hotel, and I start work on Monday ... but

... but...'

'Yes, my child?'

'What do I do then? What do the brethren want me to actually do?'

He chuckled. An oily, deep chuckle. 'Simply to be yourself, child.'

I'm 66! she thought. Child, indeed!

'That is why we wanted you. Simply to be yourself. That is enough for the brethren.'

'Very good, Master.'

'And then ... when the time is right...'

'Yes?'

'We will let you know.'

Her phone clicked off abruptly.

She realised Rupert had been earwigging. 'Was that someone close?' he asked. 'Offering their congratulations?'

'Hm,' she said. And sought refuge in her icy vampire queen persona, drawing herself back on the luxurious upholstery. She offered up a little prayer, for guidance in the days ahead. For guidance and wisdom in the difficult days ahead.

Then, suddenly, they were coming off the motorway. Rupert was announcing: 'Manchester! You're home, Ms Sorenson.'

Karla nodded, very graciously, and fished her shades out of her bag to brave the drizzle and grey.

FIVE

Colin felt conspicuous crossing Piccadilly Gardens in his Slag! t-shirt. There hadn't been time to change. He put on a good burst of speed through the lunchtime crowd of shoppers and business suits and hoped that no one would read his chest. Not that he was ashamed of where he worked. He'd just had a couple of nasty run-ins down this end of town.

He'd crossed the square late one night, where the new fountains were (the ones that somehow looked a bit lavatorial) and he'd been stopped. Not by a mugger or a junkie or a queer basher, but by four - four! - uniformed coppers standing abreast. He'd had a bit of gravel in his trainer and he'd paused to fish it out. The coppers had appeared out of nowhere and started asking him all kinds of questions. It dawned on Colin slowly that they'd thought he had drugs concealed in his insoles. He'd been quite drunk, and slow to cotton on. The coppers had packed him off home in a taxi before he knew where he was.

So, funny things could happen when you got onto Piccadilly Gardens. When you were out of the relatively safe haven of Canal Street and the gay village. It was only there that Colin knew his way around, knew all the faces and the way that the world worked. But it was only a short hop, step and a jump into a completely different country where everything was changed about.

Usually he wasn't tempted to leave the village during his lunch break from Slag! He tried to keep himself away from the shops. It was too easy to end up spending money on stuff he didn't need. Today however, because of the news, he had to venture out. He had to go and see Rafiq. Raf had to be told.

Colin quickened his pace, imagining the look on his pal's face when he told him what had happened. He hoped he hadn't already heard. Raf was hard to catch out with gossip of this calibre. He was always up to the minute because of the news sites on the Net.

Raf worked in SpoilerSpace, a comics shop on Oldham Road, just off Piccadilly. Recently it had become a trendy part of town and all the spaces above the old shops were being converted into studio flats and crash pads. The kind that had stripped pine floors and rooms that were about four feet square. Or they were one big open plan room of twelve feet square. Colin had looked in estate agents' windows with his mouth open. He dreamed about owning one of those places and he didn't care how small it would be. He didn't have much stuff to put in it. He would love it. Right in the middle of the city. His own front door. His own few, but expensive, belongings. Less to dust. A rail with a week's worth of outfits. Doing just what he wanted and keeping his own hours.

His old gran could come and visit if she wanted. But he wouldn't have to pad around carefully in the early hours, trying not to rouse her and scare the cat. His own hours! His own place! These were dizzying thoughts. He'd live above shops like these - rare vinyl record shops, swanky clothes shops, smart cafe bars. He'd pop down, out of his studio flat, and be right in the thick of it all. Urban living. No more sitting on a tram with his work clothes stowed in a sports bag, watching the city centre rooftops and wishing himself there.

It was a muggy, warm day. People on the street - the curious mishmash of types down this part of town - seeming harassed. Students and trendies and shambling old people bundled in anoraks. Some rough-looking blokes knocking about around the amusement arcades, smoking. The sweet, deep-fried smell of chips seeping out around them, mingling with diesel fumes from the buses that were shunting, groaning, pushing towards Piccadilly.

Suddenly Colin felt light and easy in his tight little top. He caught a glimpse of his reflection in a hair stylist's window and thought: Well, there goes a trim, sexy bloke. He just about skipped all the way up the street to SpoilerSpace Comics. He hoped Raf hadn't left early for lunch.

70

SIX

They had been pals for almost a year. Rafiq was, at 29, a year older than Colin. They had met during Mardi Gras last summer, when the whole of Canal Street and the other surrounding streets were just one seething mass of faggots and dykes, all clutching plastic pints of lager and wearing cowboy hats sprinkled in glitter. Colin had spent the weekend with a whole bunch from work, staying out on the heaving streets between their extended hours at work.

He hadn't gone home to Salford and his gran for a full three days and, by the time he bumped into Rafiq, Colin was delirious and wild-eyed on a combination of sleep deprivation and pills.

Raf had turned up to Mardi Gras alone, disguised as a lesbian vampire queen from some ancient movie. He explained to Colin who he was meant to be representing as they sat drinking and Colin hadn't understood a word.

'I've never met an Asian drag queen before,' Colin remembered slurring, only minutes after they had first met. They were on the balcony of a pub where they could hardly hear themselves think. They were stuck out, right over the surging crowd. Music was pounding out of every doorway and window below. Rafiq had been trying, again, to tell him who he was embodying, and how he wasn't really a drag queen, and how he had fashioned the costume himself (well, with the help of his many sisters). Apparently it was accurate in every regard; a perfect replica of the silver and black batwing number worn by the devilish lesbian vampire queen in the classic Sixties movie: 'Get Inside Me, Satan!'

Colin lost the sense of what his new friend was telling him. He just kept nodding politely, caught one word in ten, came out in a light sweat of desire, kept his eyes fixed on Raf's full, purple lips and then, eventually, moved in for the kill.

Raf had been going into a detailed account of the plot of his favourite lesbian shocker when he felt Colin's face

71

pushed right up into his (Raf was considerably taller), and Colin's tongue shoving its way between his perfect teeth.

So they had copped off easily and saw the rest of Mardi Gras weekend out quite happily. When all the music had stopped and the crowds dispersed bewilderedly, and the streets in the village were left clogged with crushed plastic pint pots and takeaway cartons, and the days started inching out of the summer and turning milder and autumnal, the two of them met up for tentative lunches and drinks now and then. Then they found, to the surprise of both of them, that they had become friends.

They hadn't been back to bed. It had been all right that weekend. Nothing too spectacular. Now it seemed beside the point to even mention it, let alone repeat the experience. So they had seen each other naked and they had fooled around. So what? It got that side of it all out of the way and they knew that they both wanted something else, somebody else. That's all there was to it. They could concentrate on the friendship: an easy, low-maintenance relationship and Colin found himself pleased with that. Raf was a good mate and they were lucky. It was like having a seven-foot tall, stunningly attractive minder when they went out together. And if they were out and hard up for a shag, they could always try it out again. Just like keeping emergency pizzas in the freezer. It might not be exactly what you fancied, but if you'd missed the shops, you knew what was in there.

When he got himself a fantastic studio flat in town, he'd get a fridge freezer, too. He'd have all of that stuff. One day.

SEVEN

'God, it would depress me, working here,' Colin said.

He glanced around again at the dark interior of SpoilerSpace and whistled. There were only a few, shifty-looking punters hanging around the magazines and he didn't care if they heard him passing comment. What they looked like to him was Fans. Fans didn't have feelings like other people. And it didn't matter what they were Fans of, particularly. Some cult kind of thing - TV shows, comics, science fiction, films. Colin had observed quite a few of their sort since meeting Raf.

There was a certain fleshiness to Fans: a certain not-giving-a-bugger about what they were dressed like and a slight air of unwashedness. They were shuffling about and poring over the racks and stacks of fanzines, videos, cds and rare collectibles. Monsters, heroes, aliens, villains. Just weird. Just awful. It embarrassed Colin, even being here in SpoilerSpace Comics. It wasn't his scene at all. He hated the very smell of the shop: new paper and body odour. Plastic and dust and dirty hair.

All in all, a strange place to find the immaculate Raf. Next to the short girl who was going to take his place at the till during lunch hour, Raf looked taller and skinnier than ever. He was just finishing up and had flashed Colin a brief, brilliant smile.

Colin watched him. It always struck him that Raf was one of those gay boys who really could have, should have been born a girl. There was a particular delicacy about him; a slightly-aggrieved tinge to his beauty. All he'd have needed was a tiny sideways nudge, genewise, to make him into what he should have been. A stunning woman; a real diva: slender of limb and tall of hair. Raf carried with him a not unattractive air of melancholy, as though holding back his resentment at what nature had offered him. Colin never asked him about it. That would seem too crass. As far as he could see, Raf made the best of things and Colin respected that quietly. But he thought his pal should really be a drag queen. He'd been so good at it, and yet he cracked on that his Mardi Gras vampire rigout had been a one-off thing. And never again. Colin wasn't sure he believed him. He could just see Raf at home, with all his many sisters. All of them crowding round, dressing him up in secret.

Raf was telling his tiny assistant: 'If any of those fucking Doctor Who fans come in, demanding this month's book, just tell them the delivery's late and they'll have to wait.' His voice was soft and breathy. The contrast with the girl's voice was marked. She rasped back at him: 'Sure thing, Raf. Doctor Who fans are the worst, aren't they?'

Sadly, Raf was shaking his head. 'Unfortunately not, Vicki. There are far worse Fans out there. But we get them all. We're the ones in the firing line when they come out to feed their funny appetites.' Suddenly he looked up at Colin. 'I know what you're going to say.'

'You're a Fan as well!' Colin complied.

'I know, I know. But ...' Raf sighed heavily, shrugging his slim shoulders. 'But not like that. Not in that mouth-breathing, mad completist kind of way. You don't know what it's like.' Then he decided he could leave the dim shop in the care of the tiny girl. 'I'm training her up to deal with them,' he said.

Colin and Raf crossed the busy street to the cafe opposite.

'I didn't follow your text message at all,' Raf complained. 'What were you on about?'

Colin wasn't very good at texting. HAVEYOUSEENTHEPAPERSYETTHISMORN-ING?KSORENSON
COMINGBACKONTHETELLYI-
NMENSWEARITHOUGHTYOU'D
BEDEADPLEASEDWHATABOUTLUNCH?XXXC

EIGHT

Their favourite cafe was vegetarian, but ironised and swishy. They ordered burgers and beans and raspberry milkshakes (syrup rather than real fruit) and sat in a red vinyl booth at a table painted with elaborate swirls of colour. Serge Gainsbourg was singing with Bardot through crackling speakers. It was hot and clammy indoors, but this was their usual place to talk.

With great ceremony Colin unrolled the relevant pages of the Daily Mirror for his friend to see.

'Fucking hell,' Raf said at last.

'Good, eh?' Colin was gratified to be the one to tell him first.

'But ... I thought she'd gone for good! She said she'd retired! That's what she was saying ... back at SlashCon last autumn.'

Colin nodded. He'd been there too. And he'd heard her say just the same thing. Last October he'd trekked down to Birmingham with Raf for a weekend and had been a reluctant atttendee at his first ever convention. It was a bewildering, drunken occasion. A hotel swarming with amateurs, professionals, maniacs, Fans. All of whom wrote fiction (most of it mucky) based on their favourite TV shows and movies. Raf had run around excitedly, meeting and greeting people and talking about his own Slash Fiction, which he published on his website. Although pleased and surprised to discover his pal was reasonably well known in this rarefied world, Colin had soon grown bored. He'd ended up shagging a Buffy Fan with a scraggy mohican and one of those odd, tapering, Walnut Whippy-type cocks.

But Colin had been there with Raf when Karla Sorenson had taken up her throne as guest of honour and queen of the convention. She'd arrived in full lesbian vampire drag and the Fans had whistled and hooted with delight. She had read aloud the winning story in the convention competition (not Raf's, to his great disgust) and answered questions about her long and distinguished career in Horror.

'She definitely said she was turning her back on it all,' Colin said. 'No more performing for me, she said.'

'And now she's going to be on five nights a week!' Raf looked as worked up as Colin had ever seen him.

'Have you seen Menswear?' Colin asked. The waitress was bringing their tofu burgers and their plastic beakers of frothy shake.

'Course,' snapped Raf. Everyone had seen it. When it first started it had been big news: the producers had announced that they intended to push back the boundaries of decency. TV drama would never been the same again. And, at first, there had been a certain breathless fascination in seeing how far they would go in making a really dirty soap opera. The first glimpse of bare breasts, the first naked arse, terrestrial TV's first flash of a full-blown hard-on: all of these tidbits were dutifully logged and discussed in the media. The queer press had given the show quite a lot of coverage, too, splashing screen grabs of naked male flesh and dwelling on the presence of Lance Randall in the cast. Manchester's local press had gone overboard on Lance. His show was filmed here and this was where he lived: amongst them all, in the city's own queer village.

'Fucking hell,' said Raf again, his voice turning deathly. He couldn't even look at his lunch. The Daily Mirror rattled and shook in his slender fingers. 'You know what this means, Colin.' He looked up into Colin's amused eyes.

'Hm?' Colin picked up his burger. Sautéed mushrooms dropped out, splashing in his baked beans.

'It means she's coming here. Karla's coming here. To live and work. Amongst us. In our city. Of all the cities in the world ... the queen of the lesbian vampires is going to be here..!'

Colin wondered if Raf was going into shock.

'Lance isn't very pleased,' he told him.

Raf stared. He knew that his pal often saw Lance Randall, because the actor's apartment was right next door to Slag! bar. 'You've already talked to him about it?'

Colin nodded, chewing and smiling, glad he had even more to disclose. 'He was in the bar this morning. Swigging gin first thing. Looking mightily pissed off. I think it's cause she'll be the star of the show now and not him.'

'Well, that's right,' said Raf. 'He isn't in Karla's league, is he? Course he's not. Just because he's flashed his tired old bollocks about, it doesn't make him a star. Karla, though ... she's the real thing. A proper, honest-to-goodness old-fashioned star.'

'Don't be too hard on Lance,' said Colin. 'He's a nice guy.'

Raf shrugged. 'Can I keep the paper?'

'Sure. He fancies me, I reckon.'

'Lance does?'

'Keeps trying to get me up into his flat. Asking me to come up.'

Raf frowned. 'Yeah? I thought he said he isn't queer. That's just the character he plays on the telly?'

Colin smiled. 'You've not seen the way Lance looks at me. His eyes lit up when he saw me this morning.'

Now Raf was looking strangely at Colin. 'I wonder ...' He grinned. 'I wonder if he can get me in,' he said. 'To meet Karla. In person.' He drummed his hard nails on the laminated table. 'I bet he can.'

'To be honest, Raf ... I wouldn't be happy asking him.'

'Not even for me?'

'He hates her, Raf. Really, the way he looked this morning, when he heard the news ... I reckon there's gonna be trouble. There's gonna be fireworks.'

Raf was tutting and ripping the relevant pages out of the Mirror. 'How could anyone hate Karla? She's a wonderful, wonderful woman and human being. I just know she is.'

NINE

Karla was used to the very best in hotels. She knew what service was. She knew what luxury was like. Proper luxury. Not just a free bathrobe and a few tatty flowers on the console table. She'd been to LA and had her eyes opened. That was back when they were grooming her for Hollywood. She'd also been to Cannes in more recent years, when the critics had decided that - 25 years after the event - the sleazy films she had starred in were High Art after all, and not just trashy soft porn. So the high life was what she was used to. These days she took a certain level of comfort for granted.

Well, why shouldn't I? she thought. I've paid my dues. When I was starting out I had to stay in some grotty old dives. God, back when we were actually making those films we were sleeping in camper-vans in north Wales. Drizzle and asthma and early morning calls to go traipsing around in slate quarries with my bosoms hanging out. That's what's earned me luxury today, and it's a long time coming.

I deserve a bit of pampering now. Today of all days. I've got them a shitload of publicity for their poxy show.

She was thinking furiously, to block out the shapes and spectres of the Manchester skyline all around her and to abate her nervous fears. Part of her mind was pushing away the memories of her last time here in this city, of all her early years here. She was coming back as an utterly different person. She was protected, she told herself. She was safe because of the invincible person she'd become.

They say Manchester's come up. Everything's world class. Property prices through the roof. The Commonwealth Games, all that. Maybe now it's big enough for me.

Karla was keen not to feel that she was slumming it. But she needn't have worried. When she arrived at the TV station's hotel, the Prince Albert, she found that even her extravagant expectations were met. She eased herself out of the car, let Rupert the chauffeur take her bags, and composed herself. She put on a gloss of simmering dissatisfaction. It wouldn't do to look too keen and excited. She mustn't seem too grateful for this second bite at the cherry. She was a mature and famous lady and, like the city itself, had been redeveloped quite a few times over. She had to be both exquisite and blasé.

Karla shrugged on this carefully constructed mien and strode like a panther onto the veined marble flooring of the Prince Albert's foyer. She made sure she drew glances and comments as she went.

Fame like hers, she'd once told HIYA magazine, was like an old pair of flashy shoes. Your arches and toes could still be deformed by them, and they could make your feet really stink. But once they were broken in, you could fetch them out again and again, and walk comfy. No bother.

TEN

The porter had seen the Daily Mirror that morning. He said so in the lift. He looked wary of her, hardly daring to breathe. He was wondering whether she'd mind if he talked to her.

He was dressed up like a little monkey, in an old-fashioned porter's uniform. Small hat, epaulettes, gold braid. Karla liked that. A bit of tradition. Respect. He was standing by her luggage. She'd brought a minimum of luggage. She wasn't sure how long she'd be here and, besides, Flissy would get her a great deal. She'd buy all new. First day off, she'd be down Kendals and King Street. All the Manchester stores she could never have afforded to shop in, back in the old days.

She realised the waiter was talking to her, asking about the show. And before she knew it, she was answering him. Even telling him she'd never watched the silly programme in her life. Only heard how naughty it was. Her voice was coming out in her slow drawl. Treacle poured onto sizzling flesh: that was the sound of her voice. Dulcet. She was talking like a vampire lady. Putting on the old shtick. She looked the porter up and down. Golden mirrors all around the lift. Very flattering.

The porter was a little overweight, just a bit tubby and hairy. She liked that, considering him as they rose slowly to the suite at the top of the Prince Albert. He was standing close to her, the luggage between them. She watched him swallow his nervous saliva down. She pushed out her breasts. Made it seem that they were filling all the unoccupied space in the elevator. She couldn't help herself. She just did this kind of thing automatically. She watched his sharp adam's apple bob and steady.

When they got to her suite and he grappled with the key card she tipped him generously. He demonstrated a few things. Where the light switches were, the phone.

By then Karla had lost patience and interest in him. She needed her lie down. The porter was wanting something he could show off to his mates about. Something to mark him out. She pictured him in the staffroom, somewhere in the basement, perhaps, where all the porters and chambermaids sat smoking and drinking sweet milky tea. He'd be telling them how close he'd come to making it with the vampire lady. It would be the most exciting thing in his life so far and all the others would listen close.

She looked at him and caught a glint in his eye. Cocky little thing. He licked his lips, hands clasped behind his back.

Oh, well. Give him something to do. Might as well.

'I wonder if you could you do me a very great favour...?'

'Of course, Ms Sorenson.'

'I need to get in touch with my producer, Adrian. Could you get onto the studio for me?' She handed him the note with the office's number on. 'I'm too tired to see anyone just yet. But perhaps they could send me some tapes of the show? I could do some homework here in the hotel.'

The porter nodded briskly.

'Oh ... and one more thing. My co-star, Lance Randall.'

The porter blinked in recognition.

'I'm a very old, very dear friend of his family. He'll be delighted to know that I'm joining the cast of his show. Do you think you could ask Adrian for his home number? I'd like to contact him first, before we have to meet in the studios.'

The porter nodded, committing all of her instructions to memory. He was trying very hard.

'What's your name?'

'Kevin, Ms Sorenson.'

'Well, Kevin. I'm not sure how long I'll be here. But while I'm back in Manchester, the Prince Albert is going to be my headquarters, at least for the first little while.' She flicked her eyes around the airy, muted room and smiled, Her gaze came back to rest on Kevin in his scarlet porter's outfit. She dipped that gaze momentarily and was gratified to see that hard little knot of flesh in those uniform trousers. 'My headquarters ... and my lair.'

'I'm sure we're very honoured,' he said.

'I would like to count you among my personal staff, Kevin.'

He nodded and his adam's apple was trembling again. As if he was daring himself to do something rash. 'Perhaps,' he said. 'You ... you could ... do ... that thing.'

Karla frowned. 'What thing?' she asked, knowing full well.

'The thing you used to do in all your movies. When you made someone into your ... servant ...' Kevin smiled weakly, eagerly. 'Maybe you could ... do that to me.'

'Oh, yes,' Karla said. And she stepped towards him.

It didn't take long.

ELEVEN

There was a view from her windows that she didn't recognise. She'd thought she still knew this city well. This was the centre, right by the TV studios, right at the end of Deansgate. Still, she didn't recognise the view. Where the sludgy old canals once lay parched and dilapidated, they'd put flatblocks with balconies. There were restaurants under the railway arches. A Harry Ramsden's on the road to Eccles, by what appeared to be a casino. It would take some getting used to.

The suite they'd given her wasn't all that bad. Flatteringly posh enough. Orchids were set out on the bedside table, along with her morning's press cuttings, and a little note from the producer, Adrian. Slimy, but beautiful penmanship. Public schoolboy type, she knew. Call him, he said, when she arrived, safe and sound.

Now she was up here, though, all she wanted was a lie down. A calming nap. The Brunchtime show, the press attention, and the ride up here had worn her down. All her insides were jumping about. She had to get a grip. She could blow it all by being too nervous and too keen. Let Adrian the producer with the beautiful hand wait a little while. Let other people get on with their jobs now. Flissy had her agenting to do, more negotiations with the TV people. All Karla had to do was be ready, sit tight, and keep her gob shut for a bit. Everything would fall into her lap.

But first, an afternoon nap, and still the same dream. It had pursued her here to the North, to her grand new setting. The dream that had gone on for years.

That awful old man with the bald and freckled head. He was looming over her, lording it over her. Two long ears like rashers of bacon stuck to the sides of his head. An ugly man, radiating ill will and temper. Something magnetic about him, though. Something that made you look twice and that drew you in. He was so cultivated. He knew about opera and art and the Left Hand Path. So mannered, so polite. And he talked very quietly, so that you had to lean in to pick up what he was saying to you. And by then you were lost.

He was a Count. That's what the make-up and costume girls had told her. A real Count, born. It wasn't a fake title. When he came to visit the cast and crew on location there were whispers, flurries of excitement.

North Wales in February. 1968. They were camped in a slate quarry, as far away from the Sixties as anyone could be. Everything dreary and damp. Spirits low on the set of 'Get Inside Me, Satan!' The Count was coming and some-how that cheered everyone and boosted morale. The regal presence of this bald, malign old gent.

The freckles on his head had been the colour of Brussels pâté. In her light sleep in the afternoon, all these years later, Karla shivered at the sight of him again, running a cool fin-ger over those freckles on the dome of his skull. He came back so clearly in her dreams. She had never forgotten a single detail of his compact, bristling figure. He was the author of the novel, and he'd had a hand in the shooting script. A clawed, twisted hand. A great personal friend of the producer, the backers of the movie. A friend of so many influential people: well-connected, powerful. Of course Karla had needed to get to know him. She was the star of his show. She was meant to be breathing life into what everyone agreed was the Count's greatest creation.

He was also a millionaire. Had been one even before all those worldwide bestsellers. The greatest, most successful Occult writer the world had ever known. Sitting in Karla's trailer in a Welsh slate quarry. Opening the brandy, talking with her as they sat in front of a hissing gas fire.

Not that he ever claimed to be an occultist himself. He explained this to her patiently, mildly, spreading his pointed fingers as he warmed his glass.

'Oh, no. Never. In fact, my various novels and literary endeavours exist for the sole purpose of warning the fool-ish public of the very real dangers in dabbling with such powers.'

'I see,' Karla said, drawing her legs up on her ocelot banquette and considering him over the rim of her glass. He was like a little gargoyle. Not so powerful here, in her mobile home from home.

'There are evil charlatans out there, Miss Sorenson,' the Count said. 'Replaying the old rituals and misusing the ancient texts. They do it simply to seduce young men and women; to exploit them to their own vile ends. But, besides the charlatans, there are also some genuine cults and occultists and these are to be avoided even more strenuously. It is these people I write about and it is against them that I counsel caution.'

'Well, I can't see me being in any danger from Satanists,' Karla smiled.

The Count raised an eyebrow. 'You speak too rashly. Here, in this place, you are embodying evil itself. This brings you very close to the dangers I am describing. You must watch out for yourself, Karla.'

She shrugged, lightly, and laughed at him. For a second, his eyes blazed at her.

'Sometimes I feel these are the last days,' he said, his voice thickening. 'The world is going mad. Hedonism is everywhere and the old, sensible hierarchies and orders are being chipped away and eroded day by day. I am compelled to make a stand, personally, publicly, against a society that has started to believe that everything should come easy and free to them. A society that has started to celebrate decadence ... and evil.'

'They're the ones that buy your novels,' Karla said. 'And who want to watch movies of your books. Have you ever thought about that?'

His face darkened. 'Of course I have. It's a terrible irony and one that is offensive to me in some ways. I myself am a symptom of my own worst fears.'

For a second he looked a pathetic figure. Karla watched him. Then his eyes flashed again.

'I find the paradox of my importance both delicious and

highly profitable.'

The Count had arrived in his smoke grey Daimler and he stayed in their quarry for three days. He brought three yorkshire terriers, gallons of champagne and brandy, two thousand cigarettes, his trusty Remington travel typewriter and his ancient hag of a wife, Magda, who hobbled about the place in a floor-length mink. Magda had squawked in dismay at the bleakness of the quarry, the quality of the catering, and the fact that the Count paid her less than no attention during those heady days of shooting.

The Count was mucking in eagerly with the young people. The crew were long-haired, in filthy jeans and afghan coats. They looked malnourished and they were stoned. The cast were blue-skinned like the slate itself. They were dressed indecently and their performances elicited shivers of salacious disapproval from the movie's author. They were doing such a good job. He strode around the valley floor, stepping nimbly over cables, rubbing his liver-spotted hands and snorting gleefully through his pugilist's nose.

He was especially delighted with Karla Sorenson at the peak of her devilish perfection.

His delight was something that she basked in. That covered her like a second skin.

It was a sensation Karla remembered and relived in nightmares all this time later. Even when she put her head down for just forty winks.

She still had time to reach the inevitable ending of that dream. The end of the three days of filming. When the old Count's wife met her own spectacularly grotesque end. Karla could still see it all and the dream wouldn't let her wake until she'd witnessed it all. Over 30 years later, it was tattooed on the insides of her eyelids.

She had to fight herself awake. Panting, sweating, flustered.

I'll never be free. That was her first thought, whenever she woke.

There was no protection in splendour, no succour in luxury. The old demons would always have their way.

But here, now, in the suite at the top of the Prince Albert in Manchester she was resolving: they wouldn't stand in the way of her career. They wouldn't come between her and this next reinvention of herself.

She had too much work to do.

TWELVE

It was going to be a wasted day. Lance decided that he deserved it. He'd had rotten news. The worst. And all he could do in response was lavishly waste the whole day.

No one was talking to him. That afternoon he tried to get in touch with the Menswear office. Again and again. They weren't saying anything at all and Adrian the producer wasn't coming to the phone. Lance supposed he was too busy buttering up that depraved old hag.

What he should be doing, what he was scheduled to do, was learning his scripts for next week. They had been couriered around at lunchtime by a motorcycle boy, who'd come clattering up the iron rungs of the fire escape just like he did every Friday. Dropping off the thick wodge of scripts - five fat volumes - and getting Lance to sign for them. Creaking in his motorcycling leathers, grinning through the visor of his helmet. Generally Lance looked forward to the courier's weekly appearance, even though the package of laser-printed words and words and more words meant a whole lot of work for him. Learning by rote had never been his strong point. Lance preferred things to be spontaneous.

There wasn't the slightest ounce of joy in the courier's advent today. Lance signed with a sigh, barely looking at him, and the lad went away perplexed. Missing the usual banter and tip. Sometimes Lance even made him a cup of tea. Not today. And the scripts still lay in their padded envelope on his dining table, untouched hours later.

I should open them, he thought. I really should. I don't want to fall behind. I can't. I can't slip behind and let that prehistoric bitch steal my thunder. Next thing I know they'll be looking for excuses to kill me off. I'll get fewer and fewer scenes each week. I'll be dwindling away. I'll rip through page after page of script, looking for what meagre lines I've got left to me and soon enough there won't be any at all ...

He'd seen this happen before, to unpopular members of

the cast. Those who proved difficult, demanding or just inept. One minute their character would be hale and hearty and at the centre of the show. Next, they'd find themselves hooked up to life-support and all the cast was gathering round them. They'd have to play dead with tubes up their nose, ekeing out their pathetic, final scenes.

Then, with Lance out of the way, Menswear would become the Karla Sorenson show. They might as well change the name now, and have done with him.

Gradually, that afternoon, he sunk into a terrible gloom. He was determined not to drink, however. He'd had a tiny sip first thing, but that was only to steady his nerves. He absolutely refused to get stewed. He'd just sit quiet. Being depressed. Doing nothing. Having what the Americans called a Mental Health Day.

Hm.

He went to see if he had any more empty bottles to sling down into the alleyway, but they were all gone. Even my empties are deserting me, he thought miserably.

Now he was even wishing he hadn't been so deliberately frosty with the motorcycle boy. He hadn't done anything wrong. He didn't deserve to be snubbed. Lance could have asked him to stay a little while. Pass some time chatting. Just chatting. Taking Lance out of himself, out of this crushing mood.

It wasn't just gloom and pique, he realised with a start.

It wasn't just professional rage.

Lance sat bolt upright on his white leather settee and tried to snag the threads of emotion tangling through him. He tried to put a name to them. And when he could he found, with a desolating pang, that upmost amongst them ... was fear.

I am afraid of Karla Sorenson, he thought. She terrifies the life out of me. And then, when he thought about going to work next week, into rehearsal and meeting her and greeting her and having to put on a falsely welcoming face - there was this awful black dread coursing through him.

She will be the death of me, he thought. Just as she was for Mum. That's what she's come to Manchester for. She's here to take my very soul.

At this, he sat quiet for a bit. Completely motionless. Then his eyes started flicking around the room.

He hurried through to the alcove just off his rumpled bedroom, to stand before the consoling studio portrait of his mother.

'I - I need advice,' he stammered. 'I need to be brave.'

He stared up into her silver grey eyes. They were so understanding. They even seemed to narrow in concern across the years. Mum was smiling at him benignly from beyond.

When she spoke her voice was liquid, musical, rushing through the glass and into him.

'Then brave you must be, my son. It is all true. Dark forces are gathering in Greater Manchester. But you must fight on. Menswear is your show and proud I am of you for being its star. You must never slip, Lance. You must be professional at all times. Do it for me, my darling son. Learn your lines. Don't let them see that you are hurt and afraid. Prove to me that you can do it.'

Dry-mouthed, Lance watched the silvery sheen depart from the portrait's limpid eyes.

'I will, Mum,' he said hoarsely. 'I'll do everything you say.'

He wanted to shout out to her. To beg her to come back to him.

But he knew he had to be a big boy now.

THIRTEEN

'That's amazing, Raf.'

Vicki said this about three times as Raf divulged his news.

'That's really amazing.'

She didn't get a chance to say anything else as he gabbled on. It wasn't like him, really, to gabble like that. Usually he retained his poise and cool. That was what Raf was all about. He was like a supermodel, the way he stropped and strutted about. Up and down the dusty aisles of SpoilerSpace Comics. He never broke out of that studied calm, never dropped his cool. That was why Vicki regarded him with awe, the way only someone half his height and nearly twice his weight could do. Raf was her hero.

She looked down at herself. Down at her Yoda t-shirt. Couldn't see over her boobs. Oh, he was a different order of creature completely. He was a supermodel and she ... I have a look of Ken Barlow, she thought glumly.

'Are you taking in the magnitude?' Raf asked her sharply.

'Yes,' she said. 'Oh, yes, Raf.' Thinking: if only. She looked up into his face.

'We have to mobilise,' he seethed, staring off into space, beyond the racks of comics, way beyond the snuffling punters. 'We have to plan this step by step ... like a military operation.'

Vicki had missed something. Hang on. Go back. What had he been suggesting? What were they planning? And did it even matter? She'd follow him to the ends of the earth, she decided. You gorgeous skinny boy bitch.

He was staring at her. Eyes like Frappe Latte from Nero's. Strong and cool. And a bit milky.

Snap out of it, Vicki, she told herself. He doesn't want anything from the likes of you. You are just his stout lieutenant. Privy to all his odd little schemes.

'We have to get to her,' he said. And took a deep breath. 'We have to get to Karla.'

'Perhaps we could ask her to come to the shop and sign some merchandise?' Vicki suggested.

Raf sneered. 'Merchandise? Sign? Her?! Her, of all people, come to this tatty dump and scrawl her name on tat, on absolute awful fucking tat for this lot?' He gestured to the few customers. They were keeping their heads down.

'We stock some of her DVDs,' Vicki mumbled. 'And posters and stills and that ...'

'Ha!' gasped Raf. 'You think I'd share her ... that'd I'd share Karla with the kind of ... people we get in here? That I would share her with FANS?'

Vicki flushed and blushed. She lowered her eyes and thought: I'm your fan, Raf. It was the first time she had put it to herself like this. But it was true. She felt about him like some people felt about Angel off Buffy the Vampire Slayer. But at least he was real. At least he was standing here in front of her, here behind the glass cabinets of the sales desk. He was bristling with ferocious energy: real and just inches away from her sweating palms.

'I won't share her,' Raf said quietly.

Yet you did, Raf, Vicki thought. Last October. At that convention down in Birmingham. When you came back glowing and gleaming and just about struck dumb. Like someone who'd had a conversion. You shared her then with a huge crowd of the unwashed. You'd seen her in the flesh, but you were just one of a sea of faces.

Wasn't that enough for you? And what are you planning now, with your eyes like the ice clinking in a Frappe Latte? Suddenly Vicki felt a stab of nerves. What lengths was he prepared to go to? He was looking and sounding like some kind of stalker. Vicki knew what stalkers were like. She'd had a few of her own, working here. Really. Even me. She was proud of the fact, even though they'd turned her stomach, each and every one of them. Still. It was nice to get the attention.

The thought of that convention made her cross all over again. That do last October when Raf had swanned off with his new pal in tow. That Colin. The one who'd turned up this lunchtime. Raf said there was nothing going on there. Just a good pal. Mollifying Vicki. Not his best pal. Just another pal. Vicki didn't like the look of Colin, with his spiked red hair. Never had done. A real Canal Street puff. And fancy turning up here at lunchtime in a t-shirt that said Slag! all over the front. He'd get his head stoved in. No sense. Bad influence on Raf, Vicki was sure of it. Sure to drag him into silly gay boys' world and Raf wasn't very happy there, was he? He always came home depressed when he was out on the scene. Vicki couldn't see what any of them saw in it.

Anyway, Colin didn't like or know anything about the kind of stuff, the kinds of films that Raf based his life around. Vicki had snorted when Raf told her the story of how he and Colin had met during Mardi Gras. How the superficial twat hadn't even realised who Raf was meant to be dragged up as. 'God, Raf!' Vicki had laughed. 'It was so fucking obvious. You might as well have had a big sign round your neck saying 'I am meant to be Karla Sorenson, the well known lesbian vampire queen.' What is he, blind? Who was he dressed as?'

'No one,' Raf had laughed. 'Nothing. Just some dancing little gay boy.'

Vicki had tutted. Raf didn't have any sense sometimes. He'd never been able to find his own level; his own context, if you like. If only he'd take Vicki's advice a bit more. She'd sort him out. She supposed maybe it was to do with his being Asian. It must make things so much more confusing for him.

Vicki's mother loved Raf to bits. Vicki had taken him for lunch there once. Dragged him all the way down to West Didsbury. 'Oh, do bring that delightful girlish Asian boy back again, Vicki, love,' Mum had said, only recently.

Vicki brought herself back to the present. Raf was enlisting her.

'I need you to come out with me,' he was saying, deadly

earnest.

'Where?'

'What have I been saying?' he snapped and then controlled himself. He needed her. 'Slag! bar,' he said. 'Tonight. Colin's promised me that he's going to have a go at Lance, but I can't trust him to do anything useful. He's too flaky. Not like you.'

Bit of egregious flattery there, but Vicki wasn't complaining.

'Lance Randall's always in Slag!, according to Colin. Never out. He lives just next to it and he's a complete lush. He's our weak spot. He's our way in to Karla.'

'Lance Randall off Menswear?' Vicki gasped. She was a fan of his too. She could wear her Lance Randall t-shirt. 'Are we going to meet him?'

'Too right. And,' Raf smiled tightly, 'one of us is going to seduce him.'

'Isn't he gay?'

'God knows,' said Raf. 'He reckons he isn't. Anyway. You glam yourself up a bit. We'll meet at nine on the rooftop bar. Colin's going to try and introduce us and then we're in.'

'So what am I there for?'

'Support.'

'Oh,' she smiled, brightening.

'And,' Raf added, 'if he turns out to be that way inclined, fanny bait.'

Vicki, shocked, started to laugh. 'You're awful, Lance.'

'Yeah, I know. But it'll be a laugh either way. You up for it?'

She beamed up at him. 'Course I am.'

FOURTEEN

Colin didn't want his gran thinking he treated their place like a hotel. He made a habit of popping back home for tea with her every day. Even when his shifts at Slag! were tight, he still thought it was worth going home. Even when it seemed like he only had time enough to turn round and get back on the bus.

He couldn't let his gran down.

She wasn't lonely or bored. Wasn't that type. She had stacks of mates and no end of gentlemen admirers, as she called them. Colin's gran wasn't one for being left at a loose end. Tea-time was sacrosanct though, and that was when she made time for Colin, and the least he could do was be there for it.

He caught the bus back to their estate and the whole trip out of the city centre passed in a blur. He was thinking about Raf, about Lance, about what might happen. He'd never seen Raf so animated about anything.

They were on the ninth floor of a block overlooking the river. You could see right across the city from there: all the dark, blocky roofs under the streaky blue brown of the sky.

When he got in Gran was frying bacon, grilling halved tomatoes, fussing in their narrow kitchen. The light was subaqueous, strip-lit and the air thick with cooking fumes, from a grill pan neither fancied scouring out. She was in a high-necked dressy dress, spangling with silver threads and a pinny tied over the top to catch the splashes of fat. She'd had her hair done. A pale blue wash through the fine scalloped waves.

'Are you off out, Gran?'

She gave a small jump and shriek and glared at him. 'Sneaking up on me. You could have been anyone.'

'I yoo-hooed down the corridor.'

'Not loud enough, Colin, love. My heart's doing twenty to the dozen.' She had Radio 2 on, rattling away on the formica table, the extendable aerial poking out through the window. Gran thought the reception up here exceptional.

'You look very nice,' he told her.

She touched her new hair distractedly as she poked her spatula at the bacon. 'Do I? Thanks, love. It's an Old Dear's Night Out. Special do at Harry Ramsden's. All the fish and chips you can eat and an old time singalong. Not really my thing, but I swore down to Effie I'd keep her company.' Gran's face was squeezed up in a grimace. She had a terrifically lined and seamed complexion. Somehow it looked good on her. Colin never understood that. She used about a million different moisturisers and youth-enhancing skin treatments but she still always looked 'like a used bloody old paper bag,' as she put it. 'Still, I'm characterful, that's what I am. Full of character. And people like that, don't they, chuck?' She was very slim too, and bizarrely sprightly for her age.

'Are you working tonight, lovey?'

He nodded and his gran was looking at his Slag! t-shirt, pursing her lips.

'I hope you look after yourself down there,' she said, peering under the grill, knowing she was talking out of turn. 'There's stuff in that local paper. People coming to bad ends. They found another boy dead, floating in the canal.'

Colin knew. He'd seen the bunches of flowers strapped to the lamp post by the canal wall. Photos covered in clear plastic taped over the 'missing' posters.

'He was a rent boy.'

'Does it matter? He was still someone's son.'

'Didn't mean it like that, Gran.' He got the plates out of the cupboard. The ones with the hunting scenes trim. 'I meant that rent boys come in for more danger than the likes of me, working the bar.'

'It's still a dodgy place down there,' she said.

'It's just a tourist trap now. It's like...' He laughed. 'It's like the Alton Towers of the gay world. It's OK.'

She peered at him thoughtfully. 'It's a funny old place,' she said. 'That whole stretch of canal, from Piccadilly

Station to Deansgate. And it always has been a funny place. It attracts all sorts of people.'

He knew better than to say too much when his gran got into one of her mysterious moods.

He helped her dish up tea.

FIFTEEN

They sat in the living room to eat. Gran's massive, evil-looking cat was stretched on the sheepskin rug. The telly was blaring. Local news. The newsreader was the one that neither Colin nor his gran could abide. He tended to read things out and then raise his eyebrow in scorn or incredulity. 'He makes his feelings too plain,' Gran would grumble. 'He should be more impartial.'

'Thinks a lot of himself, that one,' Gran added today. She pointed at the screen with her knife dripping egg.

The living room was crammed with china figurines. Every available surface was cluttered and arranged. An avid collector, Gran couldn't resist the adverts in the Sunday supplements. Commemorative plates, ludicrously cute puppies and babies, ladies in crinoline skirts. She'd cut out coupons and fetch postal orders and wait for treasure to arrive, giftwrapped in tissue papers. Colin found himself having to be very careful, moving around at home. He couldn't begin to imagine how Gran would react if one of her babies were smashed.

'Hang on,' he said. 'How come you're having your tea now? If you're having fish and chips later?'

She scowled again. 'You know,' she said quietly. 'When I'm out ... I only ever ... pick.'

He nodded. It was true. Gran didn't like eating in public. As far as Colin knew she had always been like that. She would sit down to dinner with people and she would pretend to eat. She'd slice things up smaller and smaller and keep talking and hardly touch a thing.

'And I enjoy having my tea with my handsome grandson, don't I?' she smiled. 'That's what tea time's for, isn't it?'

For a second he thought she was going to lean over and pinch his cheek. Poor Gran, he thought. What would happen when he eventually moved out? Into that mythical urban apartment of his? On the day that his real life actually began. What would happen to her then?

She'd starve.

He blinked away a vision that had risen before his eyes. Bizarre. He'd imagined walking up into Lance Randall's rooftop pad (and he was picturing what all the furnishings would be like. Fantastic) and Lance was asking him, very seriously, almost pleadingly, if he'd care to move in with him immediately, to share his lonely, starry life and to make everything wonderful and complete. Colin blinked again and shook his head like an Etch-a-Sketch to clear it. Sad bastard.

His gran's eyes were on the telly again. Riveted. Her mouth had dropped open, showing what she'd been chewing - and that wasn't like her at all.

'What is it, Gran?' Colin thought she was having a stroke. He wouldn't know what to do.

She pointed at the telly. 'It's her!' she said hoarsely. 'What's she doing on the local news?'

Behind the bootblack hair of the ironic newsreader there was a blown-up still of Karla Sorenson.

'BACK IN MANC' the headline said.

SIXTEEN

No one in the world called her Gran but Colin. Her real name was Sally, but she liked being called Gran in the privacy of their flat. It was like a game they were playing. Sally pretending to be this old person, to do old person's things, to have old person's cares. It did her good to have Colin fret over her. She liked the way those tables turned: when he was sixteen, suddenly thinking he was the most grown up, the most responsible of the two of them. That must be eleven years ago. Since then, she'd consented to become the wrinkled-up, ancient child and he called her Gran and he fretted. Fretted that she didn't get out enough, fretted that she stayed in too much. Fretted that she fretted over him and also that he was too young and she was too old and they'd have no common bond other than all the shared blood and these few square metres of living space.

Up here on the ninth floor, from where you could see right over the city centre.

Was it perverse to like him fretting? This orphan she'd taken in at eleven and brought up as her own. After the death of his parents ... No, she doesn't want to go over that again. Not just now. He's an orphan and they've lived together since he was eleven. Legal guardian, the whole shebang. They don't even talk about her son, his dad, his mam, death. They never talk about it all.

The fact he worries about his old gran means he cares. It shows that his heart is still here and he listens to her. She is still a figure in his life. Even now, when his life holds so many distractions. And life has so many distractions. Sally knows well how easy it is to have your head turned. How easy at his age - and at any age.

Oh, what does that mean, precisely: to have your head turned?

Turn again, Dick Whittington.

It means you've been flattered or duped into turning your back on where you came from. You've forgotten your roots, your family, your friends. You've abjured - that's the precise and brutal word - all those at home who know all about you, who know you too well and who love you still. They continue to love you with that irksome, embarrassing ferocity, fondness. Only those who know your faults and foibles can show that kind of love.

And having your head turned ... that means you can chuck all that back in their faces. Dick Whittington, too big for his boots.

Karla, Gran thinks. That's just how that silly mare turned.

But not Colin.

***

Colin has his own Dick Whittington moment. His Ladybird storybook of the old tale was one of the few books that came with him from his parents' burned house to his gran's flat. And it was that book - with its weirdly photo-realist paintings on every right hand page - that gave him his very first erotic frisson. It wasn't long after moving in with Gran. He kept looking at the pictures of the pauper boy and his handkerchief of belongings tied to a stick and slung over one shoulder. His cat trotting along at his side. A jaunty stride down the dirt track to the city, passing milestone after milestone. Dick's devil-may-care expression and his glossy black hair. He was off to seek his new life. And there was a moment, mid-story, when he flung off his tattered and dusty clothes to bathe in a river as his puss guarded his stuff on the bank. Colin kept lingering over those pages.

***

There was a time about then, when he had a stomach-ache in bed. Gran brought him Lemsip in a bone china cup and the pain drilled away, faded, came back again, all one night. She was so reassuring.

She said: 'Ah, you get all sorts of pains, all over the

place, when you're the age you are and you're growing. There'll be more to come yet. And you'll never know what they were about. But they won't do you any harm, Colin. They're all just natural.

'Do you know what I think, lovey? I think it's more than just growing that's hurting you. I think it's the very feel of time moving through you. It's invisible and most of the time none of us can feel it. But the age you are, chuck - you're just that bit tender and susceptible to time.

'So it twinges a bit and aches sometimes, winter mornings maybe, when you wake and twist round when you sit up in bed and it's nothing to be scared of (though I'm glad you told me - there's nothing worse than needless worry). It's just time moving through you, Colin, and it means you are ready to join the world...'

'Join the world, Gran?'

She pointed out of his window. At the pink and yellow lights of the city. The low orange cloud under the black.

'I mean, of an age to meet the rest of the world of grown-ups. Out there. To take the everyday pains and knocks and not be scared by any of it. You're hardening up. Becoming a person. A person of your own, Colin.'

SEVENTEEN

Later that evening, Sally walked her usual route along the canal, out towards the main road. She let the rippling lines of light on the water calm her thoughts; the plaiting and twining of reflected streetlight on top of the mucky sludge. There'd been a suggestion, at one point, that the Old Dears should book one of those trips on a barge for a night out, and eat their chips as they sailed along the canal. They'd decided they didn't want to chance it. Less danger to ancient bones just sitting in the restaurant on the ring road, having a singsong.

She called on Effie, as planned. Her old friend still lived in the same place. There were some nasty-looking shops open down her way: everything for a pound, places with handmade signs advertising their meagre wares. There was a kebab place right underneath Effie's flat. And Sally didn't care what Effie said; you could smell those meat fumes rising up through her floorboards and through her new carpets. It was like dog food, but Effie claimed to be oblivious. The whole area had come right downhill and Effie refused to see it. When she looked out on her street through her old sash windows, she still saw the place as it was thirty years ago.

'It's not so bad,' she always said.

'You don't see things as they really are, Effie,' Sally would tell her.

'If you'd had your way, you'd have had me up one of them tower blocks in 1967, same as you,' Effie said, with just a hint of spite. 'Well, we all know how that turned out. People scared for their lives. And you! When you first moved up there, you cracked on it was like living in Milan!'

Sally would purse her lips. She remembered. At first, she'd been a great supporter of that whole notion of living up in the sky. And she'd liked having her own terrace with plant pots stood out. It really had seemed like living on the continent.

'I like to keep my feet on the ground,' Effie would say

smugly.

Sally hated her best friend's name. On numerous occasions she had told her she thought it was awful. She thought it sounded rude.

'Indeed it does not!' Effie had said hotly. 'It was my mother's name.' And that was that. She wouldn't have a word said against her mother.

Effie was 75 if she was a day and, to Sally's eyes, she still went on like a rather prim, Victorian child. Look at her tonight, preparing for a fish supper at Harry Ramsden's: fussing with her lacy collar, patting it over her cardigan, blinking into her mottled hall mirror.

'I suppose you saw the news tonight,' Sally said glumly. She was fingering the sleeve of her new frock, as if testing the silver-threaded black for quality. She always felt too flashily dressed when she came to call on her friend. 'The local news with that big-headed fella reading it?'

'I did,' said Effie. 'Though I try not to, as a rule. It's all murdered taxi drivers and initiatives to make people more tolerant. I can't stick it.' She was pursing her lips, aiming her lipstick, clacking the top palate of her teeth.

'Did you see her?' Sally asked, meaningfully.

'I did. You knew her, didn't you?'

'When I was a kid. Before I knew you, even. We were kids together. Daft as brushes.'

Effie eyed her. 'You'll forgive me for saying so, Sally. But you look like you've got 20 years on her.'

Actually, she wouldn't forgive her. Sally was seething as they tottered down Effie's front stairs to street level. Damp and musty and reeking of aspidistra. 'Karla's had all the money and the life, hasn't she? She's had all the hard knocks pampered out of her. Injections and stretching and all the luxury treatments. She has every right to look younger than me.'

Effie was fishing in her huge handbag for her multiple sets of housekeys. 'I think it's supernatural,' she agreed.

Sally watched her wrestle with the locks. 'What makes

you say so?'

'A woman her age. Looking like that and taking her clothes off.'

'She was never shy, that one.'

Now they were out on the street. The kebab smell was very strong out here. Neither had eaten a kebab in their lives. They agreed that they couldn't see the attraction.

'There's something unnatural about her,' Sally said. 'Really.' They moved off towards the busy road.

'She's still an inspiration,' said Effie. 'To all of us old duffers.'

At this Sally fell quiet for a few moments. Effie cast a sidelong glance at her friend and saw that she was stewing with anger. 'What?' she asked.

'She's no kind of inspiration.' Sally's voice was low. 'She's wicked through and through.'

'Oh, come on.' Effie was laughing.

'I mean it.' Sally looked at Effie's thinning perm, the pink scalp showing through. 'I could tell you things about her that would make your hair curl naturally.'

This made Effie self-consciously pat her head and the two friends went quiet as they negotiated the complicated crossing of the ring-road.

EIGHTEEN

Number Withheld. The green display of his hated new phone was lighting up green. Someone wanting to talk to him, but not wanting him to know who they were.

But somehow Lance knew exactly who it would be. It wasn't many who had his private number.

Early evening in his luxury pad. He had tried to insulate himself against the world by drawing the screens across his tall windows and by gulping down bloody red wine. He'd ignored the sounds of the street stirring, storeys below him, and the heady, bassy thump from the bar next door.

Still someone was badgering him. Someone with his private number. And withholding their own. At last he snatched it up. 'Yes?'

'Lance?'

Her usual throaty warble. Yet she sounded almost hesitant. Her unplaceable accent had turned tremulous, as if she wasn't sure what reception she'd get from him.

'Who is this?'

'Your new co-star, sweetness. I want to ...' Then she went quiet. There was a slight hiss on the line, underneath her voice. He wondered how close she was.

'You wanted to what?' He kept his voice hard. He wanted to sound unperturbed. He was pleased with how steady and hostile he was being.

'I wanted to check with you, that all of this hullaballoo wasn't too much of a shock. I want to know that ... you're OK with me joining your show.'

He snorted. 'I don't get much choice in the matter, do I?'

Inside he was thinking: I'm actually speaking to her. This is really her.

'Oh, Lance.' She sighed. A long hiss. 'I hope ... we can work together on this.'

'Hm.' He was unimpressed.

Now she was trying a different tack. 'Your mother would be so proud of you.' She sounded more confident. 'I just know it. Look at you. So handsome. So successful. A big, popular show of your own ... pushing the boundaries ...'

'I know what my mother would think, thanks, Karla,' he snapped. 'I don't need you to tell me.'

'Of course, sweetness. You're right. You were very close to her. I'm sure she's looking down from heaven in complete approval. And I'm certain that she'll be delighted that fate has brought us together to work on the same wonderful show.'

He bit his tongue for a moment. Then: 'Why are you here, Karla? Really?'

She gave a gruff chuckle. A tarry wheeze bubbling in her throat. 'Honestly? Well, I need the money. My residuals are drying up.'

'I see.'

'It's as simple as that.'

He sat back on his couch. And listened to the quiet hiss again. 'It's slumming it a bit, though, isn't it? A poxy late night soap opera. You're a film actress. A movie star.'

'Used to be. But you flatter me. I'm nothing that special. Just your average jobbing vamp.'

'Mm.' He refused to be amused by her.

'So ... Can we? Can we agree to get on? To work together for the greater good and have a pleasant time?'

The last time Lance had seen this woman had been at his mother's funeral. He was a kid. Karla had taken over all of the arrangements. Lance could remember broiling with pent-up rage through all the proceedings. Standing on the sidelines, dressed like a dummy in clothes that felt stiff and too grown-up. Clenching his hot fists, glaring through his fringe at everyone. Then, eventually, when they were alone at the end of the day, he had screamed his frustrations at the flustered Karla. A banshee wail of grief that had frightened them both. You killed her. It was you. All of it was your fault.

And how had he known that? What adolescent intuition had forced him to that terrifying conclusion?

If Lance was honest with himself, he didn't really know any more. The truth of it had settled and silted down into his bones over the years: Karla was solely responsible for the tragedy. No question about it, no doubts. He was sure of it and because of that he hated her guts. His mother was dead and Karla was still swanning about in the world. He hated her now as much as he had that night of the funeral, thirty years ago, when she had tried to comfort him - purring, murmuring, pressing his head to her bosom - pillowing him with unctuous, surrogate love. He still held himself separate and hard: keeping his hatred within.

'Lance?' she prompted.

When he spoke he sounded weary. He knew she would hear that in his voice. 'We'll have to work together, won't we? The decision's been made. I'm not leaving. There's no choice, now.'

'That's true,' she said. 'But I'd like to think that we could get along as friends, as well as colleagues. There's an awful lot of history between us, Lance.'

He was silent at that. Biting his lip. Not trusting himself to reply.

'Look,' she said. 'Sleep on it, sweetness. I just want you to know that I am delighted. I'm pleased that we're going to be seeing a lot more of each other. I've always been very fond of you, you know. No matter how you talked to me or about me. No matter how much you seemed to despise me. Right from you being a little tiny boy. I've always shared in a little bit of your mother's love. We're connected by that.'

Lance swallowed dryly.

She went on, wrapping up the call. 'So I'll see you on Monday, at work. There's a photocall in the morning. They want us together. OK?'

He struggled to speak. 'OK,' he said.

The line went dead.

NINETEEN

Kevin the tame porter gently took the mobile from her and closed its flap. He looked at her expectantly. 'I take it that went rather well.'

Karla pulled a face. She wandered over to her picture window and gazed at the redeveloped wharfs of Castlefield, all lit up for the evening. 'I have an inkling it did,' she purred. 'I might have mollified him a bit.'

Kevin the porter was perplexed. 'Why on earth would he need mollifying? I don't understand.'

Karla smiled. 'He's an artist, Kevin. He's temperamental. Besides, he holds me responsible for his mother's death. He always has. And I've always known that.'

The porter's eyes were gleaming at this. 'Were you? Responsible?'

Karla felt her face twitch and then sag. Then she asserted self-control: Kevin might well be in thrall to her, but she still had to keep up her act. 'Of course I wasn't. What do you think I am? Lance thinks he knows everything. He's always been like that. But he hasn't a clue. He doesn't know what it was like back then.'

The porter nodded dumbly and knew that he shouldn't ask anything else. Not for now. He knew there was only so much he could get out of her. He would just have to take titbits as they came, and feel grateful for them. It wouldn't do to push her too far. For now, he had to feel privileged just to be here; that she had let him come this close.

The phone vibrated twice in his sweating palm. 'Text message,' he said, and smiled at her.

As she took it from him she was reflecting that she hadn't done badly today in the taking-people-over-stakes. She'd always had a knack for that. Just 24 hours and all her life had changed around completely. All sorts of fabulously sinister things were in train and she was having goose-fleshy bumps of nostalgia at the very thought.

She knew that this was all down to the intercession of the Brethren. She knew it was They who had brought about these sudden upturns in her fortunes and she was glad. She knew that their powers were boundless. The Brethren had fingers in a surprising number of pies.

This text message had to be from them. When she clicked it on the screen she was reassured to see their distinctive Gothic font:

Excellent progress, daughter. The Brethren advise that U rest well over the coming weekend and prepare yourself for the rigours of your first week back in harness. We will B in touch with further instructions.

They were always solicitous. They always made her feel special. The Chosen One and all that. Karla was obscurely chuffed by that treatment. They'd been a bit quiet for a few years and she'd wondered if they had forgotten all about her. Hey! Remember me? You've got a willing servant in Cricklewood! And she'd found herself, during those wilderness years of the convention circuit and appearances on daytime quiz shows, craving the attentions and flattery that the Brethren had always given her. She had started to assume that other, younger, more useful agents had come along.

But they were loyal, she had found. They had bided their time. Waited to deploy her again. Struck when the iron was hot. Now she was in her prime.

Karla was thrilled by all of this.

The Brethren knew what they were doing. They had been marshalling and instructing the likes of her for decades; for centuries. She didn't really know who they were or what they individually did in their daylight hours, but she had every confidence in them. She was their daughter and she would do their bidding without question.

But no one told Karla when to take it easy. It was all very well for them to text her, saying rest up over the weekend. But she was all fraught now, all keyed up. Ready for action. As she erased their message she was even bridling slightly. All these years without them, she was damned if they were coming back and telling her what to do every minute of the day. She was used to looking after herself.

'You seem cross,' Kevin the porter noted, fiddling with his golden buttons.

She shrugged him away. Made him pour her a drink. Crème de menthe.

'I can't keep you here forever, Kevin,' she said, settling into a high-backed chair. It was like a throne and the fabric was warm on her bare back. 'I mean, it's very nice having you jump at my every word, but you must have other duties to perform, for the other guests.'

'The management have placed me entirely at your disposal.'

Have they indeed? She couldn't help beaming at this. 'Pour yourself one,' she said. She watched him unsurely sip his drink. She nodded for him to sit on the end of the bed. She let the awkward silence settle between them.

'Do you have family, Kevin? A girlfriend?'

The atmosphere in the room was cloying; snarled and snagged like cobwebs. He coughed on the fumey drink.

'Married. Two kids, three and eighteen months. Boy and a girl.'

'Family man,' she smiled, clunking the ice in her green glass. 'Nice.'

'And you?'

She stared at him. For a moment he seemed almost insolent. Sitting there on her huge bed, mussing it up. Asking her personal questions. But there was a guilelessness about him. She had to remind herself: this man was in thrall to her. He couldn't do her harm. Her own powers were augmented by the forceful wills of the combined Brethren. Nothing could touch her now.

Yet her voice came out choked and harsh. 'No, Kevin. I have no family. I've no one at all.' She put a hand up to her face and covered her eyes. She felt her lashes scraping on the crêpey flesh of her palm and she heard the rustle of Kevin getting off the end of the bed and coming over to her, in one smooth movement.

'But anyone can see,' he was saying gruffly, 'Anyone can see that you deserve to have people devoted to you.' He was all concern. He was anguished with concern, she could tell. 'I am devoted to you. You know that, mistress. And others will be.'

Now he was kneeling in the thick pile of the carpet. She took her hand away from her face and looked down at him. His face was pale and earnest, and his eyes were shining a startling blue. She liked the way his eyebrows were so thick and dark, arching up into his brow. Incredulous that she could think herself alone.

'Don't mind me,' she said sadly. 'I'm apt to get like this, Friday nights.'

TWENTY

Sometimes Colin wondered why he bothered coming to Slag! bar on his nights off. It was like being in work all the time. Like all his life revolved around this part of Canal Street: like he could never get away.

The place was filling up. The nighttime drinking crowd were here in earnest. They bustled and shoved at the bars on each level and they hustled and hurried up the open plan stairs.

You had to go somewhere on your nights off, he told himself. You had to go out.

He met Raf and Vicki at the long, shiny bar, where they were already ordering shots of schnapps and looking quite excitable. They had both dashed home from their comics shop at tea time - Vicki to West Didsbury, Raf to Rusholme - and then they had dressed up. Raf was in an extraordinary suit made of some sheeny, cerise stuff, his shirt cuffs falling over his hands. Vicki was wearing a high-necked cashmere pullover, and Colin was surprised to see that it didn't have any kind of design on the front.

'We've both made a stupendous effort,' Vicki said in her rasping voice. Colin saw that she was eyeing his own outfit. He was in just another tight t-shirt. It was the same as his work one, except it didn't say 'Slag!' on the front. He stared back at Vicki until she looked away. He knew she didn't like him, and was at a loss to know why. Sometimes he thought she was downright spiteful. It wasn't even like he'd ever been nasty to her, or said anything out of turn. She had just made her mind up to treat him like a twat. He was surprised she had even agreed to come on the same night out.

Raf was always oblivious to the tensions between his two best friends. When Vicki had one of her digs at Colin, and Colin bit his lip and refused to be drawn into a barney, Raf would gaze away into the distance. Even if Colin snapped back and the two of them ended up rowing, he wouldn't be pulled into it. Raf liked to think his pals got along with each other like they got on with him: easily and smoothly and with him serene, at the centre of their attention. Any discontent and he switched off. Somehow he made this seem like exquisite good manners.

'We got you one of these,' Raf said and passed Colin a tiny plastic shot glass. Colin would have preferred a pint of lager. These plastic pots put him in mind of medication: Night Nurse or something. He gulped it down.

Raf leaned in and whispered: 'She was on the tea-time news. Did you see it?'

Colin nodded and smiled, a bit disconcerted by that rapt look on Raf's face. It was exactly how he'd been at the Birmingham convention. That's how all the Karla fans at Slashcon had been, and Colin had imagined himself in a hotel full of zombies. Zombies who filled their days and nights with amateur erotica and wistful dreams about people off the telly.

'I watched it with my gran,' Colin said.

Now's when I could tell them, Colin thought. I could tell them what Gran had said. When she was shouting at the telly and squawking at the pictures of Karla on the box. Before she bolted out of the flat to call on Effie. I could floor them both this time. I could knock their socks off if I told them both: my gran knew Karla Sorenson. Years ago, when they were kids. When they grew up in Salford together. What would Raf and Vicki say to that? When they hear that I've got another connection, another route into your precious goddess.

Yet he held off. For now he would keep schtum. It was an admirable display of restraint from Colin, he thought, and he congratulated himself warmly and silently. Usually he had this urgent need to unburden himself of secrets in front of Raf: all his messiest, most treasured secrets, for Raf to listen to, to turn over, to make of them what he willed.

Colin was glowing and mulling this over and realised that Raf and Vicki were rabbiting on between themselves. Vicki was asking, 'Do you think you'll start writing

FanFiction based on Menswear, Raf? To keep your website up-to-date?'

He pursed his lips. 'I think I'll have to.' Then he was leading them out of the heaving bar area and up the steps to the rooftop garden. Colin followed in his wake, and he kept having to nod to punters, who recognised him from behind the bar. Or maybe they just half-recognised him, and couldn't remember where from. He felt weirdly out of his context and like no one would ever remember him for just himself. He sighed and looked down at the open-plan staircase, thinking: I was mopping these stairs spotless, just this morning. And now everyone's treading all over them: muckying everything up.

The lamps and the heaters were burning and sizzling out on the terrace. The space was only half-full and, as they leaned on the balcony, over the potted shrubs, it was a bit like being on the prow of a cruise liner. They took in the view of the streets along the canal: the surging mass of people bobbing along in every direction.

Vicki was rasping away and Colin gritted his teeth at the sound of her voice. 'I feel like we are about to touch greatness. I can just sense it. Can you guys?' She gave an elaborate shudder and gazed out at the spotlights beaming beer adverts onto the low-hanging clouds. 'It's like we're about to come into contact with something ... bigger, and much more fantastic than ourselves.'

Raf raised his eyebrows like he couldn't imagine anything at all, bigger and more fantastic than himself. Colin pulled a face. 'What's that you're on about, love?'

'Vicki has got highly-developed psychic abilities,' Raf reprimanded him. 'I've learned to trust in her intuition.'

Colin sighed. 'You're only on about Lance. He's just the bloke who lives next door to the bar.' He nodded at the fire escape leading up to Lance's pad. They all looked. The blinds were drawn all the way across the tall windows. There was only a faint suggestion of light and life within. A tantalising sheen of light, Colin thought. He wondered what Lance was up to. And what state he was in by now. Colin sighed. 'He's just some bloke off the telly. That's not greatness.'

Vicki widened her eyes and blinked at them both. 'I'm not just talking about meeting people off the telly. I mean ... something more.'

Raf was rivetted. 'What, Vicki?'

She chewed her thumb. It looked dirty. 'I don't know yet. But there's something brewing here. Something stirring ... Something out of the ordinary.'

Raf peered over the balcony. 'You can probably smell the canal.' His shrewd eyes flicked to Colin. 'So. When do you think your celebrity pal will turn up?'

'I explained before, Raf. He isn't here every night. I told you, we might not even see him.'

Vicki surprised him then, by talking sense. 'We shouldn't get all our hopes up. Let's concentrate on having a nice night together.' She smiled sweetly at Colin. 'You know, I don't mind it here much. It's quite pleasant, for a gay place.'

There was a cool, slightly rancid and beery breeze slicing through the tall rooftops, ruffling the awnings and spiralling around the dark turrets of the apartment blocks clustered round the canal. Colin shivered and wondered what Vicki imagined was brewing around them; what it was she thought was stirring in the night. He was watching her narrowly and then she was whipping her jumper off over her head and messing up her hair. As she tied her pully round her waist he saw what was on the front of her t-shirt. The words: 'Lance Randall in Menswear', and a fuzzy screen-grab of him flashing his cock. Vicki pulled it tight, down over her boobs and grinned at the two of them. 'Ten quid down the Arndale. Not bad, eh?'

Colin didn't dare imagine what Lance would say.

TWENTY-ONE

Sally was less prone to dark moods than Effie. This was because Effie lived in that poky flat and Sally was up in the sky with all that light and air. Sally was sure of this. And when Effie had one of her moments of despair, Sally tended to leave her to her own devices.

Tonight, out on the ring road, at the long tables of Harry Ramsden's restaurant with all the old dears, it was Sally who was slipping into a funk. She was grateful that Effie had enough respect not to try to pull her out of it.

'You're not having much fun, are you?' was all she said. 'You're not exactly the life and soul.'

Sally just glowered. She was finding it hard to join in with the others, singing along with Alma Cogan, Frankie Vaughan. She felt a fool, sitting with these people her age, dolled up in her new black dress. Most of them were paired up and being quite exclusive, opening and closing their mouths; warbling along with their emptied plates set out in front of them. Dirty plates smeared in chip fat and tomato sauce.

And, Sally thought, I made a mistake in having those spicy pickled onions. She'd ordered this speciality side dish here before and knew full well they repeated on her. Now she had biliousness to add to her list of woes. But she knew her trapped wind was just a symptom of something deeper, and worse.

These people around her embarrassed her. She felt daft for thinking this would have been a good night out. She felt silly in advance, thinking of how she'd be telling Colin, later, that they'd had a lovely time. Even the food hadn't been top-notch. They must give the substandard fish to block-bookings, she thought: all the black bits, all the soggy batter.

She was looking at Effie and the cronies through Karla Sorenson's eyes. That's what she realised. She was wolfing down pickles that made her eyes water while everyone sang with Peggy Lee and she was wondering bitterly what

Karla would make of this lot. Karla, who had managed to escape from her own generation. Karla, thinking that she, Sally, was done up too flashy, too cheap.

'Are you having a pudding?' Effie asked her. She watched her friend crunching the last of the pickles and dabbing her fingers on a paper napkin. Sally shook her head quickly. 'That's not like you, either.'

Thankfully the music had subsided as everyone set about deciding on their sweets. Besides Effie, Sally hadn't talked to anyone tonight. Usually there was a bit of backchat, a bit of banter. Maybe some harmless flirting with the likes of that Trevor. But Trevor looked proper thick with his skinny wife tonight. He was all brushed up in a navy blazer, on best behaviour. Talking his wife into a knickerbocker glory.

'Do you ever wish you had a regular fella, Effie?' she asked, suppressing a small belch.

Effie's lips pursed. 'I do not. I've tried that once and I wasn't overly keen.'

This surprised Sally. 'When was this? Who was it?'

Effie sighed. Self-disclosure. This was the price of drawing Sally out tonight. 'It was years ago. He was the son of my mother's best friend. They set us up. He was a big soft thing who spent his time putting model warships together. A bit simple.'

'I take it it didn't last long.'

Effie shrugged. 'Almost six years. We all went to Mass together, as a foursome. And into town on a Saturday afternoon. Mam and Mrs Barnet were good neighbours for years, so I had to tag along, and so did this great gallumphing lad. Daniel. When Mrs Barnet passed away it fizzled out. Daniel wouldn't leave the house. I think he went funny. Mam didn't think I ought to go round anymore, not even to check on him. Yet she had been the one pushing us together. Trying to get me off her hands. When he went a bit daft and you didn't see him out and about and his net curtains were looking dirty and shabby, well, then she nipped it in the bud. She called the Social Services on him.'

Sally was staring at her friend. She had never heard any of this before.

'They put him away in the end. Led him out into the street. He was in his pyjamas and they were too small for him. We went out to look and I didn't know whether to wave or what. He had all of this grey hair poking out through the gaps in his pyjama top. He looked really startled, standing in the daylight, out in the street.'

'Well,' said Sally. 'That story's really cheered me up.' Then she touched Effie's hand gently. 'Sorry. But that's an awful story. How old were you?'

'I was nearly forty when they led him away,' Effie said. The singing was starting up again. 'It was my last proper chance, really. That's what I realised, a long time after.' Sally poured them both another dribble of tea. 'He was my first and my last.'

'Were you intimate together?'

'Just a bit. He was ever so careful with me. Scared he would damage me. I remember his hands had all these scars from his modelling knife. And dried bits of that flaky Airfix glue.'

'Effie,' Sally said, 'I'm sorry.'

'What's to be sorry about? It mightn't have been the romance of the century, but it was my little bit of excitement. It was mine.' Her mouth twitched. She smiled. 'I haven't lived much, have I?'

Sally laughed. 'Who has, really? How do you measure these things?' Sally was wondering: just how much have I lived? Can I really say I've had more excitement than Effie has? More chances?

'I'll tell you who you can measure against,' Effie said. 'And none of us have really lived, compared to the life she's had.'

Sally knew what she was going to say. 'Karla.' The word made her shiver. That name was the one behind all her gloom and dread tonight. It was that name that had put her

119

out of sorts.

'She must have lived enough for all of us,' Effie said. 'She's had all of our lives and more to spare.'

Sally said, 'I would like to see her again. Just once. Just to see what she's like now. After everything. And to see if that's true. See how much life she's really had. And what it's all done to her.'

TWENTY-TWO

Lance still hadn't spared his scripts a glance. He had tried watching telly and, even though he wasn't exactly expert with the remote control for all his digital channels, he had whizzed through what seemed like a hundred different programmes and nothing had grabbed him or diverted him for more than a couple of minutes. Now the sound was right down on a show in which six celebrities appeared to be swapping lives with six members of the UN inspectorate for weapons of mass destruction. All Lance could think was: no one asked me to take part. I'd have been good at that. In fact, it seemed like months since anyone at all had phoned, begging him to take part in a celebrity reality show. All those requests he had so graciously turned down had petered out completely. Maybe they all thought he was overexposed. Maybe everyone was sick of the sight of him. And maybe it was time he stopped gracing their screens altogether. Even late night TV had seen enough of him.

He shuffled back to his kitchen to lug out a second bottle of Montepulciano D'Abruzzo. He liked saying the name to himself, savouring the clipped consonants as he jiggled about in his striped sleeping pants, his bare feet on the stone floor. He had to wrestle with the elegant, wholly impractical bottle opener.

Exactly as the cork went plunk, there came a knock at his french windows. He froze, almost dropped the bottle and his heart palpitations started up. He imagined edging up to the glass doors and hissing querulously like an old woman: 'Who is it?' He coughed, ready to ask in a loud, hopefully intimidating voice. But someone outside, banging again on the panes, beat him to it.

'Lance! It's me! Let us in!'

He crouched down and did a kind of commando scramble through his own front room, barking his shins on the coffee table. There was one looming silhouette on the window: darker where its forehead and palms were pressed on the glass. Behind, two indistinct shapes - one tall and slender, the other much shorter - were hanging about like spectres.

'It's me! Colin! Open up, Lance. We're a bit worried about you!'

Worried about him? For a moment he couldn't even make sense of what was being said. No one worried about him. There was no one left around to even do such a thing.

'Who is it, did you say?' he asked, and his voice didn't come out as terse and confident as he'd wanted it to be.

'Colin! From Slag!'

He remembered. 'What do you want?'

'We were waiting for you next door, in the bar tonight. We thought you'd come out for a drink. I've got two friends ...'

Colin's voice was all breathy and gabbling. Lance couldn't keep up. Well, at least it wasn't anyone threatening and dangerous. Just that little lad from next door. He'd seen him this morning. Colin had served him with his first drink of the day. That seemed like months ago now. Even then Colin had been trying to blag his way inside Lance's apartment, angling for an invite up here. Lance couldn't really understand why. And now here he was. But in Lance's mind Colin was associated with that first, crisp twist of gin and morning consolation.

'Who have you got with you?' Even to himself Lance sounded paranoid and mad. I've got a Sunset Boulevard default setting, he thought, amazed.

'Two pals,' Colin hissed. 'They were desperate to meet you. I wouldn't have knocked otherwise. But they're both colossal fans of yours.'

Fans? Lance swallowed. He wiped his mouth with the back of his hand, just imagining the inky lipstick he'd be wearing from the wine. He couldn't let fans in when all he had on were his old housepants. He'd be making himself far too vulnerable and available. He looked down at his bare chest. His nipples had gone hard as football studs. Fans. Coming to see him.

He went whirling back to the settee to fetch his dressing gown. 'Hang on, Colin,' he said. 'I'll let you in.'

TWENTY-THREE

The hotel management had been kind enough to ask if she wanted a private room for dinner. They could sort something out, themed in her honour if she liked: something Gothic and sepulchral. They liked a creative challenge at the Prince Albert and assumed she wished to be secure from prying eyes. Karla had already said that she wouldn't eat alone in her suite. She had never liked doing that. It seemed too much like being in hospital, or a care home, and made her think of sitting up with a tray on metal legs. Stains down her nightie.

No, tonight she wanted to be downstairs. She wanted to be swish and aloof and maybe mysterious. She wanted to dine in public and let them all look at her. Let them get an eyeful of who was back in town.

So that was how the resplendent, servile Kevin came to be leading the voluptuous, silver-haired vampire lady across the foyer. Shoulders back, bust thrust straight out, drawing stares from fellow guests at eleven o'clock. She was eating late, as was her habit. She took tiny, painful steps to the main dining room. She paused in the doorway and let the maitre d' go into a kerfuffle of praise; let him busybody and fuss and waft her with the huge, handwritten menu to the best table in the place, up on a kind of podium. Everything was accomplished with a flourish. Kevin even looked theatrically dejected when she sent him off for a break. She could see how pained he was to leave her and that gratified her.

All the crockery, glass and cutlery was pleasingly chunky and spotless. The tablecloth was starchy and brilliant under her trembling fingers. She examined it all: devoting special attention to the exotic frou-frou of the table's centrepiece: some ridiculous arrangement of whorled and filigreed blooms, all dewy hoods and throbbing tongues. She took in everything through a pair of tiny, jewelled spectacles she then placed back in her evening bag, and she deliberately ignored the other diners. She knew they were looking. There were whispers from young and old alike. The heads of the weekend visitors, the well-to-do, the business class, all were bobbing up like meerkats. There was a Mexican wave of discreet interest in her presence. She even heard her name whispered and those quiet voices were molten on the air: a mist of speculation that rose above the tablecloths and up to her podium. Karla lowered her glance, decorously studying the menu.

Something light. Sole Veronique. The waiter shot over to her side and craned down to hear her whisper. She sat back to wait, and sipped cool white wine and dragged on one of her beloved black Russian Sobranies. The lilac smoke scrolled about her and she smiled to herself over her choice of dish. Once she'd had a psychotherapist - years ago, when she was on the Continent, on location for some drossy horror flick - and he had divined that she was a keen cook. Which she was, in those days. He had snapped at her: 'Tell me, what is the distinguishing feature of the dish known as Sole Veronique?' She hadn't known what he was on about. He was a bald little man, a proper ugly brute with a beard like a shaving brush. 'It is grapes!' he had barked triumphantly. 'The distinguishing feature of Sole Veronique is that it contains grapes!' Karla had been none the wiser as to how that fact was meant to help with her therapy. In the end, that man had advised her to sit in a dark, silent cupboard for an hour each day and mew like a cat. She would find a solution to all her tensions that way. And he'd put her on the strongest drugs she'd ever necked in all her life.

Karla had watched a video of that Romanian horror film only recently, (English title: 'Lick Me Out Slowly, Lick Me Out Quick') and, for the first time, she'd had confirmed what she'd solemnly suspected at the time: the viewer could tell a mile off that here was a woman living solely off fish and antidepressants. A woman who sat in a cupboard and miaowed like a cat. I've had the most ridiculous career, she thought, in both cinema and psychotherapy.

Actually, the film hadn't been all that bad. She wondered if, twenty years after these episodes of Menswear she was committing herself to had aired, they would hold up as well. She wondered if there would be special DVD boxed sets of them. If they would become Collectible or Cultish.

Karla had never had any idea of how her projects would turn out. It was the same with all of them. It was like playing the Wheel of Fortune, with divisions marked 'Lost Classic,' 'Camp Turkey', 'Kitsch Arthouse', 'Porno Trash', 'Highbrow Gorefest' and 'Nightmare Twatfest.' And there was no way of telling which way it would turn. She was always astonished at the result: what distinguished a work of art from ludicrous, forgettable tat. As far as she could make out, nothing did. It just depended on who liked it; who could find something to say about the work. She was at the mercy of pundits in the end. Pundits and time. All she could do was her same old shtick. That never changed.

At last the waiter reappeared with her dinner under a silver salver. She was pleased to put thoughts of her oeuvre to the back of her mind and concentrate on the sight of the blue-green fish suddenly revealed on the plate before her. It was languid in a thick white sauce: a glittering state of repose. The eyes of the fish had the same milky opacity as the grapes strewn about it.

It didn't look like any Sole Veronique she'd ever had before, but she was ravenous, and didn't like kicking up a fuss in restaurants. Before picking up her knife and fork she had a glance around, to see that the other diners weren't looking anymore. They weren't. They'd had their fill of celebrity.

How to tackle this monster?

She hated being given things with faces still on. It looked like it had been asphyxiated none too carefully. Its thick blue lips were very disturbing. The fins and gills and the perfect sequins of its scales looked oily, uncooked, fresh from the sea.

What the hell had they given her?

Its milky eye juddered and puckered and flinched. It was suddenly blazing at her, orange and black. She knew it was staring right into her. Out flopped a fat, bloody tongue from between those swollen lips, and the fish licked some of the sauce thoughtfully. Then it cleared its throat.

Karla dropped knife and fork with a dreadful clatter. The fish was trying to shimmy around in its pool of grapey sauce and when it could look her in the eyes again, it started to speak in a fluting, accusing tone:

'So, you're back in Manchester, are you? Well, we know exactly what you're up to. We know why you're really here. You devil woman. You should never have come back.'

Karla couldn't breathe.

'You'd better keep your hands off that boy!' the fish shrieked. 'You leave him be, Karla Sorenson! Just you leave my boy alone!'

With that, the fish had exhausted itself. It slumped back down dead onto the plate.

TWENTY-FOUR

Vicki was in awe. Though she hated letting her bluff tough façade drop in front of the hated Colin, her reaction for the first hour or so inside Lance's rooftop pad was simple, earnest, fan-girl awe. And she was secretly impressed with how cool Colin was being. He was treating Lance like he was just another person: as if he was, in fact, just a friend of his. Colin was in the kitchen, making thick, strong coffee and talking to their host. Vicki perched herself on the white settee alongside Raf. Neither of them had said anything other than a quiet 'hello' when Colin had introduced them to the drunk and mostly-naked Lance. Lance had let them in and he had looked rattled, wrecked, nervy, paranoid. The flat was dark and musty-smelling. It was the unaired den of some creature too anxious to forage.

Raf's stock of cool had sunk just as Colin's had risen. Vicki was obscurely disappointed in her best friend. He was saying thank you for the smoking coffee Colin poured and passed him. Vicki had never seen Raf so polite and subdued: sitting there with his knees clenched together. Vicki was feeling supremely conscious of her screen-grab Lance Randall t-shirt. It felt rude somehow: bad taste to be flaunting pirate merchandise in the great man's own abode.

The man himself was leaning against his breakfast bar. He'd flung his dressing gown back off and was cradling a miniature coffee cup against his bare chest. There was dark stubble on his face and his mouth was set in a grim line. There was a confused look in his eyes.

'So ... I don't understand,' he was saying. 'What are you kids doing here?'

Colin was having a good look around his kitchen. Figuring out what the various gadgets were for. 'It was really boring in Slag! Just the same old faces doing all the same old things, and I remembered suddenly how you'd said I should pop in and see your apartment sometime soon. And we were a bit worried about you, because of how you were first thing this morning. Because you didn't seem all that chuffed about the news and everything...' Colin realised he was gabbling.

'What news?' Lance croaked.

'About Karla!' Colin laughed. 'Karla Sorenson. You were taking it badly this morning. Is that why you're drinking? Is that why you've locked yourself up in here? Is it all that bad?'

Lance slapped both palms on the counter: a deliberate, devil-may-care, dead drunk gesture. He spoke as if his tongue had swollen up. 'I don't care. They can put who they want in the show. It's got nothing to do with me. I don't get any say in the matter apparently.'

Vicki leaned in to Raf and hissed, 'God, he's taking it worse than we thought.' Raf shushed her and pretended to concentrate on the TV guide in front of them.

'I think you could do with more coffee, Lance,' Colin said quietly. 'It doesn't do to get ... this despondent.' Colin was conscious of Lance showing himself in a bad light in front of Raf and Vicki. They'd be lapping this whole scene up. Now Colin wished he hadn't let them talk him into bringing them here. He felt bad for Lance, like he was making fun of him and taking a lend of his good nature. This was at the forefront of his thoughts. At the back - and thrumming along excitedly - were his thoughts to do with being up here at last: up in Lance's world, where the expensive blinds were drawn against the moon and the overspill of city centre light. The faces of his friends were basked in orange and blue. Life up here was taking on a grainy tinge, and a dramatic, filmlike quality and Colin felt like he had stepped into his proper context at last. There was a sensation of impending calamity, an undercurrent of concern, but all of this was hand in hand with his pleasure in looking after Lance. Looking at those square, broad, naked shoulders with their collarbones sticking out, he just wanted to go over and give him a cuddle. Yet the presence of his friends put him off. He couldn't do anything like that with those two there. They were like two schoolkids on that settee. It was like they were trying hard not to giggle at Lance's plight.

Lance held up his cup for more coffee. When Colin poured it, he stared down like he didn't know what he was being given. He sighed and said, 'I have to do a photo shoot for the Press. Monday morning. First thing. With her.'

Colin put the pot down and looked at him. Their eyes met. Lance took a moment to focus and then looked away.

'With her?' Colin asked.

'With La Sorenson herself. Pictures of me and her. Me welcoming her to my show. Welcoming her to the wonderful world of Menswear.' It was like he was about to cry. Colin thought that would be a bad idea.

'That's fantastic.' Raf came to life all of a sudden. He was sitting bolt upright and, for the first time, he was looking straight at them through the murky, film-stock air.

'Is it?' Lance said thickly.

'You and Karla together! It'll be great!'

Colin willed Raf to shut up. Beside Raf, Vicki was just looking dopey.

'Yes, well,' Lance croaked. 'I've got to smile and grin and point at her knockers or something.'

Then Vicki was seizing up the TV listings magazine. 'Hey - it's on. It's on right now. We're going to miss it. Don't you watch it?'

'Watch what?' Lance sounded weary.

'Menswear,' she rasped exasperatedly. 'Your own show. It's midnight, Mr Randall. Don't you ever watch yourself?'

They all looked at their host. 'Never,' he said.

'Can we?' Vicki asked. 'It would be such an honour.' She made a grab for the remote control and started waving it at the blank screen of the television. Colin felt like stabbing her.

Lance waved his hand unsteadily. 'Sure. Why don't you kids just make yourselves at home?' He pushed himself away from the breakfast bar. He reeled slightly, and Colin jumped forward to catch him. 'I'm going to the bog,' he announced, and slipped away.

At that, the telly burst into colour and noisy life. The blaze of static raised the hairs on Colin's nape. Vicki and Raf were agog: leaning forward as the show began with the familiar cheesy, loungy funk of the theme. Colin watched them watching the sequence of splashy graphics that showed the grinning heads of the major characters. He heaved a sigh. No way were his friends this keen on watching the programme. It was an act.

The last star credited in the opening montage was Lance himself. He was pristine in a black suit and lilac cravat. He winked at the audience at home: confident, salacious, and very well-built.

'Just imagine when Karla's in it,' Raf hissed. It was very nearly a squeal. He was squeezing his fingers into Vicki's pale forearm.

'We'll have to ask him,' Vicki said, 'how long the telly's behind. How many weeks it'll be, until it gets good.'

Colin put down his coffee cup and left them to it. He decided he had to see how Lance was doing.

TWENTY-FIVE

The ladies had decamped. They managed to get a bit tiddly on Pernod and black at the fish restaurant as they watched the rest of their party leave. By the end they weren't quite part of that group at all. All their supposed pals, the senior citizens, were slipping out of the place satiated on chips and batter cooked to that unique and secret recipe. They seemed pleased with their night out. It was just enough: they'd had a bit to eat and they had sang their songs and they had lapped up the good company and nostalgia.

Sally was still fending off her malaise. She was watching the sulky brute of a boy who was serving her drinks at the bar. Young enough to be her grandson: tall and sucking in his cheeks so the bones showed up; making his lips all red and flashing his dark eyes about. He was willing them to go home so he could finish his shift.

Instead he's got us, she thought. Us sitting perched on padded high stools, laughing at the framed prints of the original proprietor of the fish restaurant chain: an altogether sinister old bloke in a pinny and a straw hat. The photos went back years. They showed him and his many sons at work in the very first shop and in little vans parked on cobbled streets. Dispensing carefully-wrapped, hot newspaper parcels to women in headscarfs, men in caps. Children with scabby legs and their socks rolled down, playing in the streets.

'That was us, back then,' Effie said, with a sudden clarity. 'That's how we were. When fish and chips on a Friday were like a treat.'

Sally rolled her eyes at this and then squinched them up, gulping down the last of her Pernod. The aniseedy taste was like being on holiday. Continental. 'Listen to you. Like someone off a documentary. Going on.'

Effie flashed back. 'You've always known how to live, haven't you? How to be modern. You've always moved with the times.'

Sally could see that Effie was getting her back up. She

132

was about to say so, in those exact words, but thought better of it. Effie could be very conscious of her dowager's hump.

'Can I have your glasses now, ladies?' said the sulky bar boy and they had to relinquish them. With the Pernod, pickles and chip grease inside her, Sally felt all insulated, syrupy and thick.

They made their way out, onto the sodium-lit tarmac by the ring-road, where the only noise was motorway traffic.

'Well, I never wanted to modernize,' Effie said. 'I never wanted to live right up in the sky, however many mod-cons they chucked at me. My heart bled when they ripped up those terraces, like the one where you used to live. I think they've been daft. Changing everything they can ...'

Stuck out here, waiting to cross the big road, dallying before they could brave the four lanes of city traffic, Sally could see that her friend had a point. This was a weird place now, this part of town: to their left, the road out to Eccles and, beyond that, Liverpool. And here it was McDonalds and a Travel Lodge and Sainsburys and a casino: their rooftops picked out with neon trim. To their right, the four lanes of traffic swept under the old red bricks of the viaduct. Beyond that they could see the futuristic plate glass of new apartments. Their soft and luxurious lighting hemmed in by old warehouses done up at scandalous prices. And, ahead, the road into the centre of Manchester. The road they'd have to take before veering off towards Salford and home.

They were two relics, clumping along in their good winter coats, alone together on Friday night. Clutching each other's arms, the wind stinging their ears. The smart cars shushed by them with a noise like silk being ripped. Occasionally one would have all its windows slid down, and they would hear that very aggressive thudding dance music that seemed to be everywhere these days.

The lights went green and, linking arms, the two ladies scuttled over the four lanes, feeling dwarfed by everything.

The huge, automatic billboards showed naked young bodies and it was hard to say what they were advertising with their witty, cryptic slogans.

They had to walk along the back of the TV studios. The office block loomed above them. There, everything was produced and filmed; deep inside that tall building surmounted by the red glowing sign. Satellite dishes and antennae on that roof were beaming out programmes to everyone in the country.

It was like being in the very centre of the world. That was how they felt when they went inside that building once, on a visit. They had applied for and received studio audience tickets for that show in which ordinary members of the public became a famous face for one day. 'Wasn't it just like being in the middle of everything? Right here at home?' Sally asked. 'Like all the world was revolving around us while we were there.'

'It was,' Effie said, though she hadn't much enjoyed watching the show. She found it slow and confusing and hadn't known who people were pretending to be. She liked a proper drama, with real people in. She was very keen on murder programmes, especially those with a female detective. One who had to prove herself in a tough man's world.

As they took the path along the high, secretive walls of the studios, there were late night trains groaning and rattling over the viaducts and bridges. 'Everything crisscrossing,' Effie said. She knew they were both talking because the dark and quiet streets were disconcerting. 'Zipping about and all busy, even at this time...'

'There's that hotel,' Sally said thoughtfully, nodding across the road. 'Where all the big stars stay, when they're appearing in a TV show.' The two of them had gone there for tea and cakes that day of their visit to the studios. They'd hoped to see some celebrities and they hadn't struck lucky. They'd both read about that American pop star who'd held an impromptu concert in the bar. They imagined him in his spangly shirt, singing at the piano, all sweaty-faced and egged-on by drinkers. Alas, they'd seen nothing so exciting, but they'd been impressed by the splendour of the Prince Albert.

'I wonder if that's where Karla's staying,' said Sally. 'I bet you it is. They'd put that one in the best place.'

Effie looked at her. 'You said you wouldn't mind bumping into her, now she's back.'

Sally hesitated, not too sure now.

'We could pop in for a tiny nightcap,' Effie urged. 'I'm chilled through, just coming this far. And you must be frozen in that flimsy dress.'

Sally considered. The old cow would be tucked up in bed by now, even if she was in residence. Chances are, they'd never cop a glimpse of her. But it wouldn't hurt, would it? Just a little tipple in the hotel bar? It might be a pleasant finish to the night. She was all dolled up, too, and that had been wasted on the old dears at the fish restaurant.

'All right,' she told Effie. 'Don't get your hopes up, mind. And if we do see her, let me do the talking. Just you remember - she's as ordinary as the two of us. She's no one special.'

'All right,' said Effie, and they set off at a trot towards the white and pale gold of the hotel's foyer.

Sally was thinking: What am I talking about? Karla's not an ordinary person at all. She never was. Not what I'd call normal.

135

TWENTY-SIX

At first Colin was foxed by the unfamiliar geography of Lance's flat. When he turned into the dark corridor behind the kitchen he didn't have a clue where he was heading. Behind him, the raucous music and canned laughter of Menswear was blaring out on the telly's stereo sound-surround. The voices of the principal characters - bizarrely, Lance among them - piped up at his back. Colin could also hear Raf and Vicki talking away. They weren't really concentrating on the show. They had started talking in earnest, now that Lance and Colin were out of the way. No longer on best behaviour, they were gassing eagerly about the advent of Karla Sorenson.

Suddenly Colin realised that he didn't want Lance to know how doolally that pair was on Karla. He saw the potential Raf had to really hurt Lance's feelings. Colin could see that Raf could be quite vicious; his tall, elegant pal had a nasty streak right through him. He could also see that Lance was soft as muck.

There was a spill of light at the sharp corner of the hallway. 'Lance?' he called, feeling his way gently along the wall, hoping he wouldn't knock into anything expensive. As he inched round the bend he came face to face with Lance's shrine.

Lance was on his knees in his alcove, whispering under his breath to the glowing portrait. Everything was lit softly by cathedral candles: soft, yellow, beeswaxy. Colin was dumbstruck for a second or two, staring at this apparition in the fussy, gold-leaf frame: this benign, almost holy, glamorous studio photo of the woman. She had broad, strong cheekbones and those 1950s kind of pointed breasts. Her long, elegant fingers were clasped together.

Her calm, silvered eyes were staring out from the glass, past the bowed, bare back of the praying Lance. Colin caught his breath in his throat, because it seemed that those silver eyes were staring straight at him. Like he'd been caught sneaking up on Lance. The eyes appeared to flash a warning at him, but it must have been a trick of the candle-light. When he stared back, he saw that the eyes were lustreless and dead.

'Lance,' he tried again, and then Lance was getting up shakily and rounding on him. The heat from his body was intense. 'Are you OK?'

His host was looking furious. It was as if he had been disturbed doing something weird. Something wrong. His fists were bunched at his sides. God, he's going to punch me, Colin thought, and took a hasty step back as Lance loomed over him. Then the wall was right at his back.

'What are you doing round here?' Lance's voice was steady and low. Colin knew that he was talking like that so the others wouldn't hear him over the telly, but it also sounded sexy as hell.

'I thought you were having a funny turn,' Colin whispered.

Lance looked down at him. Colin was suddenly very conscious of their proximity. Only an inch or two between their bodies. The older man was trying to intimidate him. Colin smelled the warmth and musk coming off his skin - the smell of someone in his pyjamas all day, all interlaced with the scent of beeswax and bitter red wine.

'Worrying about me again, were you?' Lance said. 'You've been doing a lot of that.'

'Yeah...' Colin said. Oh, great, he thought. It was like he had forgotten all of his lines. Lance was playing out a scene as if he was in some fantastic TV play - beautifully lit and sexy with menace - and his broad, warm silhouette was blocking out the light, and Colin had turned stupid and silent with fright.

Lance waited and then he let out a low, bored sigh. 'OK, then. You've made your move, Colin. I knew you would.'

Colin frowned. 'What?'

Lance was looking disgusted. 'You guys are all the same. All thinking I'm the same as on the telly. Up for it with anyone. Up for it with any randy little queen who pops by. My life isn't a porno film, whatever you might think. And it isn't a sitcom, either. It's serious, actually, and really quite dull.' He was getting het up and louder. Colin could feel spittle on his face. Just a speck or two.

'Lance, I don't know what you're on about.'

'You! The same as the milkman, the script courier, even Adrian the fucking producer. You all think that I'm at it all the time! And all thinking you can just demand your own piece of me...'

'Honestly, I don't know what you're talking about.' Colin was getting fed up with being shouted at. 'This is obviously some mad frigging psychodrama of your own, Lance. I just came round to see if you were okay throwing up and then I find you worshipping a picture of some old slapper -'

The next thing he felt was a flat-handed smack, right in the face. It was like being hit by a shovel. Colin could smell something weird, like salt and vinegar crisps, just before he blacked out and slid down the alcove wall.

Within moments he was awake again and his vision had gone sparkly and silver and Lance was on his knees and trying to get him up - he thought - to start bashing him again. Colin started shouting, 'Get off! Fuck off! Get off!' but Lance was hoisting him up by his armpits and shouting back, 'I'm sorry! I'm sorry!' and they were one big tangle of limbs. Colin tried to slap him away and Lance was pulling on him and then Colin was shaking and couldn't get his balance at all. 'You shouldn't have said that about my mum,' Lance was saying. 'I had no choice. You shouldn't have said it...' Now he was crushing Colin's arms against his body with his own hot, bare arms and Colin continued to struggle, thrashing about and shouting: 'That ABSOLUTELY KNACKED you FUCKING BASTARD! I don't care WHO it is on your photo! THAT FUCKING KNACKED! I CAN'T HEAR PROPERLY NOW!'

Then, all of a sudden, he came over exhausted. He was still and he realised he was locked in Lance's grip. The world was still rocking quite a bit and the nausea had set in.

'You are all just after my body,' Lance said, very distinctly.

'What? What the fuck are you saying?'

'Aren't you? Isn't that why you came back?'

Colin blinked. The silver stars were starting to settle. His whole face felt mushy and numb. 'No, Lance. It wasn't. That's not why I came here at all.'

Slowly Lance relinquished his grip. He let Colin stand on his own two feet. Colin wavered slightly and then drew himself up properly. His red-tufted spikes of hair were flattened and his face had started to swell on one side. He glared back at Lance and the moment went on just a shade too long.

Then they were kissing each other, hard, and their teeth were clashing, noses smashing against each other's: Colin's hands on Lance's waist, Lance's hands clamped over Colin's ears.

TWENTY-SEVEN

Obviously she couldn't eat anything. Not after that.

Whether that awful Sole Veronique had been an hallucination on her part, or whether it was a full-blown manifestation of some kind, was quite beside the point.

Karla had been shaken to the core.

She sat for some time at the best table in the Prince Albert restaurant, breathing shallowly and trying to rearrange her jangling nerves. She'd had her fish dish taken away and the waiter looked most disappointed that she hadn't enjoyed it. By the looks of it, Ms Sorenson had just given it a sort of shove across the plate, splashing some of the pale sauce on the table cloth. She hadn't even touched the grapes. Now the word would go round the kitchens; Ms S. hadn't enjoyed dinner one single bit. The waiter asked if he could fetch her anything else: she waved him brusquely, tremblingly away.

Then she drank a whole bottle of the pale green wine. Had anyone else in the room seen her staring goggle-eyed at the peremptory and accusatory fish? Had she cried out in shock and dismay when it had started to harangue her? She couldn't remember. But the place seemed the same, quite unperturbed, the murmur of conversation running under the sickly-sweet piano music. The conversation had flowed over and past her: the subject of her ravishing presence in the restaurant had been turned over and casually discarded in the swiftly-rushing flow of table talk.

Was she going crazy? What was happening to her? Nothing like this had happened to her in years. Nothing impossible or mad or reeking of the vilest sorcery had crossed her path in God knew how long. She was losing her knack, seemingly. She had no equanimity in the face of impossible things. Not anymore. She would have to get a grip. She couldn't go getting all worked up at the slightest thing. Not when she was on a mission. When everything was inching along towards culmination.

She had to be a star. She had to be at the peak of her performance. That was what the Brethren required of her.

Yet - Christ, that Sole Veronique had scared her.

At last she looked up to see that the dining room's occupants had mostly left. Only a few tables were still being used. Time for her to take her leave. She collected up her Sobranies and her wits, stuffed everything into her evening bag, and wondered where Kevin the porter had got to. She needed his stout form for support right now. Inwardly she was cursing. What was the point of having abject slaves and myrmidons to tend your whims, if they just diddled off when the mood took them?

Rather bad-naturedly Karla got up, hoisted her little bag and clip-clopped in her tortuous heels, out of the restaurant, and into the bar.

It was smoky and relatively quiet. The place was done up in some kind of naval theme, with plush blue carpets and woodwork dark and shiny as melting toffee. The brass pumps and fittings winked at her alluringly and the sticky, vividly colourful array of optics were dancing in her sights as she slouched over to the stools. She rested her elbows on the bar and felt ungainly as she sat down. She wasn't sure she hadn't heard something rip.

She clattered her knuckles and all of her heavy rings against the bar. 'Shop!' she cried, and it came out as something of a screech. 'Shop!' she tried again, and sighed and noticed that she'd drawn the attention of two elderly women sitting on the stools to her left. She'd made a show of herself and one of them was tutting. Karla shrugged and grabbed a fistful of Japanese-type snacks from the bowl in front of her.

Now the two old ladies beside her were cooing and nodding. Old hags, she thought, and looked back at the dizzying optics. 'Shop,' she said again, flatly, and feeling queasy.

Then her forearm was being grasped and held down on the bar. She screeched again, thinking she was being attacked.

It was a mottled old claw that had taken hold of her:

liver-spotted and rough as pumice-stone. She tried to yank her arm back and swung round savagely to protest.

Some horrible old woman was grinning and gurning right into her face. Karla recoiled at the stink of pickled onions.

'Karla Sorenson,' the old woman jeered. 'Well, well, lady. Just look at you. Who'd have thought you'd end up like this?'

PART THREE

FOX SOAMES WRITES

My parched tongue stirs at last.
Let these papers be disinterred from their tomb and the shackles fall from my bony wrists. Stains of rust like pollen and orange blood. But now I can gesticulate as I tell my tale.
My eyes struggle to spring open. Fused with sleep dust and grave mould. Now I can speak.
Good evening!
I speak to you from outside time.
Really.
My name has been Fox Soames. All through the twentieth century. It is a name best known for being emblazoned in silver on the sheeny covers of paperbacks. For being embossed in gold on the spines of leatherette bookclub volumes. One hundred million worldwide in hardback! A couple more millions in paper-covered editions! I was a household name! Whole families gathered to quail at my words as fathers read aloud my latest instalment. Lone readers drew closer to the source of consoling light in their darkened rooms. They all turned my pages, smoothing them out. They were all drawn inexorably across my lines, a silent word of protest on their lips as they read on and on into hundreds of nights. My readers were in the rapt, seduced, fascinated stupor of those being dragged

ineluctably into hell.

Good evening!

So imagine my not inconsiderable chagrin at being silenced and stilled for all this time. For over 40 years I produced a million words a year. I plucked them out of the air and tamed them. I hammered them out and nailed them down. My volumes were sturdy coffins buzzing with captive sentences and I delivered them proudly into the world. Great fanfare, annually. My eager audience shivered. They were addicted to my every utterance. I was sorcerer and seer. A prophet really, with a task bestowed upon me from on high.

There was a warning I had to give mankind.

That's what my millions of words represented.

That's what the skull beneath the skin was shrieking. Blatant, explicit, under the trappings of popular tale-spinning.

But readers can be very stupid, I suppose.

I met a great many of my legion of enthusiasts during the decades of my effortless supremacy. The fools. They thought I had made everything up. They thought I was indulging, along with them, in dimwitted fantasies, in vicarious thrills.

Or worse, they would take me all too literally. They thought I had actually partaken of the revolting practices I described in my novels. The dolts imagined I was advocating for all and sundry the joys of the fiendish occult practices I was in fact condemning.

Even the ones who listened, never listened properly.

So I speak to you now, from outside time, from outside space, and I am full of hope. Welcome, readers.

Good evening!

***

Here is my study.

Observe this desk, which has pursued me across the world from home to home. I find it difficult to work at any-

144

thing else. It's walnut. Take note of its freight of yellowing papers in apparently untidy stacks. Stories, articles, chapters, letters, all in various states of completion. I tap everything out on that trusty Remington. Gun-metal grey. I keep the machine oiled and serviced, clean as my army revolver - which is cocked and locked in that bottom drawer. Just in case.

The shelves lining each of these walls: look. This side, everything is mine. All 89 of my novels, in each edition, translated into every language thinkable. The remainder of shelf-space contains my reference works. Invaluable to me, in all aspects of my labours. Arcane volumes and more popular, vulgar works. All concern themselves with the occult. I make no bones about that.

Let me fill your glass. More brandy. Let us pull our armchairs up to the fire. Admire the mantlepiece. Flatter my taste. Everything here was built and fitted to my exact specifications. I am indeed a hard taskmaster where taste is concerned. Just ask my poor agent, my editor, my servants, and my dear wife, Magda. A man like me has to have things just so. This is necessary, in order to let the precious words come. So many souls are dependent on my work being completed satisfactorily. To my satisfaction. Not, as I have already hinted, for the simple purposes of entertainment. Rather, for the sake of the world.

Mind your feet. Shift yourself along a bit. You're scuffing up the circle of salt. Didn't you see it? Your powers of observation disappoint me. Here, sit within the ring of my protection. As I tell my tale, you must remain inside this circumference. It's not there for decoration.

Right. Are we comfortable?

**

Let us begin with the eating of brains.

Don't splutter so. That brandy is expensive. And don't pretend you didn't know what you were likely to hear. This evening you have strayed into the home of Fox Soames. To sit by his fireplace and to hear awful tales from the lips of the great man himself. Don't make out you didn't know it would give you the willies.

I was quite serious. My story for you this evening is concerned with an ancient and delicate procedure that both modern science and morality would declare barbaric.

But think on this. What a waste it is, that when a human body breathes its last, the precious brain - an organ miraculous in even the dullest of specimens - must also die. What a terrible misuse of material. All the lights go out suddenly, cleanly as the shutting down of the electrical grid. Blackout. And the process is irreversible. Those millions of cells - dark and shiny-moist, as dear as caviar - all die and their hard-won content, earned through the nightmarish work of day-to-day living: all of this is lost. The light is quenched.

Except.

There is a theory that those glittering cells may be salvaged and passed on to the remaining members of the tribe. Even our most brutish ancestors came to this conclusion.

You've guessed it.

My point is that those bygone hairy fellows, patrolling the frozen plains of northern Europe, were onto something after all. They weren't quite the primitive sillies modern man fancies. They lived so very close to elemental nature. They worshipped the things they felt imminently: bones, fire, earth and water. Material things they touched in their everyday business. Who amongst us can say the same thing? What, exactly, do you worship?

Perhaps not so brutish, after all.

As I discovered, when I ate - just a little, mark you - of my Great Aunt Helen's freshly-deceased organ.

Back in the 1930s.

***

She was a formidable woman, rather like a stoat. She lived

146

in a manor I was fully expecting to become accustomed to. I was her only living heir. All the branches of our distinguished family tree terminated with my good self. This was a heavy burden perhaps, for the young, trembling leaf I then was.

I would look at the glowering portraits hung in the main hall and I couldn't help wondering at the nature of our curse. All those great bald domes of skulls; the liver-spotted claws. My fiancée and I on that first night at Great Aunt Helen's stared back at those faces without much enthusiasm. We were young and feeling subtly menaced by this concentration of my forebears. My darling Magda murmured something to me to the effect that she hoped I wouldn't wind up resembling my grandfathers. They were indeed a terrible-looking lot. I shivered, as if fearful they might be earwigging on us. And their oily eyes seemed to flash in the smoky candlelight.

Magda was at her most beautiful then. Swan-necked, imperious. We were in our twenties and I was just down from Oxford. I say 'down', as the popular cliché has it, and that was just how it felt. I had slithered and descended from all that light and air and lolling around and now real life was beckoning. Here in this ancestral home everything was mouldy and fly-blown. Nothing had moved. No one had passed through the main doors in decades.

Magda had been at first a little overwhelmed in these trappings. Her upbringing was of a different order to my own. She had been rather stirred by the sight of the manor, knowing that she was destined to share it, eventually, with me. Her posture had stiffened, upon arrival, but by evening some of the gloom had crept into her. She became almost stroppy and satirical. By the time my aunt joined us for dinner Magda was quite tipsy. Bolting back large glasses of cool amber wine. Quelling her nerves and pretending she belonged.

The old lady was a shocking white. So frail, yet you knew she could lash out. There was still quite considerable force and will stored in that frame of hers.

That night the talk was cordial and general as she inquired into my education and, gently, as to my plans. She was rather shocked at my determination to pursue a career as an author. I was surprised, myself, at declaring my hopes so suddenly, so openly. It didn't do, in our world, to show one's hand so readily.

Great Aunt Helen thought my ambitions childish, and rather selfish. She wasted no time in letting me know this. 'Historically, the Soamses have had a knack for dedicating themselves to the study of the Arts. A calling, you might say.' She looked at me down her long, sharp nose. 'An almost priestly devotion that we Soamses share.'

I could sense beloved Magda growing restless and stiff at my side. She reached for the decanter once more and I could see that her movements had become blunt and jabbing. She giggled, 'Your great aunt wants you to take holy orders, Fox.'

Aunt Helen frowned. 'Not quite. I merely want to dissuade my nephew from wasting and abusing his most important gifts.'

Young fool that I was, I found myself warming to this obvious flattery.

'We will discuss this further, Fox,' my aunt promised, and raked a glance over my bride-to-be. Withering.

Then the talk drifted back to Oxford and how my rooms at St John's had been close to the main gates, their leaded panes letting in the bright light of those open skies. How I could look over the Queen's Road to the saloon bar where I met my friends at lunch time. I counted among those friends some of the more senior dons.

'Elevated company,' my Aunt raised her eyebrows, impressed, as I listed the names of my fellow scribes. 'You have been lucky to make the acquaintance of such men, Fox. These connections will stand you in good stead.'

I beamed at her, pleased that my efforts to get myself counted amongst the membership of the Smudgelings had impressed her so. 'Worming in' is what Magda generally called it. She thought me foolish for expending so much energy trying to come to the attention of Professor Reginald Tyler and the like.

'Oh, they're an awful bunch, Helen.' She was slurring now, and I saw my aunt flinch and blanch at the interruption - and the familiarity. But Magda went on. 'They sit about in that gloomy old bar, nattering on about their funny old books. Drinking the most horrible orange-coloured beer. And it's not as if they're doing anything important. They're writing stories about dragons and goblins and pixies. Children's stories! That's what they're all writing! And now Fox has caught the bug, too.'

My great aunt stilled her with a single look. 'I approve of Fox spending time with these men. For they know the power of the word. They know the magic of the word.'

I was nodding excitedly, feeling the effects of the wine myself, by now. 'That's what Professor Tyler keeps saying. To write a thing ... is to make it so.'

'Then he is a very wise man.' My aunt smiled. Not a very warm expression. 'He understands the first precept of magic.'

'Magic!' Magda laughed.

Dinner was at an end, soon after that. Out swept Great Aunt Helen, dragging the white train of her gown over the flagstones. She took the glow of my self-satisfaction with her, and both Magda and I vaguely sensed that we had disappointed her.

Then, in the middle of that night, we were woken suddenly in our damp bedroom. Magda was first on the alert, tugging at my arm.

My aunt was shrieking and ululating from her own room, down the corridor. It was an awful racket. Who'd have thought the old dame had so much breath in her?

Full of gumption and spunk and, strapping as I was at that age, I hurried down the passageway to rap upon her door.

149

'Great Aunt Helen?' I called, feeling a fool.

The shrieks had subsided into moans. I knocked again, more urgently.

'Are you unwell? Shall I call for help?' Though who there was to call out to in the middle of the Norfolk wilderness, I'm sure I didn't know.

At last her quavering tones filtered back to me. 'It is nothing. Leave me.'

And nothing was said the following morning.

Great Aunt Helen was bright and - for her - almost chatty as we picked over some decidedly rank kippers. I could see darling Magda's face screwed up in displeasure - at the quality of the fare, but also at the dirtiness of the napkins, the mess of crumbs on the tablecloth. My fiancée was hungover and not enjoying her stay so far at all.

That day - to ameliorate the atmosphere and mollify my sweetheart - we took a trip into Norwich. I had recently furnished myself with a motor-car and I was keen to get away from the darkness of the manor. I wanted the two of us to go bowling through narrow country lanes hanging with baby's breath and wild poppies. We wanted to suck in the heady, healthy aroma of the East Anglian landscape: turkeys, pigs and broccoli. Then, a few hours of watching Magda fingering dress fabric and quizzing jewellers' assistants would settle my nerves. I was, as it happened, quite rattled by Great Aunt Helen's nocturnal outburst.

'Was she drunk?' Magda asked me as she clambered out of the car. I had parked right beside the cathedral, under the sticky green shelter of a tall lime. 'She was drinking rather a lot at supper, I recall.'

'She wasn't drunk,' I said tersely. Magda was making me protective of my aunt.

'Not that I could sleep anyway,' Magda sighed. 'That mattress was sopping and stank of cats.' Then she put aside all thoughts of our uncongenial home-from-home and devoted herself to the task of exploring the shops.

***

That night Great Aunt Helen had another of her queer fits. This one was even more violent. Again I found myself banging on the sturdy wood of her bedroom door.

'For heaven's sake, Fox,' Magda had grunted. 'Would you ask her to put a sock in it?'

When I hammered and called this time, there came no reassuring words from my aunt, inviting me to mind my own business, assuring me she was actually fine. She simply kept on wailing and keening as if pursued by Beelzebub himself. Somewhere in the back of my fuddled mind I was wondering if Aunt Helen was plagued with the same vile nightmares that I had suffered since childhood. Perhaps they were just another familial inheritance.

Now she sounded as if she were in the throes of agony. I could even hear her thrashing about on her bed. That couldn't be any good for a lady of her years.

So I took a deep breath, took hold of the brass doorknob and clicked open the door.

Inside there was just a spill of milky moonlight from under the ill-fitting curtains. I waited till my eyes gradually became used to the dark. Here the noise was much worse. The old girl was really letting rip. She was squawking and caterwauling fit to burst and, as I had suspected, she was flinging herself about with abandon in her four-poster bed. I was frozen into immobility. Somehow, observing such a bizarre spectacle seemed to me distasteful, even obscene. It looked as if my octogenarian aunt was in the fevered and passionate grip of some phantom lover. Her nightgown was awfully rucked up.

I told myself: be a man. I steeled my nerves and hastened to her bedside.

Instantly Great Aunt Helen fell silent and still. Her bright blue eyes flew open and fixed me with a terrible look. She said, very distinctly: 'He will not get out of me. My head feels like it will burst with the pressure of him. I am so scared, Fox. You have to help me. You must help me.'

Then she passed out cold on her rumpled, perspiration-sodden sheets. How odd, I remember thinking, that her words to me had been so composed and exact. And I also felt as if, by stepping up to that grand bed and listening to those weirdly calm sentences, I had taken my first real step into a story from which I would never escape.

***

The following morning I decided that, if Aunt Helen attempted once more to pretend that nothing untoward had occurred, I would confront her. Magda egged me on, as she briskly powdered her face at the gorgeous dressing table. I glanced at her reflection in that mottled looking glass and received a sudden impression of how my beloved might look when old. The ambience of the manor and my aunt's peculiar habits were getting to us both. But Magda's voice held steady as she instructed me: 'Have it out with her, Fox. Otherwise I'm going straight off to London. I'm not staying in the middle of nowhere with some horrible shrieking old woman.' Then my darling heart turned her attention to her new Norwich-bought boots, which had little buttons all up the sides.

***

I bearded my great aunt in her den. She was writing letters in her study. In the wash of morning light from the french windows she looked very drawn and wan. I felt a slight satisfaction that there was none of yesterday's dissemblance. As we faced each other across her desk it was obvious that we both remembered and acknowledged what had passed in the depths of the night.

'I want to know what this is all about,' I said, palms flat and sweating on the worn, cool desk.

As if in relief, my aunt sagged a little in her chair. Her resolve was melting. She could see that she now had a man to depend upon. I was gratified by this. I was there to help her.

She asked me, 'Has Magda heard my cries?'

'She is as concerned as I am, Aunt Helen,' I said stiffly. Really, I look back and I must have been such a pompous ass. So full of myself. I was convinced I could protect my formidable Aunt.

'That girl is not worthy of you,' my aunt said. 'You know that, Fox. She has her sights set high and you have given in to her. She is the first woman who would let you do as you would with her and you have made the mistake of promising her the earth. So grateful are you for her favours. I imagine that you will regret that, nephew.'

I felt myself grow red with embarrassment, and then fury. But I couldn't get any words out in retaliation.

'She is common, Fox. All too common. Hasn't she wondered at all why I have let the two of you share a room under my roof before you are married? Has she not questioned anything?'

I was reverting to a schoolboy. I was mortified. 'Magda realises that my upbringing, my education, were unorthodox ... and she herself is a very modern girl ...'

'A whore,' said my aunt simply.

Our gazes locked and I was speechless.

'You mention your education, Fox, and how it might be seen as unorthodox. There was a reason you were sent there. All that way north, to that particular establishment.'

I frowned. Aunt Helen had never mentioned my schooling for a long time, had never gone into its particulars, though it had been her signature on the monthly cheques. Until I had left and found myself at Oxford I hadn't thought my alma mater at all out of the ordinary run of things. But recently I had seen that it was. Nobody I knew had been to such a school as I had.

Do what thy wilt be the whole of the Law. The first, most important rule of the school. The only important law in the world. Because of my education in the north, human love and sexual relations - human passions of every sort - held no mysteries or fears for me. Everything was natural and easy and I counted myself lucky to find a young woman like Magda who wasn't put off by the things I took for granted.

'You were sent to be schooled as have generations of Soamses. You were sent there for a particular purpose.'

'I see,' I said, though I didn't at all.

'You were sent there so as to be untrammelled by workaday morality. So that your spirit would be free and open to the universe.'

Her words discomfited me. She seemed so passionate and earnest. People of my generation were always put off by talk that grew too earnest. Magda and I belonged to that peer group that came between the two world wars and we were determined not to let anything matter as much as all that.

What could I say to this old woman? Protest that my spirit was indeed unfettered? I baulked at such words.

'You were put there to be educated properly. To venerate the name of the Lord of This World.'

Well, that was easy to take on board. I had never questioned the religion of my upbringing, though I had perhaps, neglected it of late.

'You have chosen one of the uninitiated as your bride-to-be,' said Great Aunt Helen, calmly licking a stamp. 'Even you must realise that she will have to be brought in.'

My throat was dry. 'Of course.' I was shocked to hear how she took it all so seriously. I had no idea what to be 'brought in' entailed. I thought, with no living relative apart from my haggard aunt, I had escaped all trappings of tradition. Apparently not.

She nodded at me with some satisfaction. 'There will be a gathering. Here. This Saturday night. People will come from all corners to attend. We can have Magda initiated then. Since you are so set upon taking her as your bride.' Her expression was rather fierce at this and I knew I couldn't argue. 'You will inform her, Fox. You will let her know what is likely to happen to her.'

'Very well,' I acquiesced. The details, however, were somewhat hazy to me. I cursed myself for never having paid much attention to my divinity classes.

My great aunt Helen's face softened and, for a moment, I could imagine that she gazed on me almost fondly. 'One more thing, Fox. To do with what I told you last night. When I was in the midst of my ... distress.'

'Oh yes?'

'It is to do with the pressure on my brain. That is the most urgent of my concerns. The demon in possession of my immortal soul is making himself a rather uncomfortable lodger. You must help me relieve myself of that encumbrance.'

I was an idiot. 'Indeed?'

'During the Saturday night ceremony. As my closest living blood relation on this earthly plane. You must take the sacred implement and punch a hole into my skull. Help me bleed the excess spirit away. The Brethren will, of course, coach you through the exact procedure.'

'Oh,' I said. 'I see.'

'You don't mind, do you, dear? I realise that it sounds rather grisly ...'

'No, no, not at all ...'

'But it has, as I've said, become a rather pressing matter.' She took up her fountain pen with a flourish, preparing to dismiss me from her presence. 'It really is quite straightforward. Our family have been opening up their skulls for generations. That is what keeps us open to the universe. To the divine word and breath of the Lord of This World himself.'

I smiled. 'Quite,' I said.

'Well, off you toddle.' She smiled benignly. 'You hurry off and tell that little strumpet of yours what a treat she has in store for her, hm?'

So then I turned on my heel and left my great aunt to her stack of correspondence. The study door snicked shut at my heels. I was alone in the gloom of the corridor, my mind

155

a sickening whirl. It was Thursday now. Saturday sounded as if it was going to be rather hectic.

And all of a sudden I felt like screaming.

***

So.

You come again to hear another of my fireside tales. You draw up your chair and hold out your balloon glass so expectantly, ready for these heady fumes.

Let us sit together in this stifling warm study air. And you profess not to enjoy stories like these. You believe you credit them with no truth nor validity in this rational age. But here you are back.

How I reel you in. Just as I did when I was a bestseller. When sturdy businessmen bought me at airport stalls and sat in a chill sweat of fear in air-conditioned and pressurised cabins, high above the earth. Or housewives, at home at the kitchen table, neglecting their daily chores for the sake of gobbling up every morsel I lovingly prepared for them. All that Satanism, all that witchcraft. Oh, they knew what they were getting when they sat down to listen to my voice. Just as, years later, cinema audiences came to sit in the dark and watch my terrible tales unspool on the smutty gauze of the screen. Boys and girls would clutch each other on the back row, chilled to the bone as adepts and ghosthunters stalked each other through the thousand wicked nights of my imagination. Those hormones stirred and thrilled and trembled in pleasure palaces the world over. A million gropings and fingerings went on in my name and the fear I inspired. A great deal of unharnessed naughtiness was spurred and engendered by plots set in motion by me.

Oh, though I sought to warn the world of the devil's dark motives, my stories themselves pushed my audience to give into their fears, their desires, their wildest dreams. I got them all going. I got them to give in.

Just as you have. Coming to sit here, beside me again.

156

You want to know more. Like they all do. And I, decrepit raconteur, savouring my brandy, thinking back to where we got to in this latest, oldest tale, I let my hampered mind drift back and back on the eddies and tides of myriad ironies...

Ah. I'd had my little interview with Aunt Helen. In this very room. At that very walnut desk. Didn't I tell you that one day I would inherit the manor?

But you have a modern sensibility. Not for you some long and weighty exegesis on witchcraft and the cabbalistic tradition. If you are interested you will simply insert a few key words into a - what do you call them? a search engine? - and pull out a few bizarre and probably misinformed virtual documents. Then you might learn how Satan had come to be Lord of This World. And how some people come to follow the Left Hand Path, as they call it. Or you might consult these volumes in this study of mine. Everything you might need is right here. Grimoires, everything. Books you might not come across or even be able to request in your local lottery-sponsored Millennium library. All of the important works are, of course, in private hands.

You want to be pressing on with the story. You want to involve yourself in the human element: the character-driven plot. And why shouldn't you? Why shouldn't you want to learn how my sweetheart took the news that she was, within the next two days, to be somehow initiated?

Of her own account, she had grown nosy and intrigued that morning. She was that kind of girl and that was one of the reasons I wanted her. She was just the type - resourceful, independent, thoroughly, thoroughly modern in every way - to support me in my literary endeavours and (I felt sure) my marvellously successful career as a writer of popular novels.

While I had been consulting my great aunt Helen, Magda had been browsing in the library. Now, she wasn't really one for books (as I was to discover) but sheer boredom and irksomeness that morning in the stately pile had driven her to the extreme measure of plucking out several hidebound volumes and glancing through them in the hope of finding something marginally distracting. She had flicked, first sighing, exasperated by page after page of impenetrable text, and then she felt herself compelled to look further. To look at the pictures, to scan through the writing itself. My Magda was shocked, awed, appalled.

I found her red-cheeked and hissing. 'These books are absolutely filthy!' She thrust one example under my nose. It quivered in her grasp and I could see a large number of other, similar volumes, splayed open on the table behind her. 'Your aunty hasn't got a single decent book in this whole place. They are all utterly vile.'

I was attempting to focus on a black and white etching on the page she held shaking before me. In that plate, a number of winged beasts were circling around a naked and corpulent woman. One of them appeared to be squatting on her, but that was about all I could make out.

'Rare editions,' I said, paling under Magda's affronted gaze. 'My family has made a habit of collecting them up.'

She wasn't about to let ancestry and tradition assuage her. Collecting up big houses with neatly-laid grounds and respectable treasures was one thing. Dirty old books were quite another.

Magda was seething. 'I knew it. She is a nasty old woman. All that crying out in the night. These evil books...' Suddenly I saw that my beloved was looking rather frightened. I wanted to gather her up in my arms and smother her back into normality. 'I don't want to stay here, Fox. I can't sleep in a place like this.'

Her eyes looked rather wild then. It was as if she was realising what kind of reception was awaiting her, should she go running back to her parents. It was without the blessing of her rather common grocer father that she had come to me and become my common-law wife. It would be hard on her to return to them, disgraced. For a moment she looked stricken and I knew what she was thinking.

But she wouldn't have to leave me. She was all mine. I would protect her. All she had seen was my eccentric great aunt's admittedly strange collection of books. Nothing to get the wind up about. Certainly nothing to flee from.

I held my Magda tight. Pushing her face into my neck. I stroked her soft, fragrant hair. I felt the warm wetness of her tears on my flesh. I let her sob gently and, when she was calm again, braced by my strength and my common sense, I told her: 'There may be one or two things I need to explain to you, my darling.'

**

Maybe you can't credit the innocence of my darling Magda back then? If only you had met her in her youth. She was quite something. She was like dew on the furled and fleshy whorls of white lilies. That distinct, almost too stuffy and sweet scent. The kind of purity that's just about teetering over into rank corruption.

She became horribly fascinated by the Left Hand Path, of course. You've guessed as much from what I have said before in my interviews and my various bestselling memoirs. She was hooked from that very first day when I - callow, stuttering buffoon that I was - explained to her my family's tradition and closely-guarded secret sidelines. She was - shall we say - agog.

Agog is one of my favourite words, incidentally. It's how I like my audience to be and it has about it a certain ring of the old gods, eh? Gog, Magog, Agog. These are the words of a shaman, inspired by divine fire, plugged into the real life of the world.

This is why I have always felt as if I were in the very centre of the world. Wherever we went upon the surface of the globe - book tours, lecture tours, exotic adventurings undertaken for profit and fun - we always felt that we were the locus mundi. Magda was always by my side, from that very first trip to Great Aunt Helen's pile to the fateful day of her death. All the invisible eyes were trained upon us, as

159

were all the vibrations on the ether.

With that weekend approaching, it really felt as if we had become the centre of things. There came a flurry of telegrams, of cryptic messages in code, announcing the imminent arrival of her Saturday guests. Aunt Helen would receive these at breakfast, smile in a self-satisfied way, and then crumple them up. A great air of expectancy was sweeping through the old house, stirring up the old servants into activity, causing them to call on other servants and soon a frenetic pace was established in the draughty halls. You could hear them in the kitchens, bashing and clashing and preparing a banquet. Delivery vans slid up on the gravel at the back of the manor. We saw them carrying whole pigs and lambs indoors. One van brought wicker cages containing live beasts - goats and chickens. They sounded alarmed and doomed in that brief moment of daylight between van and cellar kitchen. These live creatures disconcerted Magda and I when we peered out of our bedroom window to see what the ruckus was. We had a feeling we knew what they were for.

Soon, as Saturday drew near, Aunt Helen's guests started to arrive. Sleek black cars were pulling up on the drive. Impressive, expensive cars with tinted windows and little flags on their front fenders. Flags of all nations. It was like a secret summit meeting. The servants ushered these guests into the building quickly, before we could get a good look at them. The place was large enough for them to be installed before we bumped into them. Guest after guest after guest. Most ducked in swiftly, as if nervous of being observed. They were furtive, and we peered out and glimpsed the vivid peacock colours of saris; the lightly flowing robes of Middle Eastern gentlemen, and the dove-grey and ebony regalia of Nazi officers. Magda and I were a little shocked at who was being welcomed into our future home.

Of Great Aunt Helen, the gracious hostess, there was no sign. Her distinguished multicultured visitors were taken in and presumably urged to make the place their own. All of them seemed to know and to understand the routine.

Magda and I didn't.

In later years it was Magda who knew more about the occult than I did. Indeed, she proved the more susceptible to its wicked charms and had I not had my native fortitude and strength of mind, she may have been damned forever. I was her rock. And at least I know she is in paradise waiting for me. I salvaged her soul, if nothing else.

The first tangible evidence of her lifelong fascination came with her enthusiasm for the rather shapeless black satin robes with which we were presented by one of the servants. He explained that they were the required uniform for the Saturday night proceedings and then he left us with the things. We'd been taking a spin in the country that Saturday afternoon, intending to keep ourselves out of everyone's hair and, when we returned, the place was thrumming along with all these polite strangers. We sought solace in our room and had been surprised by this gift of new outfits, folded neatly at the bottom of our bed like satanic guest towels.

'His-and-hers,' Magda said, pulling a face. 'Your great aunt Helen thinks of everything. She must have known that we'd forget to pack our ceremonial robes.'

Something clutched at my heart. It was the way Magda managed to sound so breezy and blithe. She'd had the wind through her auburn hair and the fresh Norfolk air had put two spots of red on her creamy pale cheks. My beloved was treating all of these preparations like they belonged to some ridiculous game. A charade; an elaborate fancy dress party. Somewhere below us there was a band tuning up. They were making weird, unearthly sounds, distorted by the eccentric twists and turns of the ancient corridors and I couldn't begin to imagine what kind of instruments they were using.

'Darling,' I said, watching her hold up the black robes. She smoothed them over her svelte form, gazing critically

161

at herself in the looking glass. 'I rather think this is more serious than you imagine. Aunt Helen means what she says. About the ... um, initiation.'

Magda shot me a strange, ironic look.

'You see,' I stammered, 'I think I've managed to get us into this pretty deep.'

She came over and punched me lightly on the shoulder. 'Oh, shut up, Fox. It might be amusing. Just a load of her funny friends dancing about in frocks. I'm rather glad to hear that the old girl still has some life in her. It's better than sitting over another of those interminable dinners of hers.' Suddenly her green, tigerish eyes widened. 'I say, you don't think there'll be an orgy, do you?' Then she started struggling out of her outer garments and working out how to go about slipping into the donated black robes. I pointed out that one was supposed to be completely naked underneath.

'Oh!' she cried, delightedly. 'Been to one of these do's before, have you? Sly old Fox?'

I coloured. 'School assemblies.'

She was stripping with great gusto by now. She looked at me quizzically. 'That school of yours begins to sound stranger and stranger.'

'I thought every school was like that,' I said glumly. 'Now I realise that we were quite unique.'

Magda was standing in the bright light of the opened curtains. There were golden motes of dust swimming between us. I was staring at her pale, shapely body and I was growing aroused as she unlaced the last of her vestments.

'They will ask you to do certain things,' I said. 'During the initiation. And you must perform them. Once the sacred ceremony is underway, you must obey.'

Magda shrugged. 'In for a penny,' she smiled. 'I'm a game girl.'

It was I, I realised, who was having all the qualms. 'I'm not sure I can stand to see other men looking at you ...

162

touching you...' This was very hard for me to say. It went against all of my conditioning. I wasn't supposed to think of her as a possession. She was as free a spirit as I. I shook my head to clear it. 'I am afraid I may become rather jealous.'

Magda smiled indulgently.

'I know I shouldn't feel like this,' I choked. 'I shouldn't seek to restrain you ... any more than you would dream of restraining me ... men and women are equal in wills and potential, I know...'

She stepped up to me, into my clumsy embrace, allowing me to take hold of her. 'You silly thing, Fox,' she murmured. 'You know I am yours. Now, get your black satin robes on and you'll feel much better about it all.' She pulled back, gazed at me and, as she often did, in order to puncture my seriousness, pulled on my nose. 'There's something very interesting going on here, Fox. I can sense it. At first I was somewhat shocked at finding those books in the library. But I see now that I was simply being prudish and bourgeois. I was reacting as my father would, or my mother. But we are different, Fox. We really have to learn to give ourselves up to novel experiences. Isn't that what marriage is all about?'

I was wondering if she would be singing the same tune come midnight.

'Come on, Fox,' she said. 'You're the one who wants to be a writer. You need material! You need adventures! You have to look life in the face and be open to all of it!'

Her use of that word 'open' put me in mind of Great Aunt Helen and what she had asked me to do this evening. I hadn't gone into this with Magda. I had placed it in the back of my thoughts. Now it came back that, not only was I to watch my fiancée being manhandled by hordes of drunk Nazis and Arabs, I'd have to drill a hole in my aunty's brain to boot.

Oh, Saturday nights in the old days!

We didn't need television then!

***

There was a cocktail party in full swing downstairs and the rumbles and cackles from the best drawing room made us feel awkward and nervous as we paused outside the doors. That queer music was issuing from within: undulating and exotic. It made all the hairs on my body bristle beneath my sheer satin robes. The two of us held hands and Magda nodded at me decisively. We were going in and we were going in with confidence. The brightest, youngest things there. We would keep our ends up.

She thrust open the doors.

It was as if Great Aunt Helen was waiting for us, as at a surprise birthday party. We entered the scarlet room and she let out a vivacious shriek. She clutched both our arms and started announcing to the assembled guests that we had arrived, and now the circle was complete, or some such nonsense as it seemed to me. There was a tall Negro in footman's livery holding a silver salver out to us: we were given the same creamy green drink as everyone else. They were swigging this down with great abandon, seemingly quite used to the infernal taste.

Aunt Helen was full of beans. She was like a six-year-old child who had managed to organise her own party, all to her own lavish specifications. She led us in a great circuit of that room, introducing us to her invited revellers and we were soon lost in a flurry of decidedly foreign-sounding names. Aunt Helen behaved as if she were very proud of us. She was even beaming at and flattering Magda, whom I knew for a fact she held in very low esteem. She told her that black was absolutely her colour and that the robes were clinging to her in the most mischievously becoming fashion. I looked at my aunt, thinking she must have gone mad, and I realised with horror that she, too, was prancing around naked beneath her flimsy gown. Suddenly I felt sick with dread, glancing around at the other old duffers chatting and guffawing over their noxious beverages. I thought: it is one thing to be invited to an affair like this when one is young, nubile and fit. But this bunch were looking less and less appealing by the minute.

I was aware then, that my beloved was nudging me urgently, and that Great Aunt Helen's tone had become more sober and solicitous. We were approaching the orbit of a rather ugly, hawklike man, who was surrounded by fawning lackies. Obviously a bigwig.

'Grand Master,' Aunt Helen cried, in a simpering voice. 'May I present to you my nephew and his woman, Magda, whom you are to initiate this evening.' My aunt was smiling but, as she touched her brow just then, I could tell that the expression was forced. The old lady was in some considerable pain. That confounded skull of hers.

The old, bald, hawklike man was bending over my darling's slim hand and murmuring imprecations. I distinctly heard Magda giggle, though she refuted this later. Now he was whispering into one of her small and perfect ears. I could have sworn I saw his tongue flick out and it was tiny and forked.

'We're very privileged to have him preside at our gathering,' Aunt Helen hissed. 'He's a great adept.'

'Is he indeed.'

'And he's very high up in the world of publishing,' she added, with a meaningful look. 'He might well do you some good, if you insist on carrying out your ridiculous career plans.'

I smiled at this. It sounded to me as if Aunt Helen had come round to the idea of my becoming an author and she was helping me out with a little networking.

The old hawk was still nibbling away at my beloved, his head poised directly above her breasts. My aunt continued with her introductions. At the next face that presented itself I baulked and almost choked on the swizzle-stick from my vile cocktail.

'Professor Cleavis!' I burst out, glaring at the genial features that had swam out of the general hubbub. 'What the hell are you doing here?'

Aunt Helen's grin grew more rictuslike. 'You are already acquainted?'

The old don's ruddy face gurned enthusiastically. 'Yes, indeed, madam. Young Soames here was one of our brightest stars. We miss him greatly. Especially at the weekly gatherings of our small writers' circle. The Smudgelings feel quite bereft now we no longer hear his works in progress.'

Aunt Helen eyed the two of us with great interest. 'Quite a coincidence,' she said archly. She turned to me sharply. 'Professor Cleavis is on a walking tour of Norfolk. He was given my address by a great friend of his. He was very keen to join our number tonight.'

'He was?' I asked.

'Professor Cleavis is a student of many subjects,' she said. 'Including the Left Hand Path.'

'I thought it was Old English and the Icelandic sagas,' I said, quite frostily. 'At least, that was all he imparted to me.'

Cleavis chuckled at this, and gulped greedily at his drink. 'Ah, well, we don't tell our undergraduates everything, do we? Not even those special enough to be asked to join the Smudgelings.'

'Indeed,' I frowned. My mind was reeling. Cleavis was a Christian! A famous one! He was renowned for his Godbothering sermons in The Spectator! He had written whole books upon the interminable subject of his unshakeable faith in God.

I refrained from quizzing him further in the presence of Great Aunt Helen and within earshot of the grizzled Grand Master (who was still buttering up Magda) and instead I wondered dryly: 'Whatever would Professor Tyler say?'

I was glad to see Cleavis blanch and twitch at the name of his austere chum. Tyler was the founding member of the Smudgelings and no mean Christian himself. There was no way Cleavis would want Tyler getting wind of his latest field trip.

'It's the long vac,' Cleavis said dully. 'What I get up to is my own business.'

Ever the skilled hostess, Aunt Helen piped up just then: 'I am sure my nephew is delighted to see you again, Professor Cleavis. You must forgive his gaucherie.'

'Oh,' Cleavis's eyes were gleaming with mischief. 'That's quite all right. He's a very talented young man. We must allow him his rough edges.'

Rough edges! I was bridling, I can tell you.

Aunt Helen took herself off to a gilded side table, where she struck a brass gong with a large drumstick. As the room fell excitedly silent she clasped her hands together and took on a beatific mien.

'Friends,' she announced. 'It is time for us to descend to the cellars. The hour approaches.' Then she chuckled, to undercut the sententiousness of such a pronouncement. 'I've had the basement done up especially for the occasion. I trust you will find it pleasing.'

There was a scattering of spirited applause and then a general exodus from the drawing room.

The true party was about to begin.

***

This being the first of these kinds of affairs I ever attended, I wasn't sure about the form. I stood around somewhat awkwardly in the crowd once we had descended the stone staircase. At my side Magda was behaving a good deal perkier than I felt. She was looking about at the vast cellar space with great interest. Indeed, the rising tension and anticipation in the gaggle of cultists was very like that at the beginning of the sales season. It was as if we were being led into something rather like a bargain basement. Where everything would be up for grabs at shocking prices.

The walls were hung with rich fabrics in black, gold and red. Ghastly shadows were flung hither and thither by the leaping flames from ornate braziers. There were delicious aromas wafting our way: of crackling on pork, of barbe-

167

cued meats and, indeed, there were long tables laid with an immense feast. The products of the kitchen staff's hard labours amounted to far too much food for even our generous number.

There was, of course, an altar. I shivered to gaze upon that stone block at the end of the room. Although it wasn't that different to the platform from which my old headmaster had once proselytised, there was something about that ominous slab that filled me with dread. On it awaited an array of shining utensils. They looked very well cared for and surgical. On the wall behind there was a crucifix, life-sized and hung, of course, upside down.

The vicious-looking Grand Master had dropped his mask of urbanity and was clasping his big hands with glee. 'Oh, Helen, dear heart. You have done us proud.' There was a murmur of garden party appreciation from the others. I was wondering which publishing firm the Grand Master worked for. I couldn't help it. He was a powerful man. He may well hold the keys to my future success. Even with the heady scents of that cellar crowding my nostrils, I could smell the ripe promise of fresh-cut folios, calf-bound hardbacks, printer's glue.

That small band of dratted musicians had pursued us into the cellar and now they were resuming their cacophony. At this signal my great aunt took command. Her colour was high and her tones imperious. Her rheumy eyes had taken on a manic intensity as she exhorted us to eat our fill; to gorge and surpass our puny human appetites. Gluttony was the order of the day and her distinguished exotic guests fell to the task con brio. No evidence of cutlery nor napkins; they seized up whole glazed hams and roasted birds and ripped into them bare-handed like a pack of wild dogs. Soon their faces were smeared with gravy and fat and blood juices as they crammed their grinning faces. They scattered the groaning trestles in a gory, unappetising debris.

Magda was pitching in with the rest of them. She who

was usually such a picky eater. She who claimed to have the appetite of a sparrow was engaged in a tug of war over a platter of baked eels. She and a swarthy-looking gentlemen were scrapping good-naturedly and spraying green ichor all over the place as they stuffed themselves.

And then, soon enough, began the item on the evening's agenda dedicated to the orgy.

Now, I don't propose to go into all the details of this rather shaming sequence of entertainments. Indeed, I am renowned as a writer who knows just when to draw the prudent line; when to include just enough relevant detail to provide that certain ring of authenticity. I intend always to give the merest hint and flavour of debaucheries. I never wanted to be prurient or self-indulgent. I certainly never wanted to draw any of my readers to explore the Left Hand Path or any of its disgusting rites for themselves.

I was tackling a sticky chicken wing when I caught an eyeful of my great aunt throwing caution to the winds and shucking off her Satanic robes. Cries went up as others followed her lead and before I knew it, they were falling upon each other with the same unsavoury relish that had undone the banquet. I found myself caught up in their morass of heaving and squirming - and mostly bloated, raddled - flesh. Hands were tugging at my slippery frock; some of the more urgent, persistent ones seeking to pull it over my head. No prude I, of course: I'd been one of the most enthusiastic participants during Games at school. But this lot weren't doing anything for me in this particular rutting season.

I noted with grim satisfaction that Magda had been ushered away - ceremonially - by the Grand Master. She was standing patiently by the sacrificial altar. As the evening's sole initiate she was to be spared the more prosaic hurly-burly of the orgy.

So I found myself dragged down into the rubbery, heaving mass of their bodies. They were redolent and tacky with salad dressings, marinades, meat juices and who knew what else. The moaning was terrible to hear and really, I thought, those lascivious groans must have been mostly put on, or at least evidence of swift indigestion. I was trying vainly to keep myself to myself, but hands kept grabbing at me and, as in the way of these things, my human body let me down. But at least I looked as if I was taking zestful part.

Professor Cleavis came swimming through the jellylike rolls of fat and prising his way through convulsing, scissoring limbs. 'Young Soames!' he hissed to me. He was florid of complexion and his bald pate was gleaming.

It seemed to me - even in the throes of my bogus passion - that the professor was attempting to communicate something to me. Something clandestine. It was difficult to concentrate on exactly what he intended, however. I was still most distracted by the sight of my scrawny, gallivanting great aunt.

The words that eventually came to me were: 'I'm not here for the reason you think, Soames.' Somehow Cleavis had managed to sidle up to me. He was all barrel-chested and clammy, his voice terse in my ear. Evidently so as not to attract suspicion to ourselves he was stroking my inflamed flesh. I complied and waited for him to explain further, sotto voce. Rather odd, to be caressed and fiddled with in public by the fellow who taught to you to read the Nordic myths in the original.

'I am here undercover,' he said tightly, reaching for my traitorous manhood. I tepidly returned his false attentions and at first I didn't pick up the import of his words.

'Undercover?' I gasped.

As he was then - as I believe the latterday parlance has it - blowing me, I had to wait until he could tell me: 'It isn't what you think.'

'I see,' I said.

***

There was a fair bit of singing and chanting while the company regained its collective breath. I think we were all feeling the effects of those foaming green cocktails, along with the heady incense that was gusting about the place. I rather gathered that my beloved's initiation was last on the bill this evening. She was standing by the altar looking altogether piqued. I wasn't sure if that was because she felt left out, or if it was at the sight of her fiancé, struggling to get back into his satin robe, all dishevelled and bespattered as I was. Cleavis was standing right behind me, dressed again, with his fair hair awry. I thought we'd dissembled pretty well amongst all the goings on. A commendable job at seeming as if we were in the swing of things. Just then he was patting my arse and telling me we'd have a good talk about it later.

Or perhaps Magda looked piqued because now the Grand Master was handing her a golden blade and expertly stretching out a chicken on the spanking new slab. The bird had kicked and squawked feebly when he pulled it from the cage, but now it was pathetically supine. Its beady eyes were staring up at my dearest. The lamb in the basket on the floor didn't look too happy either.

Magda didn't mess about. She drew the knife across the chicken's neck with a fastidious little chopping motion. The Grand Master was ready to catch the blood in a golden bowl, which he bade Magda quickly drink.

Then, before she'd even finished swallowing and choking the filthy brew down, my great aunt Helen had hopped onto the raised dais and was announcing that now it was her turn.

She said some hasty words about an ancient and sacred tradition and how everyone present should feel honoured to see this rite performed. Beside her, the Grand Master was fondling a very odd-looking device. It was a tubular metal object terminating in what looked very like a pastry cutter.

'Good God,' Cleavis gasped, right in my ear. 'The old girl wasn't joking.'

171

Now my great aunt was calling me to the podium. There was a light ripple of applause and Cleavis gave me a quizzical look as I was pushed to the front of the sweaty rabble. Before I knew it I was up by the altar and my aunt had hopped nimbly to lie full-length on the mess of chicken blood and feathers. The Grand Master nodded at me and passed the pastry-cutting affair.

Magda was staring at me horrified. I hadn't warned her about this part. I hadn't really thought it would come to anything. Yet now here I was, poised above my grinning aunt like a drunk and imbecilic surgeon.

'The Grand Master will show you exactly what it is you have to do, Fox,' she said, brimming with confidence. 'And precisely where to punch the hole.'

'Very well,' I said thickly. My tongue was all swollen inside my mouth.

'But know this, Fox. Know this, everyone...' Her voice rose in thunderous tones. 'Fox is committing one of the rites practised by members of our family for hundreds of years. The aperture he is about to knock into my skull will free me. It will allow clear passage for dark spirits, between the universe itself and the microcosm that is my own mind.'

'And,' I said nervously, 'It won't hurt you, will it?'

She even managed a ribald laugh. 'My dear, I've had it done at least twelve times before. All around the circumference of my skull. You ask the Grand Master there.'

The evil-looking Master nodded solemnly at me.

I hefted the dullish golden pastry-cutting apparatus thoughtfully and saw how it worked. It was indeed a stamping mechanism with a round, savage blade at the end. When one pressed the switch at the other end, it would punch a disc the size of a florin out of the patient's head.

Magda let out a squeal. 'You can't do it, Fox. A bit of a feast and an orgy is one thing, but...'

'Shut her up,' my aunt seethed and the Grand Master

shot my darling a poisonous glance and she froze on the spot. Then he pointed silently at the space right between my aunt's watery eyes and just a little way up. Bang in her forehead.

I raised up the pastry cutter.

I could hear the revellers take in a quick, startled breath.

And I admit a tiny part of me was enjoying all the drama. I was at the centre of it all. And if she said it was harmless and this was her thirteenth time having it done, then it must be safe, mustn't it? It must be a fool-proof and fairly easy if unconventional operation. And -

CHUNK.

That was the exact noise of the implement plunging neatly, briefly, into Great Aunt Helen's forehead. I gulped. She was still. A thin, meagre dribble of dark blood started down her ashen face. I lifted the pastry cutter away very gently and gritted my teeth as I heard the grinding of bone sliding against bone.

There it was. I'd put a hole in her head.

She was smiling at me. Everyone was completely silent. But then the Grand Master started laughing.

'Ding! Dong! Ding! Dong! It's thirteen o'clock!' he howled mockingly. 'Thirteen times! Thirteen holes all around her filthy old noggin!' Then he was shrieking - as is the wont of these people - maniacally.

I didn't know what he was on about. My great aunt was still smiling, as if she'd had all her dreams come true at once. As if, indeed, the whole of the invisible universe was rushing into her skull and expanding there, for her benign delectation.

The Grand Master shook with laughter.

'What do you mean, 'ding dong'?' I asked him savagely.

'It's thirteen o'clock!' he sobbed hysterically. 'Too late! Too late!'

We all looked down at my Great Aunt Helen. Then, with exquisite timing, her skull flipped open and the top of her head fell off, onto the slab. Just like a big bloody boiled egg.

***

Here we are again, my dear.

Here we sit in the calm, protected space of my study. Only here inside this ring of salt are we safe from the spirits and demons that roam abroad, in the wider world.

So. You return to hear what became of my much younger, much less experienced self and his divine bride-to-be on the evening of what was meant to be her initiation. What is more, you seek to know what became of my poor great aunt Helen, after the top of her head was lifted off so cleanly by that evil device. By an act of my own hand I had revealed - to all our astonished eyes - her pale and pulsing blueish green brain itself.

The look on her face was a sight to see. She still bore that dazed, ecstatic expression, but she was frozen solid, as if someone had snapped a photograph of her.

The orgiastic crowd were subdued. The Grand Master was chuckling. He seemed to have lost possession of himself. And so it was then that my one-time professor, the bluff and learned Cleavis decided to leap into action.

Somehow I had known that there was more to it, and he hadn't really become a Satanist. Old Cleavis the Godbotherer was there for other reasons. He came up to us at a run, flapping his robes like a big black crow. 'Soames old man! This has gone far enough! We should have stopped this nonsense well before now!'

I was shaking. Still staring at my poor aunt. I couldn't fix on what he was saying to me.

'You've killed her!' my dear Magda started to shriek. 'You've knocked her bloody block off!'

Quick as a flash, Cleavis whipped up the silken braids that had been meant for restraining my darling during her initiation. Without an ounce of squeamishness he set himself to the task of binding up Great Aunt Helen's head, popping the lid of her skull back in place and then knotting the whole thing tight under her pointed chin. Then he was struggling to lift her off the stone bier. 'Fox! Help me, man.

We have to get her out...'

Just as I shook myself out of my stupor and into action, the Grand Master came back to his senses and he was snarling.

'You will not take her from me.' His clawed hands reached out to grab her withered, helpless form. His cultists were moaning, unsure of how to proceed. People like them are generally weak and easily led. They get into these hellish affairs for cheap and vicarious thrills. They simply don't expect to face real danger or nastiness.

Cleavis had stiffened with resolve. His face went puce and he thundered back: 'You can't stop us, you charlatan. You are messing around with forces that you can't possibly understand.'

I must say that I flinched when I saw the sheer, brutish insanity of the Grand Master's face just then. 'I understand all too well, Professor Cleavis. I understand exactly why you are here. You and your impotent Oxford cronies, dabbling and interfering yet again in our business.'

'Your business?' I broke in, sensing a revelation in the offing.

'Absolute domination,' the Grand Master snarled. 'The coming again of the Lord of This World.'

While this was going on we were each holding one of my aunt's limbs and we were all tugging at her. Her flesh at our fingers was slack and white.

'The same old story,' Cleavis gasped. 'And we are still here to stop you.'

The Grand Master cackled. 'We shall see. What this young fool has done this evening has released enough psychic energy from this old hag's mind to...'

'Oh, Fox,' Magda wailed. 'You idiot.'

'To do what?' Cleavis demanded.

'To summon us up some help. To put an end to our enemies.' With that, the Grand Master let go of Aunt Helen's foot and started to utter a strange, guttural incantation.

The atmosphere in that cellar was starting to turn very

odd. 'Oh dear,' said Cleavis, turning to me. 'I think he's calling up one of his demons.'

Here was a manifestation for us to contend with. Full scale, as the parapsychologists would have it, though I have no time for their awful pseudo-scientific jargon. As you know, Fox Soames is a man of action and his word, and he calls a spade a spade. And this was a great, unholy, seven foot tall apparition that popped up at the behest of the Grand Master. There was a rush of blue, incandescent, broiling flame and a hellish reek of sulphur and, oddly enough, roasted fowl.

At first it seemed that a gigantic peacock had come strutting and bristling into our midst: a gorgeous, lambent, sapphire blue. The flames licked at its dazzling plumes, and haughtily the creature gazed down at us all with its unblinking, jewel-like eyes. I suddenly knew and understood that this creature represented an evil of many thousands of years' standing. As we watched, appalled, it drew up its colossal fantail and spread those feathers commandingly, so that a whole sheath of wicked, evil eyes fixed us beneath their opulent glare.

The Grand Master was shouting: 'You do us great honour with your presence...'

Its beak was silver and dagger sharp. I felt Magda grip my forearm, as if in fear that it would reach down and pluck out our hearts. 'It's a bloody big bird!' she hissed. 'That's their great god? What's it going to do? Show us fear in a handful of birdseed?'

I was astonished she could find the nerve to even speak in such dire circumstances. But I was to find that Magda was much braver than I in the face of such things.

The Grand Master intoned: 'We call you here to protect your flock...'

It was as if the demon was paying him no attention whatsoever. As we watched, its form was shifting within those stinking flames. No longer did it seem so solid. Its form was starting to liquefy and blur. That smooth swan neck was becoming the torso and breasts of a very tall, very beautiful woman. I rubbed at my eyes, attempting to focus, and at last she resolved herself into the image of a blue-skinned naked goddess and her eyes were so very cruel.

When she spoke her voice was commanding and sensual. I had no doubt that her words were issuing to us from the very antechambers of the underworld itself. She first addressed herself to the Grand Master.

'You have let pettiness and human ambition intrude upon our plans.'

'But, mistress, how...?'

'By allowing this woman to be killed at the hand of her doltish nephew. For your own profit and amusement you have permitted her to die.'

The Grand Master's face was twisted in fear. 'But ... of course. Do what thou wilt be the whole of...'

The goddess snapped: 'You will do only what I wilt.'

The Grand Master quailed.

The goddess went on. 'What the dead woman knew is worth much more to us and our plans than anything you or these pathetic initiates could ever contribute...'

I wasn't surprised she said this. The Satanic cult was a pitiful sight by this point. At the first glimpse of a real demon they had prostrated themselves - Arabs and Nazis and all - and now they were squirming and moaning on the insalubrious cellar floor.

'She was as important as all that?' the Grand Master looked annoyed - and very worried.

'Of course she is,' the gorgeous apparition sighed. 'That brain of hers - which you have so inelegantly endangered - contains the accumulated wisdom of countless generations of Soamses. Her mind - clouded and crazed though it undoubtedly is - represents the crucible in which a rich brew of arcane wisdom has been distilled. At all costs it must be salvaged.'

'But ... how?'

I heard Professor Cleavis clear his throat, as if he were to commence a lecture. He was glaring up at the cerulean goddess defiantly. He looked smaller and less impressive than ever. 'You shouldn't be here, you know,' he said, very mildly. 'Creatures like you have no place on this Earth now. You should stay where you have been put and stop interfering in the lives of men.'

She smiled at him. It was a terrible smile. 'You are such a pious little man.'

'Really!' he fumed.

'That is how history will remember you, too,' she told him. 'Not for all your daring escapades and your secretive attempts to rid the world of Satanic cults and covens. Nor even as a distinguished scholar, fingering texts that no one cares about anymore. But as the author of a series of children's books. About plucky little children running about in magical lands with talking animals. You haven't even written them yet, but I can tell you now: they are awful. Feeble Christian parables that people will jeer at.'

'Oh,' said Cleavis dully.

She could see the future. She could look into the bookshelves of the future. Suddenly I needed to ask her about it. My throat was parched and sticky, but I couldn't help myself. 'What about me?' I burst out. 'What will I be known for?'

Magda was appalled at this. 'Fox! How could you be so selfish?'

I shushed her brusquely. 'Tell me, goddess. Will I live my dream? Will I write?'

The burning blue woman sneered at me. 'Is that all you care for? You have killed your only living relative this evening and you stand with these others in the utmost peril, and all you care for is knowing whether you end up being the revered millionaire bestseller you dream of becoming?'

I nodded firmly. 'I do.' Wedding words, I realised. I was marrying myself to this self-loving future me. God forgive me, I didn't feel at all ashamed.

The demon woman seemed gratified by this simple answer. 'My master will enjoy your hubris,' she smiled. 'You are a worthy voice-piece for the Lord of This World.'

I gritted my teeth. 'I intend to be no such thing. On the contrary, I shall warn the whole world of what you are up to. All of you.' I glared about wildly at the nightmarish room.

The woman shrugged. 'We shall see.'

So preoccupied had we been in this talk of my coming career, none of us had noticed that the Grand Master - now gone quite feral - had darted forwards and onto the stone bier. He was kneeling astride my poor, uncomplaining Great Aunt Helen.

'Fox!' Magda screamed. 'Look!'

When I looked it was all too plain to see. Nimbly he untied the cords that Cleavis had fastened. He flipped open her head (with a nasty sucking sound) and, before we could stop him, the monstrous wretch had thrust a bony fist into her brain cavity.

An awful moan of protest from everyone observing covered most of the sickening noises he made as he rooted around. For a moment I was motionless in shock: an intense wave of nausea went rolling through me.

Cleavis barked: 'What the devil is he doing?'

'Stop him!' This was Magda.

The Grand Master had handfuls of my Great Aunt's brains all mashed up in his palms. Greasy gobbets of them were dribbling between his fingers. I was fixed on those vile details as I lumbered towards him. I was weirdly fascinated by his ghoulish pleasure: his grinning face as he brought that sample of matter up to his mouth.

'If he eats them,' the goddess warned, 'he will inherit everything your great aunt knew. That should be you, Fox Soames. That is only for you.'

I had no intention of letting him eat her brains. The old dear had suffered enough.

So I dealt with the Grand Master. I still had hold of that

pastry-cutting device. I aimed it straight at his jugular.

It proved effective enough. My very first cold-blooded murder. I won't go into details. But the Grand Master was dead. Sprawled at the foot of his new altar. I remember thinking that I still hadn't discovered which publishing firm he ran.

As I crouched there, gathering up the messy remnants of my great aunt's brains, I was aware of a general exodus from the place. And of the goddess's rasping voice in my ear. She was telling me that I knew what I should do with what remained of Helen's mind. That it was my right and my duty. That it was an important business, where brains ended up. And I needed to do it if I wanted to go into the future I desired.

Then we watched that bejewelled goddess crackle and disappear. Her last words struck me, at the time, as very odd: 'One day, Fox Soames, you will have to protect your own brains, and see that they survive. They will go to a girl called Karla. She will be a goddess. She will look just like this form I have adopted tonight. Watch out for her. Make sure she receives your knowledge. This is vital. Don't let your mind go to anyone else...'

Then she was gone. Back to damned hell, or wherever she had come from. And I knew it wasn't the last I'd see of such apparitions. In that quiet instant, I knew that both Magda and I were bound for a life together of madness and black magic.

***

I'm afraid my memory becomes somewhat hazy at this point.

I passed out, I think, under the nervous strain. I was aware that I was with my darling Magda and the redoubtable Cleavis. I knew that all the Satanists had fled the building. They had not been expecting a night like this.

And I recall the next morning.

Early, damp, beautiful, golden dawn over the manor. We

realised that this place now belonged wholly to us. The sun was brilliant in dewy cobwebs through the grass. The long line of evergreens down the drive were like sentinels. All was peaceful.

Magda and Cleavis were quiet and careful. They were treating me as if I were a victim of shellshock. All three of us moved like mice around that kitchen, knowing that, beneath out feet, under the stone flagstones and down in the cellar, the desecrated body of my great aunt Helen awaited decent human burial.

No servants turned up that morning. We were undisturbed. I think they had been warned to stay away, the day after all the revels. We talked gently about what to do next. Whether to report the death. About going to Oxford with Cleavis, to report to the other Smudgelings on what had occurred. At last, it seemed, I had penetrated the secret centre of their writers' circle: the real reason for their existence. Again I was in the middle of things. We anticipated a long drive across the country. It would take us weeks to recuperate after this adventure.

But in the meantime we had breakfast.

Magda ground coffee beans. Cleavis hefted down a great big, blackened skillet and fried up bacon and sausages and eggs. Distractedly I watched them frazzle in the spitting, soupy fat. When they were done, I quietly asked him to place the pan back onto the heat.

'Still hungry, old man?' he chuckled.

I shrugged. Then I took out the parcel I hadn't been able to put down all night, since the apparition had vanished. I opened the square of altar fabric quickly and dumped the slimy contents into the hissing hot lard.

'Oh, Jesus,' said Cleavis.

I ignored his qualms, and my own.

We stared at the pulpy, wormy mass as it fried in the bacon fat and slowly started to brown. The smell was rather rich, and good.

'I am going to come into my inheritance,' I told Cleavis

and Magda determinedly. 'I am going to inherit and I am going into the future.'

They were staring at me. I turned to set out a fresh plate and a knife and a fork for myself.

I was actually starting to feel very hungry.

***

This is where the tale of the first part of my life ends. Thank you for listening to an old, old man.

Good night, my dears. Good night!

PART FOUR

THE DEVIL FINDS WORK

ONE

It seemed that Effie had a new friend. That hadn't happened for a long time. She had kept the same store of familiar faces and eked them out, supposing that she wouldn't really need to add new ones. She thought that you got to a certain age and you don't go needing to know new people. There's nothing they can bring you now.

She was, she thought, old enough and ugly enough to regard the whole thing with a certain amount of suspicion. But, when Karla rang her home on Saturday morning she was flattered. She was suspicious and cautious and thinking Karla was mad, but she was flattered as well. She had been picked out as a likely-looking friend. And, from what Karla had said last night in the bar of the Prince Albert, it looked like she was needing new friends in Manchester.

Effie wasn't used to being picked out as friendly.

And, Saturday mornings, she wasn't used to the phone ringing. It made a strange, shrill noise in her living room. She hovered in her housecoat and slippers and stared at it. She wavered over picking it up. Probably it was someone from one of those call centres. Wanting to harass her. They'd got hold of her name and number somehow. She knew these people were often situated on the sub-continent and it seemed bizarre to her, that people all that distance away cared a jot what kind of insurance she took out, or whether she wanted her windows replacing. And, often their English was atrocious. She would try to get rid of them as swiftly as possible, even though she knew it wasn't her bill they were rocketing up by ringing from India. But these people lingered and lingered and they kept you hanging on.

She hesitated, sighed, and plucked up the receiver.

'Darling Effie,' came the half-familiar voice, and she was both offended by the familiarity and jolted with a weird excitement.

'Who is it, please?'

'It's me. Karla. We met yesterday evening. In the bar.'

Effie could feel herself colouring. This woman was making it sound as if she spent her every Friday night loitering around such places.

'Oh, yes,' said Effie and started wondering how Karla had got hold of her number. During the conversation last night Effie hadn't actually said very much. She had kept out of it. She had stood to one side and then sat quietly, when the three of them repaired to a table by the picture window. Effie hadn't liked to interfere. Sally and Karla were apparently acquaintances from way back and they had a lot to say to each other. Effie had done her usual thing, nursing her gin and lime, listening, and trying to blend into the wallpaper.

'...And perhaps you would like to help me out?' Karla was saying now. Effie had let her attention drift.

'I'm sorry?'

'I was just asking whether you'd like to keep me company today, dear. I have a shopping expedition in mind. Kendals, Selfridges, and so on. I've hardly got anything with me and I need a whole lot of stuff.'

Effie listened, biting her lip. She wasn't used to shopping trips like this. Sometimes on a Saturday she and Sally would have an amble up Market Street and a take a look at

Debenhams, and Sally was very fond of bargain hunting in TK Maxx. They weren't exactly enjoyable, those afternoons, but they made you feel as if you were in the swing of things. Everyone headed into town on Saturday afternoon. It was just what you did. It got a bit busy and you could get shoved around, but it filled up a few hours.

Effie had looked before at those rather grander, more expensive ladies who went to the more exclusive shops. She had noted their carrierbags as they had loaded them into taxis on Deansgate. Just last weekend she had heard two of them going on as they went by Kendals. One of them had been saying she was keeping an eye out for some particular shoes. 'Something in stone...' she had said. Effie tried to picture that exact colour. Then she tried to imagine being a woman who could fill her afternoons worrying that she'd never find just the right shoe.

Still, those two women had been very smart people. Effie had liked the way they were bustling on down the street with a mission in mind.

So here was Karla - a woman who had made an appearance on the Six o'clock News last night - and she was inviting her, Effie, to become just that type of lady.

'Is Sally coming along as well?' Effie had to ask. She made herself sound uncommitted. She hoped she sounded like she had no end of ideas for filling up her Saturday.

Karla sighed. Such a weary sigh. Impatience, Effie thought. She's spitting into that receiver. 'She says she's spending time with her grandson today.'

Oh, Effie thought. So she phoned Sally first. Of course. That's her real friend here. And Sally's busy with her precious Colin. I'm next best, of course.

'I don't know anything about her grandson,' Karla went on. 'Do you know him?'

'Sally's just about brought him up,' Effie said. 'His parents were killed in a house fire. He's been with her since he was a kiddie, really. She's very fond.'

'Oh.' Karla drifted off for a moment or two. 'Well, what

about it, Effie?' she said, rather brusquely.

'Well,' Effie stammered. 'I'm not really...'

'It'll be fun,' Karla urged. 'We'll have a lovely lunch together and you can tell me all about your life, and I can tell you all about my ridiculous life. Come on, Effie. I need someone ... sensible like you around. To stop me from blowing all my first six months' salary on my first weekend here.'

People might recognise Karla out and about. She'd been on the news after all. And Effie would blush and feel more self-conscious than ever. It could, it would probably be, quite horrible.

But it was something different, wasn't it? Better than watching sport on the telly, in her housecoat all afternoon. She didn't even like sport. Maybe athletics. She liked the cleanness of the springy plastic mats. And the one-piece outfits the chunky, streamlined men wore. The way they put chalk dust on their hands before attempting anything. It seemed a very civilised kind of sport to her. She frowned into the mouthpiece. 'All right,' she said, cautiously. 'Shall I meet you in...'

'I'll send a car,' Karla told her briskly. 'At eleven.'

***

So then they were out in town and, Effie had to admit, she was having her eyes opened.

Somehow I never understood the point, she thought. All of this is about enjoying yourself. All these things are here for you to enjoy. This plethora. She rolled the word around on her tongue as Karla tugged her arm, easing her through the commotion.

On this particular Saturday afternoon I am taking my time. Karla is making me stop and stand and take my time. To do things and enjoy things I never would have before. Usually I hurry on, I know. I think they're looking at me. I think they're going to make me buy something that I don't want. They're going to press something on me and I'll get confused and I shall end up wasting all of my money. And I will hate myself for it.

On the cool, spacious ground floor of Kendals department store Karla made Effie pay attention to the woman at a swanky make-up counter. She made her sit on a high metal stool and stare at her own reflection. Effie had to examine little pots and tubes of unguents and cream. Then she had to listen to them all talk about her face. And she became content to let them rub this stuff into her skin and swipe it off again with balls of cotton wool. Then they talked about what lovely skin she had, actually, and what marvellous bones. And Effie realised that she was having a nice time.

Karla was fussing around her as well, giving her own expert tips on skin-care. On what Effie might do with her hair. She knew what would match Effie's striking complexion.

Very respectable and smart today, was Karla. Effie looked on her approvingly. None of that vampish black and fishnet. But, of course, that was just her acting persona. Her celebrity uniform. Naturally Karla didn't dress and behave like that on her days off. This was her mufti, as it were. Karla was in a russet trouser suit, cut very flatteringly. A cream silk blouse. Effie thought the whole ensemble did very well on a top-heavy lady like her. She had already complimented her new friend on her very discreet jewellery.

Part of Effie had worried, as she'd been driven into town by Karla's chauffeur, that her shopping companion would doll herself up and be all showy, to attract attention to herself. But instead, Effie had been pleased. It turned out that Karla dressed herself very much like Effie would, had she the resources.

They looked at clothes together, slowly ascending the levels of the store on smooth-running escalators. Effie felt fresh and strange and stiff with all this new stuff on her face. She could feel the expense of it: it felt cool on her skin.

They made comments to each other as they compared fabrics and prices and the cut of things; what might wash well and what would last. They found that many of their opinions exactly chimed in. Who would have thought it? Effie chuckled to herself as she waited while Karla tried on a number of garments. Who ever would have thought they'd have anything in common at all?

Not Sally. Never in a million years. She'd have kept us far apart. Far apart. Sally hadn't been at all pleased to see Karla last night in the bar of the Prince Albert. Not really. No matter how she fussed and went on all jaunty. She looked at Karla like something she'd never wanted to clap eyes on again. Which was cruel really. What with Karla trying so hard. And that was why Sally had made excuses today. Sally was determined not to be friends. Well. It would be her missing out. No one else.

I don't believe, Effie thought, in cutting off my own nose to spite my face.

Then she thought: but yes I do. That's what I've always done.

And then she was confused.

They went to look at shoes.

Karla praised Effie's small, rather elegant feet, with their high arches. Said her own were diabolical. Effie perched on a little leather stool with one foot stuck out, angling it about. 'Oh, I don't know...' she laughed, as if Karla was being ridiculous, paying her the compliment. Though really, she had always known her feet were one of her more special features.

Karla seemed pleased to see Effie laughing. She urged her to try on different pairs. Some of them had heels Effie would never consider braving. She wondered how she would look, strutting about. Karla was very good though. Whenever she suggested that Effie slip into something more stylish than she was used to, she never made it seem like criticism. It never felt as if Karla disapproved of how Effie looked now. Even trying to walk across the thick carpet in a pair of heels that would pay a year's Council Tax, Effie still never felt old womanish and silly in Karla's eyes. That was the very last thing she wanted to feel.

Sally was impossible to shop with. When she went digging through the scraps and mismatched rails in TK Maxx she didn't have an ounce of dignity. She'd be elbowing people aside and having a good rummage. Effie always stood on the sidelines, pretending she wasn't there. 'It's all good stuff,' Sally had told her severely, on a number of occasions. 'These are all designer tops, you know. Knocked down.'

'Hm,' Effie would reply. She never did say much when they were out and about. She'd be thinking: have I locked the front door properly? Did I leave the gas on? Was that iron still plugged in? These were the kinds of thoughts she had when she was with Sally.

The two of them never went anywhere like this for lunch, either. In the basement of the new Selfridges there was what Karla called a sushi bar. More high stools to sit on and there was a conveyor belt going round in front of your nose like a miniature railway. All these dollies' dishes, brightly coloured, sliding by, like things Effie had never seen before in her life.

'This is an adventure,' she said, not knowing where to start.

'You might not like it,' said Karla thoughtfully. 'We should have gone somewhere else, really.' She peeped over at the small dishes. To Effie, everything looked as if it was very tightly rolled or wrapped up in parcels, or dyed unlikely colours to seem like something else. 'I just wanted to try it in here,' said Karla. 'They never used to have places like this in Manchester. Not in the old days.'

Effie perked up at the mention of the old days. 'Oh, we used to have all sorts,' she said. 'There was always everything here, if you looked for it. Even sushi, I bet.'

Karla laughed - a lovely, deep warble of a laugh.

'It's not different,' added Effie. 'It's just dressed up a bit smarter.'

189

That stopped Karla chuckling and Effie regretted sounding a little sharp then. But now she needed help, sorting out which utensils to eat with, and how to hook the dishes off the shunting conveyor belt. Karla helped out, trying to work out the system for her. It was delightful, really - all this fiddly, picky food. There was even a tap in front of them and when you held one of the tiny cups underneath, it would rush hot green tea into it for you. It was that pungent, oriental-type tea that you could only sip at.

As they picked and fiddled Effie decided that she had to brave it.

She looked at Karla's famous face beside her (odd how no one had recognised her in her respectable garb today) and she asked outright: 'When was it, then, the last time you saw Sally? Years ago, I suppose?'

Karla glanced at her and started messing about with the slivers of pink stem ginger that they had both found rather overpowering. She was trying to take the tiniest piece possible, jabbing at it with a toothpick. 'What has she told you?' Karla asked.

'Nothing much,' Effie shrugged lightly. 'Not a lot. She's quite deep, really, our Sally. Doesn't give much away. All she's told me is that you two knew each other as kids...'

Karla smiled. Really, when she smiled, she looked so much younger. And at these close quarters you could see how marvellous her skin was. There was an almost unnaturally healthy sheen to the woman.

'We were evacuees together,' Karla said at last. She went hunting for her cigarettes and lighter, then realised that she wouldn't be able to here, where everything was fresh and raw and new. 'Yes, that long ago. A long, long time. We went to the same family, up in the Lake District. We'd lived in the same street, you see. Known each other all our lives. At that point, in Kendal, it was almost like we were sisters.'

'Sisters!' Effie was starting to tackle a purple-tinged slab of tuna. It was on a bright green plate.

'Oh, yes. I don't suppose she put it that way, did she?'

190

Effie jabbed at her fish. 'Like I say, she doesn't let much slip, our Sally.'

Karla tossed her beautifully streaked mane of hair. Effie wondered if all of it was real. 'I was the mucky kid on the street,' Karla explained. 'Deprived, I suppose they would call it now. Abused, maybe.'

Effie kept a respectful silence, as she would if anyone brought up that curious word 'abuse'. It was something she had noticed had crept into the language, these past twenty years or so. The word had taken on an increasingly frightening, serious charge and the respectful silence that had to follow its use had to be proportionately intense. You couldn't mess around with words like that. It was something she had heard from people of even her own age: that they could look back on their lives and start thinking and using that word. It seemed to make them feel better somehow.

Karla was going on. This was the next stage, Sally thought grimly. When the person starts telling you the details of their purported abuse. Then you have to measure it up, along with them, against the known scale of historical neglect and maltreatment. And you finish the conversation by agreeing between yourselves that no life is easy; everyone suffers; there are degrees of different hurts. But Karla was an actress, Effie reminded herself. She'd use her training to elicit even more sympathy than that which Effie was prepared to show.

'Sally and her mother were both very good to me,' Karla was saying. 'My own mother was hopeless. When the war finished at last and we were sent back to Salford, I found my mother in a terrible way. She'd always been a drinker, of course. Always running after the men. Before the war she'd been relatively glamorous. There was always a queue of new uncles down our street. She got a name for herself, not that she cared. Well, by the time I was back home from the Lake District I'd grown up quite a bit and suddenly I was the one having to look after her and do for her. The

191

supply of booze and the uncles had started to dry up for her. She had turned into this proper old woman.' Karla laughed and shook her head. 'God, she was probably twenty years younger than I am now. But she'd never looked after herself. Back then, people didn't look after themselves, did they? Not in the same way. Not like now.'

Effie nodded slowly. She was thinking about the adverts on the telly that had models saying they pampered themselves and titivated themselves all day long. And that you, the viewer, should do just the same. 'Because I'm worth it,' is what they kept saying. Their endless self-serving mantra that seemed like an excuse, a justification for all their nonsense. No one seemed to quibble with that. Everyone believed that they were worth it too and the thought of that scandalised Effie sometimes. The money and time that people lavished on themselves. Her own face was burning under its new mask of dear creams.

'Anyway,' said Karla. 'We were on the run after that. We went from room to room, boarding house to boarding house. We only ever got places with one room. Shared a bed. Did our laundry in the sink in the corner. We had to climb out of the windows, sometimes. Just to get away from paying the rent we owed. The two of us - shinning down drainpipes! Chucking our cases down into the alley! Sneaking away. Well, we had nothing. And as time went on we couldn't stick each other. We rubbed along so hard and so long we brought out the worst and hated each other.'

'How terrible.'

'So that was when I lost touch with Sally. When me and my mother were moving around so much. Flitting. Keeping away from the law. Sally's mother was quite respectable, you see. A nice person. A proper widow woman. And I think she'd have thought we'd gone beyond the pale. Decent people didn't do flits like we did. Decent people stayed in one place. They faced their problems. They didn't have their problems chasing them. I was too ashamed to walk down our street, you see. I couldn't even walk down our original street, where I'd been happiest.'

Effie nodded.

'I think perhaps Sally and her mother might have thought that I'd drifted into the same way as my poor old mum. With the dirty men and the gin and all.'

Effie looked shocked. 'Would they have assumed that?'

'Oh, they thought that I was a wild one. They definitely thought that. And I was, but not in the way they suspected. I was full of fire and energy and determination. I was wilful and ambitious. But then, I had to be, didn't I? I had to be if I wanted to haul myself out of the muck and to become an actress. You can't do that by just staying at home and living the quiet, respectable life. You've got to stick your head over the battlements...'

'You knew then what you wanted to be?'

Karla smiled. 'It was like a little voice had told me. Whispered it to me. A little demon on my shoulder, bending in close and hissing. When it came to my ambitions I was on automatic pilot. No question but that I was going with my demon. I knew where I was headed.'

Effie loved to hear about other people's ambitions, even when they hadn't worked out. She found them the most fascinating thing about anyone she met and she was always amazed at how gladly people would discuss them. Karla was turning out to be no exception. This was like being on a chat show. Here was Effie, firing off the questions, and here was Karla being so unguarded. She was opening up complacently as they nibbled at their delicate dishes.

'So you never saw Sally again after that? After you left your street?'

'Oh, yes,' Karla nodded slowly. She toyed with her chopsticks, tapping out a little rhythm. 'I don't know if she'd remember. But we saw each other again when I was about nineteen. Just out of the blue we bumped into each other. We were both having tea at the Midland Hotel...'

'How glamorous,' Effie smiled.

'It should have been.'

'It used to be lovely then,' Effie sighed. 'When was that, the Fifties? High tea at the Midland...'

'I really wanted it to be lovely and special,' said Karla. 'And Sally was the last person I expected to see sitting there. It was a shock to both of us. Of course, we recognised each other straight away. I was there with a man.' She smirked at the look on Effie's face. 'It wasn't anything like that. He was a theatrical agent. Piggy, they all called him. He was the first one to show any real interest in me. For the right reasons, I mean. Well, he'd made it plain that I held no interest for him in any other way than professionally, as an actress. So I thought: well, Piggy chum, you'll do for me. So we were having high tea together, to seal the bargain, while the ink dried on the contract we'd both signed. He was going to represent me! He'd seen my promise and would let the whole world know. He'd sworn to make me a star.'

'It sounds like a film,' Effie said, rather moved.

'That's exactly how I'd always wanted it to be. Sat there in those grand old chairs, with the waitresses fussing around us and those silver salvers and doilies and the little cakes and fancies ... Well, I was Bette Davis and Katherine Hepburn and Joan Crawford and oh, everyone, all rolled into one.' Karla was looking into the distance, down the length of the conveyor belt and laughing wistfully at herself.

But she made it, Effie reminded herself. It wasn't just some silly kid's dream. Karla really did eventually become famous as a film actress and now she's a household name. All across the world they know her. Effie herself had seen Karla's name flash up across the screen at the cinema and on the telly, though she'd never admit to watching those kind of late night films. Horror wasn't quite Effie's cup of tea.

'Piggy even ordered champagne. He wanted to do things right. It came in a bucket, all frosted up and they had these long-stemmed flutes. First time I ever saw them, and the champagne tasted dry and sweet and grown-up and strange and everything I'd imagined it would. It was exploding in my mouth after the first sip and I was determined not to cough or choke or to show myself up in front of Piggy.'

'Fancy calling him Piggy!' Effie laughed.

'He was an ugly brute of a man, bless him. Bright ginger hair coming out in tufts everywhere, his ears, his nose. He had this little red Hitler tash and a combover. And he'd wear green checky outdoorsy clothes, hunting and fishing type of wear. He'd put on airs to make you think he was posh. I don't think I was ever fooled. But I never doubted that Piggy could get me into the business. I knew he was the real thing.'

'And Sally was there?'

'Right at the next table. It was a shock to both of us. There I was, all hell-bent on my success and my future and celebrating and all, and here's this young woman at the next table, doing exactly the same thing. With a young man. Well, I'd already cast a glance in his direction. He was an agreeable, beefy-looking soldier type. I'd had a pang - I admit - of envy. Why did other girls get to hook the good men? And I hadn't paid much attention to the girl that this handsome chap was with. Then I did. And it was her. All grown-up and staring back at me with this funny look all over her face. A look that was like - What right have you got to be here, Katy MacBride?' Karla gave a sudden bark of laughter. 'It was exactly the look she had on last night, actually. In the bar at the Prince Albert. As if she still thought I didn't belong there, or anywhere. I was still the mucky kid who'd been dragged up and who lived down the end of her street.'

'Sally isn't like that...'

'She is to me, Effie, dear. I'll always, always be muck in her eye.'

195

TWO

Colin had a new friend, too, that Saturday afternoon.

But at first he was alarmed.

When he woke up his breath stank, he only had yesterday's clothes with him, and he remembered that his pals had made a show of him in Lance's front room last night. They had left bad-naturedly when it became clear that they'd be leaving without Colin.

He woke up and there was a host of awkward thoughts waiting for him. He vaguely took in the fact of the crisp sheets' luxury and the presence of a warm, heavy, sleeping body lying only inches away. He listened to the oddness of the city sounds just outside the window and he tried to orient himself. But soon enough all the difficult thoughts came rushing up. And then the headache and the swooning dizziness.

He imagined dressing hurriedly in his dirty clothes and setting off for home on the first bus he could find. That's how it would happen. Without even time to wash, and he'd be sitting on the bus with his hair sticking up daft. Everyone who saw him would be thinking: slag. They'd know what he'd been up to, and they would be right. And worse - Lance would be awkward with him forever now. They had done something Lance would have started to regret the moment it began. Now Colin would be forced to regret it as well. He would be forced by the way Lance would avoid him in future. He'd stay away from Slag! bar. He'd slide his eyes away uncomfortably should they happen to bump into each other again. Ever again. That was it now. Something promising nipped so brusquely, so disastrously, in the bud.

Beside him Lance was beginning to emerge from a heavy sleep. He slept like an animal, all selfish and abandoned, hogging the space and the bedclothes. He had pushed Colin right to the side. Colin had balanced there, in shock, feeling begrudged, cool under a slippery sheet.

He would have to handle this very carefully. When

Lance woke up properly he would have to make sure he was tactful. They had ended up doing exactly what Colin had promised only the day before they never would.

'Oh, hi,' Lance said, coughing and sitting up gently. He'd grown an awful lot of stubble in the night. Suddenly Colin was conscious of the burn of it, all over his body.

'Hiya,' Colin said and was stuck then. Usually their conversations had a shape. Barboy and customer. Usually at this point they'd be talking about what drink Colin would fix for him. Then some general chitchat about the morning's news. There was a pause now, as if they were both thinking this, and Colin looked at the blue and tastefully pale walls; the muslin billowing softly at the window; the heavily framed prints - Picasso line drawings, quite suggestive.

Lance rolled over the other way, away from him. Colin stared at the hard ridge of muscle down his side as the sheet slipped back. Colin was sitting with his knees drawn up, rather demurely.

'I'll make some coffee in a bit,' Lance told him, without looking round.

Colin frowned. 'I think I remember Raf and Vicki leaving. Did they?'

Lance was quiet for a bit. 'Yeah. I don't know what they came round for anyway. Kids. They weren't too happy with you. Not going with them.'

'Oh.' Colin looked at Lance's smooth shoulder; the top of his head.

'Fuck 'em,' Lance said. 'They're not nice friends for you.'

'What makes you say that?'

'I just didn't like them,' Lance said, yawning. 'That Raf is just a sniffy queen. I don't know why you bother with him.'

'I don't, really,' Colin said, his heart leaping with betrayal.

'You're better than that,' Lance went on sleepily. 'You're

not just some ... little queen, coming up to have a look - at what I've got, and where I live. You're not like that.'

'I'm not?' Colin was losing his voice. He suddenly felt exposed. What was he supposed to be like? He had expected - and usually was - chucked out on the street by now.

'No,' said Lance and turned round to look at him. Before Colin knew what was going on he was being hugged hard and aggressively. It was almost a fatherly kind of thing and that made him feel very odd. Then Lance was rolling him around and he was forced to unbend and lie straight again, pulled back into the bed. Lance was pressed against him, pushing against him, and fragments of last night's events were starting to come back to him, bit by bit, as they went about doing them all over again. Like doing them again would convince them, confirm them.

It wasn't like sleeping with anyone else. Colin remembered that much from the thick of last night. The novelty of it all was still rolling around in Colin's head like a penny about to drop, and he could feel it knocking away inside his body like all his joints had come loose. He had been tenderised, sensitised - and maybe a little roughed up.

Right now Lance was lying right over him: all the weight of this older man was pressing him right down and bearing on him hard. It was like having the full brunt of someone's attention on him. A stare that refused to blink away. The torture of an endless Chinese burn. Colin wasn't used to that quality of attention. He knew he was labouring these points to himself as he ran them through his mind. He was too conscious, too panicky, worrying if he was doing the right things. He was too callow, too inexpert with this mature man's practised body.

I'm too used to the teenaged sex I've been having, all through my twenties.

He had only come out at nineteen. Only started doing stuff at twenty. And 'doing stuff' was how he still thought of it, what he still called it to himself. And he only ever 'did stuff' sporadically anyway: when he got lucky, or when he got drunk; when randomness, loss of inhibitions or chance collisions in hectic circumstances paid off for him, or forced his hand.

All these encounters were starting to seem slighter than they had even felt at the time. More furtive, less comfortable. Less meant, somehow. A whole lot of games of sardines, murder in the dark, or ping-pong. Lots of squash with mismatched partners. Or maybe that most insultingly simplistic game of all: 'Snap!' Maybe that's what all his previous sex had been like. 'Look! Snap! I've got just the same!'

Was making love with Lance making him retrospectively dismiss his own sex life thus far? So soon? Maybe it was just sleep deprivation, anxiety, hangover. They were conspiring to make everything up till this moment seem utterly useless. This moment with Lance Randall and his perfect, even, TV star teeth nipping gently, playfully down the length of Colin's neck. Making this weird electricity he'd never felt before run round past his ears and over his scalp. He felt the length of Lance's cock nudging under his thigh and he struggled to free one hand and take hold of the famous Randall equipment. He felt it pulsing in his grip and Lance raised his pelvis neatly to let him take a tight hold. It had the girth and heft of a small and frightened animal. Not frightened, Colin thought, gripping harder and starting to stroke him hard: alert, aquiver, preparing to strike.

Lance laughed. 'What are you doing?' His voice was right in Colin's ear. 'Don't wank me so fast.'

'I'm gonna make you come...'

'You sound like someone awful out of a porno film,' Lance said, and his hand brushed down, knocking Colin's away. 'We've got time. Don't push it. What's the hurry?'

Colin swallowed his reply as Lance started kissing him again. So what had been the hurry, after all? And what was his problem? Why did it have to be a race?

199

Colin remembered nights of vague and quite drunken sexual shenanigans, when it seemed that making the other bloke come first was the only object. And not out of any kind of gallantry. It wasn't in order to concentrate on their pleasure. It was to make them feel that they weren't being short-changed. That they were getting something out of this transaction. It was to stop them regretting it.

And it was as if that were the only way to make them feel or seem vulnerable. That was the truth. As if at last, now that I can see your face above me as you come on me, on my chest and all hot in my face and trickily in my hair - I have managed to solve the puzzle of you. I have managed to fettle you and best you, here in your own bed.

It wasn't like that with Lance. Lance seemed to know that's how it usually was, and he was determined that this would be quite different.

I feel and seem vulnerable, Colin thought. I feel and seem involved. I feel and seem like I'm not thinking about anything but the fact that Lance is kissing me now. And I can respond and not think it through. I could stop thinking altogether if I wanted to. And I won't try too hard to please him. And now what's he doing? And what should I do back?

'Colin,' said Lance, quite patiently. He was smiling at him, but there was a glimmer of exasperation there, at the back of his eyes. 'Jesus. Don't you ever relax?'

***

They had coffee in companionable silence.

Lance threw open all the windows in the living room, letting out the fug of last night's smoke and the wine fumes and the bad moods of the last couple of days. Colin had started to pull on his own, worn clothes and Lance had looked at him appalled. He reached into a drawer and threw him an expensive pair of new pants. Now Colin was sitting on a corner of the settee with his bare legs drawn up, balancing a large coffee bowl in both hands. His knees had marks of old scars on them. He wished he had something to cover them up.

Lance went to sit on the armchair, away from him, in a kimono-type thing. He was looking at Colin oddly as he sipped his scalding coffee. 'Well, you did it.'

'Hm?' Colin knew what he was going to say. All of a sudden, he knew. He swallowed the froth of his coffee too hot and it went down in a boiling lump.

'All that stuff you've been saying for ages. I knew you were just after ... what we've just done.'

'I really wasn't!' Colin burst out. 'Really. It just all happened ... spontaneously, didn't it? That's how it seemed.'

Lance grinned slowly, ruefully, as if he didn't trust what either of them were saying at all. 'It seemed to. It was weird. I thought I'd grown out of being impulsive.'

'Yeah, well.'

'When we were in the hallway, I just...' Lance shrugged. 'I just wanted to get you into bed. It seemed the right thing to do.'

'It was,' Colin smiled back. Then he thought it was incredible, ridiculous, that here they were just grinning at each other across the room. Lance was usually so guarded. So private.

'It's been a long time,' Lance said, 'since I've had anyone properly in my life. Anything serious.'

'Serious? Is that what this is?' Colin laughed. Then he thought: Shit. Lance is looking deadly earnest.

'Yes, I think it might be. Don't you?'

'Um,' said Colin. Oh, great. Um. What a brilliant contribution.

Lance was quite straightforward about it. 'I know my own heart and mind. I'm quite a plain and centred person. And I think I know when I might be falling in love.'

Was he taking the piss? Was this some kind of perverted revenge for his having succumbed to a one night stand? Because that's all it was, surely. Colin wouldn't have dared expect anything else. And now he didn't know what to say.

He felt silly, sat there in a new pair of somebody else's white pants and listening to this. So he didn't say anything at all. He thought - if I close my eyes I'll see all my golden chances passing me by. But this bloke could still be taking the piss and trying to be cruel, couldn't he? He could still be about to laugh in my face and then chuck me out down the fire escape, back down on Canal Street, where I belong. A stab of hurt, there, amongst all the broiling, caffeine-fuelled confusion, as Colin thought: It's always other people's flats that I'm in. Even when I'm at home. Where is my home?

Lance was still looking at him. A clear-eyed stare. Like he was being completely honest with him. Oh, Jesus.

'I mean it, Colin. You've had quite an effect. Already.'

'I thought you weren't gay.'

'I hate that word. It's trivialising. I don't think it means anything, really. I never did. And so I don't think of myself as anything in particular. So I'm not tied to anything. That's how I've always found it best to carry on. I've been with women and I've been with men. I've not really been in love. Didn't really trust anyone. And everyone - I suppose because of the roles I play on the telly - they think I'm a right dirty get.' He laughed. 'Maybe me and Karla have a lot in common, after all. Mind, she really is a dirty get in real life, believe me.'

Colin's head span around for a bit. Oh, God, and I only brought Raf and Vicki round because they wanted to use Lance in order to get close to Karla. She's the one they want to see. I was using Lance! Raf was making me do it. That's how it was last night. I was exploiting my slender link to Lance. I never dared hope - I never thought there'd be - anything like this -

Lance was on his feet now, sturdy and determined in the silky kimono. Oh, help, what's he saying now? He came to sit on Colin's settee. He lifted up his hands, all helpless, like he didn't know what to do with them. A dumbshow of exasperation. He slapped his palms down, hard, one on each of Colin's scabby knees. Colin jumped. Those eyes, again. Boring straight into his. Shit. Stop looking at me like that. Suddenly Colin didn't know whether to laugh or cry. Actually, he felt more like crying. What was that about?

'I feel like the male lead in some old Victorian costume drama,' Lance said. He was sounding husky, for God's sake! He was making himself all emotional. But he was an actor, wasn't he? He could turn this shit on at will, couldn't he? 'And I'm paying court to some delicate flower of Victorian maidenhood. That's what you bring out in me. That kind of ... tenderness. You look pale. And vulnerable.'

'Like a girl?'

'Yes. Sort of.'

'Oh, great!'

'I don't know. I'm simply trying to say, to explain to you...' Lance shook his head. His palms were still cupping Colin's knees. His fingers were flexing. 'When I was making love to you, just before, it was strange. I had this feeling ... that it was all too quick, all too easy... I wanted to do it all differently. I didn't want us to be gung-ho and wham-bam. I didn't even want it to be sex. You were offering up so much of yourself. But with all of your defences up. A fractured, broken kind of bravado you've got. So there's nothing sacred in actually giving yourself up; in submitting to me...'

Colin blushed. I submitted to him? Then he thought - Well, I did. I always do. I'm like a frigging puppy.

'And I didn't want all that. Not all at once.' Lance grinned and tweaked Colin's chest. 'All that can wait. I want...' He sighed deeply and struggled with the words. 'I think I want to cherish you.'

It was on that word that Colin started to listen to him properly. It was a word he'd never heard anyone actually use. Not in a normal conversation.

THREE

Sally dusted her nick-nacks all Saturday afternoon.

She had gotten hold of one of those feather dusters from the shopping channel, the ones with all the attachments. They employed static electricity in a very ingenious way to lift household dust off in long, easily disposable strings. Ideal for going round her porcelain dolls and her commemorative plates. Even so, they took a full afternoon to care for. Sally didn't like detritus about the place.

So she beetled around, keeping herself busy, telling herself she wasn't waiting for Colin to turn up.

She hoisted out her old records, wanting to fill the flat up with music she hadn't listened to in years. They were oily, purple, black and brown and crackling with their own accumulated dust. She slid open the window so the syrupy strings of Mantovani went out into the open air, all these storeys up.

She wasn't waiting for Colin to come home. It might have been nice, to tell him the tale of last night and maybe spin it all out to make it more dramatic than it was. He'd have liked that. But he wasn't here and that wasn't to be helped. She wasn't going to worry about him. That would do no good. He'd have hooked up with one or other of his pals. She had a number for that Raf, who was supposed to be such a mate of his. Maybe she'd try it later.

I should have met up with Katy when she called. Karla, I mean. But really, I did think she had a cheek. It's not like we're long-lost best buddies. Karla was acting like this is some TV show where they reunite loved ones. I've wondered what happens on those programmes, once the cameras stop running and the audience go home. Oh, everyone looks so glad to see each other. Often they've been flown in from somewhere far-flung, like New Zealand and no one's seen each other in decades. It's all tears and hugs and make-up running. Then the presenter steps to one side and sings a sentimental song about time and distance and love never changing. I always think, Well! They've kept apart this long. They can't be that keen on each other. And when the show's finished they'll slip apart again and there'll be Christmas cards but they'll peter out eventually. Everyone ends up back where they started.

Yet maybe I should have seen Karla today. At least she's making an effort. Last night at the bar of the Prince Albert she took me by surprise. She was affable. She was all right. She was treating me like a friendly face she didn't mind seeing.

It stirs up all sorts, a reunion like that. As we talked I kept thinking about my mam and our street and her mam and how they ended up. Just the sound of Karla's voice put me back there. Her accent was coming out stronger, the more we talked. She was dropping her airs. I could hear my mam telling me I had to keep a watch out for poor little Katy MacBride. Well, she's done all right for herself. Now she's going to be on the telly every night. That's the ultimate accolade, isn't it? Isn't that what everyone wants to do these days?

Back then, she really faded out of our lives. We knew they had the bailiffs after them and it was all moonlight flits they were doing, from one set of digs to another. We'd hear bits and pieces. They had all sorts of people after them for money. Her mam had sunk really low and I bet we never even knew the half of it. She was dragging Katy through the dirt, is all my mam would say about it. Still, Katy stuck by her mam. Even when she could have bolted. She stayed with her.

I saw Katy and her mam in St Anne's Square once about that time. They didn't see me. It was Christmas and all the stalls were out, the crib by the church and the lights. Hot chestnuts and all that. The theatre crowds were coming out of the Royal Exchange. And here's these two coming along, looking a bit shabby. Shabby but flashy, that was her mam. She'd cleaned herself up a little, but she looked tarty, like she was back on the game again. I didn't go over. They were sitting on a bench by the church and my feet marched me smartly away. I didn't want people seeing me going over to them. Katy was in a green woollen coat that looked old. She was smoking right there, in front of her mam. I could see her looking into space, or at the crowds as they came out of the theatre, down the steps. Her eyes were flat, hostile, envious.

I don't know how she got into acting.

My mam used to say, How do you think? Well, they call it acting. That's not what I would call it. They start off as street walkers. Round Piccadilly Gardens. That's what it really is. Or in them hootchie kootchie shows. I know the kind of thing. That's not like acting Shakespeare, is it? It isn't Pygmalion or any of that lot. Can you imagine Katy learning her Shakespeare? No, course you can't. She'll be up on a stage somewhere, in front of a whole lot of dirty men. And she'll be showing her bum. That's the kind of acting she'll be doing, bless her heart.

My old mam wasn't far off the mark, was she? Katy certainly went on to show off her bum. And everything else.

One time I even went to see one of her films. This must have been the Sixties by then. She hadn't been doing them long. She was the bright young thing. I was with Mick. Ah, bless him. It wasn't his kind of thing at all. Queuing outside the Odeon. He liked a war film. He liked men's films. He couldn't see why I was suddenly wanting to go and watch a horror flick, a monster film. He found the whole thing highly suspicious. But I'd read about it in the Evening News. Local girl nabs star part in vamp shocker. 'Blood in the House of Love.' Well, it was a lurid title and I could understand why my Mick was embarrassed queuing up outside.

It was a whole load of teenagers out on dates standing with us. It was freezing and dark, the wind slicing up Oxford road with the buses. There were a few funny-looking characters waiting with us, too. The dirty mac brigade is what Mick called them. He was a man of the world, my Mick. Merchant Navy, all that. He didn't hold with nonsense. He'd seen quite enough. Now I was making him sit through this silly, overblown film. On the backrow, like we were kids. As if we'd gone to sit on the cinema's ratty old plush to neck and fondle each other because there was nowhere safe to do it at home.

Yet we were respectable. Married for years by then. Getting out like this into town was a proper treat. It was unusual for us.

God, I never really think this far back. It doesn't do. I shouldn't. What good can it do?

And I never sit in the flat by myself, thinking about Mick. Standing outside the Odeon with the snow starting to come down. In his long coat with the collar up. His old hat on. Pulling a face at me because he'd rather be at home. He'd rather we'd just gone to the boozer on the corner.

The film was horrible, of course. It was more horrible than I'd expected it to be. The house of love, indeed. There was precious little love in it that I could see. Plenty of blood, mind. That was when Technicolor was all the rage. You saw colours that you'd never see in real life. That old gothic castle was brilliant blue and the night time forest was a sheeny purple and green. The blood when it came on the screen was ketchup red and we were glad we never got hotdogs.

All the flesh was unrealistic. Here came Katy MacBride like a sleepwalker, moving up the stairs of the castle in a lightning storm and her skin were like alabaster. I'd never seen her so clean in all her life. Her nipples came out like cherries on a bakewell tart.

In the seat next to me Mick was getting flustered and eventually outraged. 'This,' he hissed, 'is a mucky picture, Sally.' I could see he had squashed his choc-ice in surprise. The yellowy cream had melted down the sleeve of his good Friday night shirt.

'I didn't think it would be this bad...'

'It's an XXX!' he said.

'That's Katy MacBride,' I told him. 'A good Catholic

207

girl.'

'That one? That's the one you know?'

I nodded. She was the sleeping victim of a vampire queen. She was tossing in a four poster bed and the camera was poking its nosy way between heavy swags of velvet to catch a glimpse as she rolled and heaved, all nightmare-stricken on her counterpane.

Then in came the vampire lady: a guest in Katy's father's castle. The vampire queen was sexy too, but in a disquieting way.

'Not something I can put my finger on,' Mick said later. 'But I thought, that's not attractive. That's not sexy. And I were right, weren't I? Doing nasty business with other women. I didn't know what you'd brought me to see. It were like a ... medical film. Deviants and all sorts.'

Always upstanding, my Mick. He never liked talk of anything perverted. He'd just leave the room. He wouldn't have the News of the World in the house. He didn't like mucky men's talk in the pub and the pals he had knew better than to start on like that when he was around. A proper, old-fashioned gent, my Mick.

And he wasn't standing for this. Women kissing women. He watched as far as the point when Countess Dracula or whoever she was slipped out of her robes of satiny night and then he was up on his feet as she leant forward to caress the breasts of the girl on the bed. She was nibbling at Katy's neck and the two of them were moaning so hard the speakers were vibrating. Then they pressed up together and Mick grabbed hold of my hand and he was pulling me up out of my fold-down seat. He never said anything, he just yanked me up and dragged me along the aisle, scattering choc-ice wrappers, the lot. We were treading on everyone's feet and I kept saying our excuse me's, and there were all these hisses and boos from the seats behind us. Mick wasn't to be deterred. He wasn't staying for any more of this filth. I tried to duck and crouch down. Our silhouettes were marked out against those colossal, pale, female bodies on the screen as they went tumbling over each other; one shot fading into the next in the endless melting and shifting of a cinematic love scene. I even caught a glimpse of Katy's face as she drowsed in the vampire queen's embrace. I saw her eyes widen hugely as she succumbed - and got her fatal, sexy bite on the neck.

Then, next thing I knew, we were out in the foyer, which was overwarm and carpeted in bright blood red. All the light and all the red made me feel a bit queasy. Shame, I suppose it was, too.

Mick was furious with me. 'Who on earth writes rubbish like that?'

The funny thing was, I knew. I actually knew who had written the script, and the original novel upon which 'Blood in the House of Love' had been oh-so-loosely based. His name had appeared in the opening credits, in golden Gothic lettering a foot or so tall. He had been the other reason I had wanted to see the film that night. Fox Soames, the famous writer of the Occult. Fox Soames the rescuer of children. He was someone else I knew in real life.

I didn't have time to explain any of this. Mick was whisking me out into the hurly burly of Oxford road on Friday night. My head was still swirling with lurid pictures and the snow was stinging my face. We found a pub where everything seemed familiar, smokey and green-tiled and chockablock with folk. Everything was normal. And as clear and settled as a pint of bitter.

***

The phone was ringing.

The record had finished ages ago and Sally found herself in a trance, stroking her feather duster.

'Hello?' She hoped it wasn't Karla again, trying to persuade her.

It was a funny voice. Queer-sounding. 'Is that Colin's grandmother I'm speaking to?'

Her heart started thumping. 'It is. Is he all right?'

'Oh, he's all right, all right,' said the tight, brusque voice at the other end. 'I just thought I'd ring you and tell you what he's been up to.' Something malicious in that tone, Sally thought. She didn't trust this person one bit.

'Who is this, please?'

'I'm Rafiq,' said the voice quickly. 'I'm Colin's so-called best friend.'

'Oh, you're Raf,' Sally said, cupping the receiver and squinting. He sounded to her like a spiteful girl. 'Well, what's happened to Colin? He's not in trouble, is he?'

'Only with me,' Raf sighed.

Sally felt her hackles rising. 'Are you going to tell me about it or not, Rafiq?' There was odd chatter in the background at his end. It sounded like he was in a shop of some kind.

'Your grandson is a real slut,' Raf said at last. 'He makes out he's better than everyone and me and that I'm the dirty one. But at least I was home in my own bed last night. Do you know what he did last night? He was doing everything he could to schmooze round that Lance Randall off the telly. We were up in his flat and Colin got as drunk as he possibly could and then he was all over the fella. It was downright embarrassing. He made a right show of himself and I'm ashamed to call him my mate. Me and my friend Vicki had to leave, we were that taken aback. Well, your grandson stayed there. In that flat. I thought I'd better let you know, in case you were bothered. But that's where he is. Hobnobbing with the stars. I expect we'll see him in HIYA magazine next.'

Eventually Raf ran out of steam.

'Well?' he said. 'What do you think of that?'

Sally was pursing her lips. 'Did you ring me up to give an old woman a nasty shock?'

'Pardon?'

'And you call yourself Colin's best friend?'

'I am! That's why I'm telling you...'

'Stop it. I don't want to hear any more from you. You

sound like a nasty, spiteful boy. I shall tell our Colin what you've done. How you tried to mix it and make trouble for him.'

'What? But he's a starfucker! A tuft-hunter! He'd sleep with anything that's been on the telly!'

'That's got nothing to do with me. Or you,' said Sally calmly. 'I'll thank you not to ring me again in future.' With that, she slammed down the phone.

Then she bit her lip. Oh, Colin. What have you been up to now?

FOUR

Vicki was staring up at Raf in admiration.

He'd handled the phone call fantastically well, standing there at the till, while she saw to the queue of customers and earwigged. He hadn't let himself lose his temper with the hysterical old woman. He had simply stated the facts. And he was quite right. Colin was indeed a terrible star-fucker. It had sickened them both to watch him licking around Lance last night.

That Lance. What a loser. Vicki couldn't believe how sad and pathetic he'd turned out to be. His flat wasn't all that special, either.

This morning Vicki had binned her Lance Randall t-shirt. She planned to record over all her Menswear videos.

'That's told her, anyway,' Raf said, simmering with anger. 'God! What a horrible old bitch. No wonder Colin's as fucked up as he is. Being brought up by her!'

'Yeah,' said Vicki. 'You know I never liked him, anyway.'

Raf let out a great, dramatic sigh. There was still a queue at the cash desk. He looked at the next fat, greasy punter, who was holding out a pile of fanzines and a plastic model of something off Star Trek. Raf grabbed them off him and shoved them in a bag while Vicki rang them into the till. 'He's got the tiniest cock, you know,' Raf said. 'Did I ever tell you that? That's one of the reasons I'd have nowt to do with him in that department. He couldn't do anything for me. I need a great big strapping one I can get my gob around. I could hardly find his. He was useless in bed.'

'That's £32.74,' Vicki told the sweating punter, her eyes gleaming.

'Really,' Raf went on. 'I think, if you've got a cock that small, why even bother? Chop the fucking thing off. No one's gonna be impressed. Become a woman why don't you. That's got to be better than going about with nowt to show off as a man. No, I think anything less than eight inches semi-erect is a waste of fucking time. It's an embarrassment. I don't want it. No - you can take it away! Stick

212

it up your own frigging arse! You might as well go home and stay home or hack the bloody thing off with your nail-file. I wonder what that Lance made of it. It's bound to have been a disappointment.'

'I bet,' Vicki grinned, watching their customer shuffle away.

'All he had to do was quite simple. His instructions were easy. All he had to do was tap Lance for information about Karla, But no, he's much too selfish for that. Once we're all up there in that flat, he forgets all about us. We don't matter to him anymore. We're just his mates.'

'So what do we do now?' Vicki asked. She was keen to move on, past the subject of Colin.

'I hate losing friends,' Raf said. 'I really fucking hate falling out. But sometimes it just has to be done. You can't let people shit on you like that from a great height.'

Vicki thought back to the look on Raf's face when it became clear last night that Colin was going to be staying with Lance. Raf had looked ... affronted, was the only word for it. He'd looked sick with disgust.

They had left with all haste and hardly a word and walked down Canal Street and into Piccadilly together to get their night buses. Raf had been so furious he'd hardly had a good word to say to Vicki, either.

'Look at me!' he'd burst out eventually. 'I'm young and I look fucking fantastic and I'm slim as a whip and look at who the fuck I'm stuck with at the end of Friday night! And that Colin is...' He had clamped his gob shut at that point and glared at Vicki as she stood hunched in the bus shelter under an advert for mobile phones. She could have been quite hurt at what he was saying, but where would that get them? Of course she wasn't who he wanted to be stuck with. Of course he was gutted, and wasted.

A thought had struck her then. 'You didn't fancy Lance, did you?'

He tossed his head, eyes blazing back at her in contempt. 'Of course not. But if anyone was going to shag the old cunt, it might as well have been me. I could have got Karla's number out of him.'

'You'd have ... shagged him?'

'It's just a shag, isn't it? You can easily put it out of your mind. Specially when there's something important at stake. You can suffer that much. It's usually over quickly enough.'

Vicki shrugged and sat heavily on the plastic seat. She was wondering if Raf wasn't becoming a little obsessed with this idea of Karla Sorenson. Still, she had to admire him as he stood there, silhouetted by the new lavatorial fountains and hugging himself, all rigid with ire. The way he talked so casually about shagging. It was marvellous. It was liberating to Vicki. 'Maybe you can still go and pick someone up,' she suggested, trying to sound casual. 'You said, down by the canal and that, it's easy enough...'

'That's not the point,' he snapped. 'I'm not bothered. For fuck's sake. If I just wanted to come, I'd get you to jerk me off. It really isn't the point.'

Vicki was holding her breath in shock. But then her bus was pulling up, all its windows lit and all its seats empty. And Raf was still looking at her like she would never, ever get the point.

***

Now he knows that she's actually here in his city, Rafiq wonders what he would say to Karla Sorenson. Any day now he might bump into her in the street. Or in a queue in a shop. She had to use shops. She was human, same as him. In the foodhall at Marks and Spencers, picking rolls out of baskets with plastic tongs. On an escalator in Harvey Nicks. Him going down, her sailing upwards through the middle of the building. They would meet in the middle where two hypotenuses bisect, with all those cabinets of luxury items laid out, seemingly hovering in mid-air around them, like angels. And for a second they would meet on the level, and look into one another's eyes.

214

Raf couldn't imagine how she would be dressed. He didn't want to think of her looking dowdy, unimportant. Or looking any different to how she did in the theatre of his sporadic Fan Fiction, and that was an amalgam of every sluttish, gorgeous, vampiric ensemble she'd ever donned for her movies of the Sixties. Only not cheap. When they met face to face she'd be in some expensive version of those past incarnations of Karla. He'd invented these outfits and dolled her up quite lavishly in the endless stories he had written about her.

When he went back and read these stories of his - his fanfic, his slashfic, his adventures in glorious hypertext - he was disappointed, of course. The exact look and feel, the precise sensation was never there in the text. Everything he ever imagined never transmitted itself into the writing. The words were bold and crass and lifeless. As he wrote his vampire lady tales, he thought them redolent and heady and shimmering and fleshly. When he read them back - when they were already afloat on the worldwide web - they seemed flat and minimalist and sometimes silly. Not much detail. Not much plot. A bit cartoony. Fanwank.

If he met her to talk to in the city one day, he'd say: I feel like I know you because I've tried to get inside your mind. I feel like I know all about you and I suppose that's a very daring thing to say? The words would leap out of him and the sentences would be fully-formed: the thoughts perfect and exact. And she would smile and nod at him and she might have heard such things before. It might be par for the course. Raf was no fool. He knew what fans were like and what they thought. How they contented themselves. How they consoled their fevered selves. He knew he was no better than that.

Except. Except she would see something special in him. In just that quick eye-contact and those few phrases. She would see the natural genius there. The beauty. The flash in his eyes that matched hers completely. That marvellous ironic glint she would occasionally give to the camera, to

215

the audience, during her close-ups. A tiny thing, a tiny glint, that most of her viewers would miss. A wink to the wise and the initiated, that ironised her whole perform-ance; that sent the whole thing up. Even in the most terri-fying of scenes, and the most sexy, Karla would swivel round to the camera and give this tiny little sign that she was taking absolutely none of it in earnest. It was the kind of sophisticated, self-crafted gesture that Rafiq adored.

He had practised his own version for hours in the mir-ror in the bathroom at his parents' house. His sisters bang-ing on the door, needing to be in, and he was rehearsing, perfecting, what he called The Glint.

It was the means by which superior beings recognised each other. A glamorous, coded little signal that simply said: Well, here I am and what a dump this is we both find ourselves in. What a tawdry, dreadful world we have to survive. And we are better than this, aren't we? Me and you. We were made for far better things, my dear. Our raw material was superior to this tatty dross from the very start and we've moulded it and pounded it and rarefied our-selves until we became this advanced and superior and delightful and aren't we glad? Hello, my dear, this is how we work out in the end. And just look at us both! Aren't we great? Glint. And - heavens! - she was glinting back at him. Even as he genuinely bared his soul in a way he would never do with anyone other than her, the two of them were glinting like mad at each other. They were still sending it all up. Oh, nothing mattered. Nothing but us. Oh, don't mind me, my dear. I'm so glad to meet you. Soul sister. Soul brother. Glint. Glint. I'm so pleased that I've come across you, in that actual flesh.

FIVE

Ask Colin what the photo shoot was like and he wouldn't have been able to tell you. Lance took him to the studios but left him outside. He was wanting to involve Colin in his life and Colin thought that was good. But he thought he'd be meeting everyone right away and getting introduced, but after they took a cab from Canal Street, bombed over to the studios on the edge of Castlefield, Lance bundled Colin into a pub for the morning. A nice, old, traditional pub where, Lance said, they look after you and the barmaid was Thai. He said that was where the cast and crew often went for lunch when they were filming or rehearsing and, if Colin looked out, he might see some famous faces while he was waiting.

Then Lance was off and it was clear he didn't want Colin around while he was having his piccies taken. Piccies of him and Karla all wrapped around each other for the local and national press. Whether that was to spare Colin's embarrassment or Lance's, Colin had no idea. But Colin ended up spending late Monday morning in a bar full of heavily varnished tables reading the wrinkled Sunday supplements, passing time, swallowing down bubbly lager before it went warm.

Lance had been wearing a beautiful suit. Really nicely tailored. You could see. So nice it was hard to see what colour it was. That subtle. He'd been off like a shot. And he'd seemed so keen on Colin up till then.

This was Colin's first still moment. His first time alone after a weekend of seismic activity. Lance's sudden - well, what? Affection, enthusiasm, this rush of unconditional love - it had knocked Colin sideways. He'd had uninterrupted hours lavished upon him. He was dizzy with tiredness; freshened up on new booze and fags and the expensive unguents and creams kept in the Japanese style bathroom and now he was rubbed raw, through the unfamiliarly sustained contact from someone who actually gave a shit about him. It seemed. And now, after sitting alone - the varnish on the pub table so thick it made the pint glass stick - Colin was actually missing the bastard.

Then Lance came back. Flushed with being the centre of attention. His job done. A successful, tidy operation. When Colin looked, it was as if you could see the flashbulbs preserved in Lance's dilated pupils. He said Karla hadn't been too much of a cunt. That was the way he put it. Not as much of a self-serving cunt as he'd expected. A professional, she'd been focused on the task in hand. Dragged up as vampire lady numero uno, of course and flapping around the place with her bazoomas thrust out to catch all the free publicity. She was enough of a pro for that. So she hadn't been impossible.

'I needn't have worried,' Lance said. 'Maybe I overreacted. I should have known she'd behave. I didn't even mind when she draped her raddled body all over me. She was right. That shot will make the front page of the Manchester Evening News. It's just work. We can do that much.' He declined a drink - hastily, surprising Colin. Colin's lagers had gone to his head and he'd figured that wouldn't matter: Lance being such a boozer, he'd soon catch up. Make Colin feel less lonely in his headachey Monday lassitude. But Lance wasn't drinking. He had plans for Monday afternoon, and Monday night. He laughed and wouldn't tell Colin what the evening plans were - but this afternoon, he announced solemnly, he wanted to take Colin home.

'What?'

He wanted to see where Colin lived. He wanted to meet his gran. He wanted to announce to her in person that he had fallen in love with Colin. And that he wanted to look after him and take him off her hands.

Was I ever in her hands? thought Colin dazedly. Was I ever a burden to anyone? And do I ever want to be in anyone's hands again?

***

Lance had to sign to get into our tower. Eric on the desk downstairs made him do it, to seem extra vigilant in his job, but also because he wanted an autograph. As Lance bent his head over the desk Eric raised both eyebrows at me: I was bringing celebrities home!

I didn't say anything. We took the tiny lift up to the ninth floor. Lance was looking around with interest, though there's nothing to see in the lift. I know. I've been trapped in there before.

'I didn't think you'd have a security guard,' he said. 'That's good. I could do with one in my flat.'

I smiled, but I'd been watching him ever since we'd got out of the taxi. He was determined to find everything about the place I lived in quaint. We had left his gorgeous, taste-ful place in the world far behind. Now I felt awful coming back to mine.

I let us into our flat and straight away he was onto how roomy it was, how surprisingly airy: how these council flats were little palaces in disguise. We were standing in the poky dark hallway. I could hear my gran jumping up from her armchair, having heard us come in, realising I had com-pany. She'd be dashing about having a tidy, in the seconds it took us to get down the hall. I could hear the rustle of her knitting bag. She liked to use a plastic carrier bag to keep her wool and needles in. I'd bought her a number of lovely, smart, purpose-made knitting bags over the years that she said were too nice to use. They'd go in the cupboard and she'd stick with her Tesco carriers. They got punctured by the needles and eventually fell apart. She'd be so ashamed of them she'd have to hide them behind the sofa, all in a panic, when company came. Like now. We walked in to find her kneeling on the settee, bundling things out of the way.

She straightened up and did an amazingly composed double-take. She greeted Lance like she was the Queen at a garden party, gently taking his hand.

'I knew the face was awfully familiar,' she smiled, as he

219

introduced himself. 'Of course! You are one of my very favourite actors, Mr Randall. But I'm sure Colin has told you that already.'

Lance grinned at me quizzically.

'I had no idea Colin had such illuminous friends,' she went on. 'Now, what can I fetch you? Colin, lovey, sit him down. Make him feel at home.'

'I was just saying, what a lovely place you have here,' Lance said smoothly. He gazed at the UPVC windows, taking in the whole view of the city centre. 'Panoramic,' he said approvingly. 'Do you realise what you'd have to pay to get this these days?'

'I've been here since the late Sixties,' Gran said proudly. 'I was one of the first to move in, up in the sky. I've never regretted it. Colin's lived here all his life, haven't you, love? He doesn't know what it's like, to be anywhere else.'

***

One of the really great things about Gran is the way she can suddenly make a party out of nothing. That afternoon we had salmon sandwiches with cucumber, biscuits with cheese and cocktail onions, and then three kinds of cake. The best china came out - the Royal Doulton that had once been my mother's, all gold and rose trim. My gran has this great sense of occasion and an ability to get the tone just right. Out came the hostess trolley; doilies appeared on the nest of tables; a Mantovani record started playing, seemingly of its own accord. Without, it appeared, any discernable effort on her part, we were having high tea and enjoying ourselves: sitting in a huddle and eating cake.

This was completely typical of Gran. I could see that she had won Lance over completely, in a matter of minutes. Through the proceedings I would catch her eye now and then. She looked shrewd and amused, wanting me to see that she'd cottoned on to my game. She knew that Lance and I were somehow together. I could see in those glances that she was pleased and bemused and worried and sad and eager to get it right, all at the same time. Also, she was annoyed that I'd not given her fair warning of our arrival and that I'd been away since Friday night. Though she lavished attention on Lance, there was an edge to her dealings with me during our tea. It was brittle as the brandy snaps I never even knew we had in the kitchen cupboard.

'We've got something else in common, Lance,' Gran confided. She was using his first name easily now, and eyeing his expensive clothes like she was trying to see through for the labels. 'Besides Colin, of course.'

'Oh, yes?' Lance smiled. I was impressed at how unflustered he'd been through all of this.

'Hm-m,' she sang, pouring the last of the tea from the bulbous Royal Doulton pot. That meant the sherry would be coming out of the sideboard next. 'Karla Sorenson,' she said, brightly.

He paused and blinked before he said, 'Really?'

'She's your new co-star, isn't she?'

'Indeed she is,' Lance said levelly. 'In fact, I've just come from my first dealings with her on this show. A publicity photo shoot.'

Gran clapped her hands. 'How wonderful! Did you see it, Colin? Did you meet her?'

'Uh, no,' I said. I was slicing up the rest of the swiss roll.

'Well,' said Gran. 'A photo shoot. No wonder you're so smart, Lance. Did she behave herself then, hm? She was always a bit of a livewire, Katy.'

Lance frowned at her.

'Oh, I knew her well before she was Karla,' Gran laughed sagely through the crumbs. 'I remember when she first started appearing in the movie magazines and the papers and that, and they were going on about her being a big new British Star, and I couldn't understand why she'd taken this funny name. Foreign-sounding. Then, she was putting on that daft foreign accent as well. Like something out of the Iron Curtain.'

'So she's really 'Katy', then?' Lance smiled.

'She was when she were on our street, years ago,' Gran told him. 'I was evacuated with her, you know. Did Colin tell you?'

'No,' he said, looking at me. 'He didn't.'

I shrugged. Shrugged like my head had been in such a whirl these last few days I hadn't had time to think straight.

Gran was over in the sideboard. 'After I saw her on the news I went through some old things,' she said, tugging open the stiffest drawer. 'I knew I had this somewhere.' She held out a small, faded photo so we could both see. It was so old it was just about falling to pieces. Most of the cardboard backing had come away so it was like a scrap of dirty cloth she was making us squint at.

'That's you? With her?'

Gran gave him a wry grin, almost flirtatious. 'We were all young once upon a time, Lance.'

I'd never seen Gran as a little girl. You could see it was her. There was still something stern and pinched in her rounded face.

'Who's the two grown-ups?' I asked her.

The photo had been taken outside a terraced house and everyone was screwing their eyes up against the sun: the two little girls, one dark, one blonde, and the wrinkled, bearded, hobbit-like man and a skinny, really tiny woman in an apron. It was a photo before the days of flashes, when they had to go out on the street to get their picture taken. Something very touching about those photos. Something you don't see anymore in people's collections of snaps: whole families bunched up together outside their front doors. This is our house. This is where we all live together.

'That's the Figgises,' Gran sighed. 'I haven't looked at this in ... decades, it must be. Funny how they stay looking just the same. Brings it all back exactly. They look smaller, and younger, actually, than I remember.'

'They look like proper country people,' said Lance, peering intently at the worn snap.

'I suppose they were,' Gran said. 'Like people out of another age.'

'They're who took you in?'

She nodded. 'And we thought they were the funniest looking things we'd ever seen. Me and Katy, getting off the train in Kendal, just praying that it wouldn't be the Figgises we were going to. They looked like the weirdest ones of the bunch. Well, we knew we'd end up going with them, to their narrow little house. Still. I suppose they were kind enough to us. I can see that more clearly now. When you're a kid you resent everyone. Even those trying to take care of you.' She looked at me.

'So the girl you were put with, that was who turned into Karla?' I was gobsmacked. I'd heard Gran's stories about the war, but I thought the girl with her had just been some girl she'd lost touch with. Not Karla. I didn't know they were that close.

'For a while we were like sisters,' said Gran. 'Till I ran away.' She laughed gruffly, and took the photo back. She shoved the drawer closed with her hip and returned with the sherry and three sparkling glasses.

'You ran away?' I certainly hadn't heard this bit before.

'Towards the end of the war,' she said. 'If we'd kept a proper eye on the news and all that, we'd have known we'd be sent back to Manchester soon. But I ran away, anyway. Katy stayed with them.'

'Where did you go?' Lance asked.

Gran was pouring the drink. 'I was rescued, I suppose,' she said. 'By a couple who vaguely knew the Figgises. Moved in the same circles, you could say. They lived in a big house in the Ribble Valley. A really big house. A mansion.'

'But why did you need rescuing?' I asked. 'Was it Karla's ... Katy's fault?'

'Not really. She got mixed up in what the Figgises were messing around with. Them and their friends. By the time I realised what it was all about it was too late. Katy was in pretty deep and there was no getting her out of it. I had to leave her behind.'

'What was it? Drugs?'

Gran laughed softly. 'Drugs? Back then? Jesus, Colin. It was hard enough getting hold of sugar back then. Drugs!'

Lance was sitting forward, all alert. 'It was magic, wasn't it? Black magic.'

Gran glanced at him, a suprised look on her face. Then she nodded very slowly. 'That's what it seemed like. To me. And to the Soamses, who were the couple who rescued me and took me in and eventually returned me to my mam here in Salford. The Soamses had been involved in their coven, too. That's what the two of them did. Infiltrated suspect covens. And to them the Figgises' lot seemed harmless at first. A few rituals in the woods and dancing around by firelight. They said they were trying to defeat the Nazis through white magic. They wanted to turn back the possible invasion by larking about in the trees and on deserted beaches. Well, it wasn't just like that. The Soamses discovered that they were into something much nastier. And I was best off away. Even though the Figgises seemed so nice. And Katy stayed behind and, I suppose, got into it even deeper.' Here Gran looked perplexed. 'That's the kind of world it becomes impossible to leave. Once you're in that far, you can never get out. I've always thought that. Fox Soames thought that. He told me to watch out for the person Katy would turn into. He told me to watch my back.'

I stared at my gran.

'It's no accident, all them creepy films she's been in,' Gran said vehemently, mistaking my surprise for scepticism. 'Everything she's done has been about the black arts. Everything. She's spreading the word.' Gran's voice had gone rather thick. A terrible pall was spreading over the tea table. 'She was even in films based on novels by Fox Soames. All he wanted to do was warn the world. He knew she was up to no good. He tried to get her out of all that.

And every film she was ever in, everyone she was around, all of it were cursed. Fox's wife, Magda Soames. She died. Killed in an accident when they were visiting the set. When they went to sort Karla out. Magda karked it. And I think it's all down to Karla. All the electricians, script writers, extras and co-stars who've died while she's been around, working on a film. It's too many. She's damned.'

Lance set down his tea cup. 'I know,' he said. 'I know exactly what you mean.' He looked at me hesitantly, and then back at Gran. 'I've tried to warn people. For years. I've tried to tell them. I've seen at first-hand what Karla can do. No one believed a word of it.'

Gran nodded in satisfaction. 'Well,' she said. 'I'll back you up, Lance. I know. Everything she touches turns to ash. I know because I was there when she first gave her soul to Satan. When she was just a kiddie. I know the damage she can do.'

I couldn't believe this. They'd switched into a different mode, all of a sudden. My gran and my new boyfriend. Suddenly they sounded like vampire hunters.

Lance had gone white. 'She tried it on me. She tried it on my mother first. My mother died. And I was in Karla's care. She tried to take my soul, too.'

SIX

Lance didn't care if he sounded paranoid and mental. He felt a bit sorry for Colin in the midst of this conversation. Poor Colin, who was already so bewildered at Lance coming on so strong and being so keen for the past few days. Lance wouldn't have blamed Colin if he'd backed off right then and wanted nothing more to do with him.

But didn't Colin see? There was serendipity here. Or fate, or destiny. Some force was bringing them together. Look at the three of us, Lance thought, having tea together and there's no real reason for it. Just that me and Colin have happened to have started seeing each other. I had no idea Colin's gran knew Karla and had a piece of that woman's past in her safe-keeping. Why would I even suspect that?

Lance suddenly felt as if he was being told something. He was being warned and protected by an invisible force. A force opposed, perhaps, to the dark forces that Karla represented.

And that was why he was with Colin. That was why he had thrown in his lot with the boy so quickly and easily. He knew it hadn't really been like him, to behave like that. It just wasn't him at all. This force knew that Lance had to meet Colin's gran. It had duped Lance into falling in love, just to get its own way. All for the greater good.

Lance had been prepared to forget about Karla. He'd got so embarrassingly worked up at the thought of her coming to Manchester. He couldn't see past that. He'd got scared. He'd thought she was coming here to do him in. To reclaim him, body and soul.

But Colin had been his distraction. When he woke up with Colin on Saturday morning, all that horror had gone. Dissolved out of his mind and bloodstream. It was like waking up with the sun streaming into the room. He realised that he didn't have to dwell on the past at all. That woman didn't have to be allowed to take over his life and fill all his thoughts. And when he saw her today he'd thought: Well, she's just a harmless old woman after all. Just a jobbing actress. She's nothing to me.

But this was too weird. This link to Colin's gran.

Lance didn't believe in coincidence. He just didn't. He thought all things happened for a reason. There was a pattern somewhere, here in this.

He was used to finding patterns. In his day-job he was a soap actor. He read his scripts every week and his fate was dictated by the panel of writers who sat in the conference room above the studios. By now he knew all their tricks. He could see their plot lines and their schemes and leitmotifs spiralling and stretching out ahead. He could sometimes anticipate what was coming. Every soap actor he knew kept on the ball like this. Agog for meaty storylines. Alert for getting the chop. Lance was particularly skilled at guessing what was in store.

And that was how he felt now. Karla had them all tangled up. She was drawing them in closer. She was behind all of this, as she always was. She was plotting.

Colin and his gran had to work hard to calm Lance down. He was getting himself into a right flap. He really did sound paranoid to them as he stood up and paced around the living room, gabbling away and looking out at the cityscape. Colin had never seen him so perturbed and rambling. He was letting his words run on ahead of his mouth and not being very clear at all.

***

Gran fetched out more sherry. Lance looked to her like a drinker. Someone to whom something very stiff and very dry wouldn't come amiss. He thanked her and slumped back down.

'Sorry,' he said. 'It's just ... She brings everything back up for me. I thought I'd dealt with it all.'

'Katy's like that,' said Gran. 'I've had all weekend, roving over the old days. She's just one of those people who can get to you.'

'Lance,' Colin told him. 'It doesn't matter. She can't hurt you. She can't affect anything. We aren't being drawn into anything.'

He looked up at Colin, anguish in his eyes. 'But that's my second surprise,' he said. 'Remember I wouldn't tell you what the plans were for this evening?'

Colin nodded.

'We're going for dinner,' he said heavily. 'With Karla. We arranged it at the end of the shoot this morning. We got a bit carried away and decided it was the best thing to clear the air. She's booked a table for us. Me and you and...'

Gran tipped the sherry into his glass again. 'And I'm coming as well.'

He smiled unsteadily. 'Karla's bringing some other people. Friends she says she's made here already. A porter from the hotel she's staying in...'

'She didn't waste any time,' Gran sighed.

'And another friend,' said Lance. 'Esther, or Ellie, or something.'

'Effie!' Gran burst out. 'Effie's supposed to be my friend, the cheeky mare!'

Lance shrugged. 'Anyway. That's what's happening tonight. A nice Italian restaurant near the town hall. She seems to be drawing us together...'

***

Lance couldn't bring himself to tell them the full story of Karla and his mother. He gave them some of it, in the remainder of that afternoon, as they prepared for their evening out. The rest of the tale he kept, as ever, to himself.

My mother, he said, was everything Karla isn't. I know I idolise her and always have. I probably go too far. You've seen the picture in my hallway, Colin. You said it yourself, I've got a shrine to my mother.

She was classy. She was graceful. She used to stand by the scoreboards and the glittering prizes in evening dresses on TV quizzes and she became very popular. Then they sacked her because she had me out of wedlock. The sponsors wouldn't have her on anymore, even after the bump went down. That's how it was in those days.

So it was just me and Mum together and she had to work. Her agent was called Piggy and he said she needn't worry. She had the British Film Industry to fall back on. Studio comedies and thrillers and, eventually, horror. Business was booming. She was able, she was gorgeous. She could sing and dance and she could scream. Sammi Randall could look like dynamite in anything she was given to wear. She appeared in the very last Ealing comedies, the earliest Carry Ons, and she was in the Hammer movies through their heyday. Never starring, always to one side, maybe one or two lines if she was lucky. But she was there to provide an alluring backdrop to the main action. It was enough to get by, to keep us both in babyfood and shoes and tea bags through the Sixties. While everyone in London was partying, she was home learning her scripts and bringing me up. Slowly I became aware of her public life.

My favourite moment of all the many moments she occupies in those movies comes in the dinosaur flick she made. She manages to look fabulous in a furry bikini, as a cavewoman with a Doris Day coiffure. She has one line and it's in perfect, clipped, King's Road tones: 'Well, I don't mind roasting a pterodactyl, but how the devil do I stuff it?'

This was where she met Karla and how Karla came into our lives. They became friends amongst the polystyrene rocks of the set of 'Prehysteria!' the cavewoman musical. Karla was the star of the show, of course.

They all caught fleas off the furry costumes. They were covered in itching bites and the script was, of course, an insult to their intelligence. But they were a team of women making a British film together. No Christopher Lee, Sid James or Peter Cushing in this one. Just lots of leggy extras in furry bras and pants fighting rubber tyrannosaurs and thinking they were making a feminist movie. Naturally they had the time of their lives.

Karla took Mum under her wing. I remember Karla coming back to our flat a few times, along with members of the crew. Mum's fee had gone up, and it was Karla who taught her to take charge of her money, and helped us look for a better place, closer to her. I was about twelve and I remember sitting up late in my pyjamas, watching these exciting film people drinking and smoking and dancing round our new house. It was like the party had decided to come to us.

Karla remembered Mum when it came to her next star vehicle. 'Get Inside Me, Satan!' The one they filmed in a quarry. Another vampire queen extravaganza, written by Fox Soames. The best of its type, say all the movie books. Soames himself and his raddled boozy wife even came to see the filming. They lived with all of us in those grotty mobile homes in a valley in North Wales. I was there too, of course. Mum took me everywhere. I thought everyone lived like that.

Mum was one of the vampy slaves of the evil vampire queen, but she came back to our caravan every night to make me beans on toast or a poached egg, and to read me to sleep.

This was when Karla was at her height. The height of her fame and popularity, and also her powers.

That film marked the turning point. That was the film that was cursed.

It was the one during which Magda Soames died. I can remember seeing her shuffling about between the trailers and across the set in her mink coat, acting all grand and sniffy. She thought she could order everyone around because her husband was the great writer, Fox Soames. None of us rabble would be there if it wasn't for him.

There were all sorts of rumours that he was having an affair on the set. That was the real reason he was there, the dirty old sod. And he had the effrontery even to bring his wife. No wonder she was so foul-tempered. By then the production had already hit a few snags. Quarrels about decency with the studio, electrical faults. Several cans of rushes had mysteriously combusted en route to London. Costumes had shrank. There were dozens of retakes. Everyone was becoming fractious. The director was young. It was his first feature. Everyone knew he was supposedly gifted and brilliant, but they were starting to doubt his mettle, his pragmatism. His was another name apparently cursed by that film. He was killed the following year in a water-skiing accident. When you put them altogether, that's a lot of people dead who were connected with 'Get Inside Me, Satan!'

And there I was, at my tender age, wandering about and watching all the grown-ups at work and play in that freezing valley. It was like running away and joining the circus. I remember walking about late at night between caravans, stepping over humming cables, keeping out of the arc lights. I wore slippers and a woolly checkered dressing gown Mum had bought me for my birthday. I thought I was the bee's knees, everyone knowing who I was. Everyone being so proud of Sammi Randall and her cherubic son. Thinking she was an angel and a great actress, destined for great things.

All the time we had the devil in our midst. Well, I always thought that was Fox Soames. I thought he was surely the epicentre of the evil storm they brewed up in that Welsh valley and then committed to celluloid forever. He certainly looked the part: suave in his velvet suits and that gargoyle's face. Half-cut all the time on his brandy and champagne, furiously smoking black Sobranies and bullying the young director in his officer class tones.

My mum had read his novels of the Occult. In our caravan she had a shelf of well-thumbed paperbacks. She was thrilled to be in a film of his, and to actually meet him. She asked him to sign her yellow-spined, luridly-covered Pan paperbacks. He did so ill-naturedly, I remember, and he peered down at me with a wicked scowl, as if a mere child had no business on that film set.

It was being around that world, in all that industrious confusion of the filming, that made any other career but acting unthinkable for me. I sensed magic - not necessarily black - in the air on those cold Welsh nights.

If what I've been told by Sally today is correct, then Soames was only there to warn Karla. To rescue her from her wicked life. He wasn't the driving force at all. And, of course, he was dead himself, within a couple of years. Dead of the booze and a broken heart, they all said - though a few wags suggested he'd been dragged off to hell, having fleeced the devil for millions through the sales of his novels and movies. Now the devil was after his percentage. Others said that it was the cursed movie that got him: claiming yet another victim.

They can't even show that movie on the TV anymore. They banned it. I remember it being on once and I thought I'd tape it, because of Mum. But when I played the tape back the next day it was snooker. I've never been good at setting the video. The newspapers went mad about people being found dead, frozen solid in their armchairs. About power failures and pets going mad. Heart attacks and so on. It's not actually that scary a film, from what I recall.

Can the essence of evil really be trapped between the frames of a film? Squashed into the cans and the reels and ready to seep out again into the world?

Some of the fanatics suggest that. Ghoulish creatures, fans, of course. I keep an eye out for their speculations. The internet seems to be seething with conspiracy theories and what they call Fan Fiction about 'Get Inside Me, Satan!', Fox Soames and, of course, Karla Sorenson. Some people who weren't even born when that trashy film was made have let the damned thing take over their lives, their whole imaginations. Recently they've been saying that missing cans of unused film have turned up. Found in a church bring-and-buy sale. These were the ones that were meant to have been burned. And there's rumours that one unscripted sequence has Karla turn on my mum and curse her out, vilely. I remember her coming back to the trailer that day, furious and upset they'd had a falling out. Of course, the fans make more of this supposed out-take. Pointing out it must have been a real curse from La Sorenson, because my mum was dead within a year, as well.

This is how legends grow up, of course. That's the legend I've grown up in the shadow of. No matter how ridiculous it sounds to people, I still can't escape it. And this afternoon the legend seems more palpable than ever. The legend that Karla Sorenson brought true evil into that film and all our lives and, as a result, Magda and Fox Soames, the director and my mum all died.

They found Magda on the rockface, broken up like a doll and her brains spattered all over the scree. She'd climbed up the rocks in the middle of the night, pissed out of her mind in a nightie and her mink. We all heard the scream as she flung herself down on us, and missed. She'd been driven crackers, the inquest implied, by her husband's single-mindedness, his ruthless dedication to his career and his bizarre, unswerving conviction that the devil was at large in the world. Magda's capacity for rational thought and self-preservation had been utterly destroyed. The old man himself slunk away, ruined by guilt and grief. No more novels, no more stories.

I remember Karla being weirdly unfazed by all of this. When the young director gathered the entire, shocked company together and addressed them all in a shaking voice and led them in prayer, she was standing to one side, looking aloof and bemused. Almost scornful: that they thought they could ward off the evil in their midst so easily.

They struck the plywood sets. We decamped back to London. The director had decided we ought to leave, even before the studio demanded that we come away at once. They had enough exterior footage by now. They could adjust the script, rejig some scenes, do the rest on interiors, back at Pinewood, after Christmas. Nobody wanted to stay in Wales.

That was the last I saw of the company. I was sent to school. Karla had told Mum that I had to go. She was ruining my chances by keeping me with her. I had to get an education. Once more I had something to thank Karla for. It was hard, being torn away from Mum. We'd never been apart before. We both wept a lot over that. But the holidays were over. Mum paid some ridiculous fees. I went away from her and we both couldn't stand it.

Mum tried to fling herself into work. Floating about on the studio sets as a lesbian vampire. She sent some very funny letters to my school. How they had put her in a harness on wires and hauled her up over the fake forest and castle set and she'd had to flap the wings of her diaphanous nightie and bare her savage fangs.

The others boys would listen as I read out my letters in our dorm. Maybe it was easier for me to settle into a school like that, because my mum was famous. Some of them even had pin-ups of her by their beds. Or posters of Karla, actually, in her furry bikini from 'Prehysteria!' - and Mum standing in the background.

We had hissed, whispering conferences late at night in the dorm, on the subject of those racy vampire ladies and I was, naturally, the acknowledged expert in the field. I had been amongst them and everyone wanted the inside story of 'Get Inside Me, Satan!' Had Soames really been in love with Karla? Had they really conspired to murder Magda? Had I seen the woman's ruined body on the valley floor?

I became quite popular in my new school. I jazzed a few stories up for them. I told them there was real black magic involved of course, and real blood, and real sex. And that I had seen it all. We all became very excited about it. I got a lot of respect because my mum was a lesbian vampire. God, I even had my first ever bout of mutual masturbation over one of those posters from a horror mag. Me and whichever boy it was, getting worked up over those wicked ladies, working each other up to a froth on my truckle bed.

Very odd, maybe, letting someone wank you over a pin-up of your mum's best friend. Or maybe not. To the other boy she was a star and she was ineffable. A purely fantastic creature. To me she was Karla, who'd turned up at our house the day after Boxing Day, with a goose, some satsumas and three bottles of Prosecco. She was Karla who had persuaded my mum to send me away.

There was something extra thrilling and taboo about gripping on hard to my new friend's smarting, sticky cock and thinking about Karla in this whole new way. It was a kind of revengeful way, it seemed. When I came the first sight of my spunk frightened me, making the other boy laugh. I wanted it to be like holy water, burning into that cheap poster of the vampire lady.

**

Colin came out with the question in the end.

They were back at Lance's flat. Lance was changing into another beautiful suit. Colin had packed a few things into a holdall and was holding up different tops and discarding them, one after another. They were in the pale blue bedroom and Colin's gran was through in the living room. She was quite content to sit in the white armchair and wait. She thought Lance's flat was magnificent.

Now Colin was looking earnestly at Lance.

'How did your mother die?'

He looked away, smoothing down a shirt. 'Brain tumour,' he said at last. 'By the time they diagnosed her it was inoperable. It had been growing there steadily, for a while. Giving her those headaches, blurring her vision, making her forget her lines. It was Karla who made her go to her doctor in the end. Harley Street. They rushed her in. Few months later she was dead. She died while I was at school. I never saw her at the end. Wasn't with her. She never even told me she was ill.' He looked at Colin. 'Karla knew. Karla was with her at the end.'

Colin almost wished he hadn't asked. There was something very lifeless in Lance's voice. As if he had never told this story before, but now he had to tell it to Colin because Colin had asked and Colin was important to him. Colin felt awful.

'Karla told me all about it, when I came back, too late. Karla told me all about my mum at the end. Stuff I didn't know because I wasn't there. It was like that woman had taken possession of my mum's last weeks. Months. Caring for her, she said. Well,' Lance flapped his hands. 'I don't know.'

Colin didn't know what to say. To him it sounded like Karla had just been helping out. She had been a friend. Lance couldn't blame his mother's illness on her, surely?

I can't say anything, Colin thought. Lance has lived this story over and over inside his head for all these years. If it's helped him to blame Karla, well, maybe that's OK.

All this black magic stuff ...

Colin didn't know what to make of that at all. His gran had knocked him sideways with her own revelations. It was the last thing he would have expected from her.

No. It was better for Colin if he kept his mouth shut. He was out of his depth here.

'Wear that one,' Lance told him, just as Colin threw down another t-shirt. 'Come on. Your gran will think we're up to no good in here.' Then Lance grinned at him. 'You aren't getting fed up with me, are you, Colin?'

'What?'

'Older man. All this ... baggage.'

'No! Course not!'

'And tonight, of course, you'll be surrounded by all these old fogies. Not your usual night out...'

Colin shrugged. 'So?' Then he thought. 'Well, maybe...'

Hm?'

'I was thinking I should phone Raf...'

236

Lance pulled a face.

'Oh, don't look like that. He's been a good mate to me. And he's obsessed - really obsessed -with Karla.'

'Jesus,' said Lance. He could see he was beaten, though. He'd have to give Colin what he wanted.

'I just feel bad because Raf was so mardy on Friday night. And I've not rang him. But it would make his year ... his whole life ... if I invited him to dinner tonight, with the rest of us...'

'He won't make a show of himself, will he? Screaming and squealing at her?'

Colin smiled. 'Raf knows exactly how to behave. He'll be perfect.'

Lance sighed. 'Give him a ring then. The more the merrier, I suppose.'

SEVEN

'Out again!' said Effie. 'I was out for a meal on Friday night. Look at me now. Out again on Monday.'

She arrived at Karla's suite flustered. She was hoping she looked right for this evening. The suddenness of everything had thrown her. She had had to resort to her very smartest wardrobe. This meant hunting through the outfits she never wore. Expensive, slippery, pristine things she kept in polythene storage, ready for holidays she might one day take, or funerals, her own and others'. This was just such a dress: dark, plain, with its folds and seams so stiff they seemed to be squeezing her into a different shape. The shoes were ones she had never worn and they pinched.

'I'll pay,' Karla told her.

'Oh, I didn't mean that,' said Effie. 'There won't be any need for that. I'm delighted to come along. I'm delighted to be asked. But you must understand, this is something I don't do every week.'

Karla shrugged, hooking her earrings on. She was in a black trouser suit and she looked businesslike. There was something brusque in her manner. When Effie walked into the suite, gazing around at all the space, Karla didn't rush over to welcome her. She had asked Effie to come along and Effie had arrived. She didn't need petting or fussing over. Effie was glad, in a way, to be treated this casually, to be taken almost for granted. It was as if their friendship had moved on a stage already. Still, she felt awkward, standing by the door.

She caught Karla's eye in the dressing table mirror. In that moment she saw that her new friend was nervous. That was what the brusqueness was about.

'We have to ask the chauffeur to take us past the front of the town hall,' Karla said. 'According to Adrian, the producer. He phoned a little while ago. He says there's something I have to see. Something the City Council have done.'

'Oh,' said Effie. 'I wonder what.'

Karla shrugged again, examining her make up. Then she

turned to Effie and sighed. 'Oh, sit down, will you? I can't stand people hovering about me.'

As Effie hastened to obey there was a knock and the door came open to reveal a young porter in his scarlet uniform and golden braid. He was carrying a sports bag and looking keen. Effie thought he must have come for room service, until he closed the door and hurried in, as if he was used to making himself at home in the suite. He went to Karla and kissed her proffered cheek.

'He's my assistant, Kevin,' Effie was told. The young man was just about standing to attention beside her.

'Assistant?'

'The management have loaned him to me. Isn't he nice?'

'I suppose so...'

'He's chaperoning us this evening, aren't you, Kevin?'

'I am, Ms Sorenson.'

'What do you think, Effie? The two of us arriving on the arm of this young man?'

Effie had never arrived on the arm of anyone before. She thought it sounded a bit cumbersome, the two of them having a hold of him.

'I told him to bring his best suit,' Karla said. 'Have you, Kevin? Are you going to make me proud?'

'I hope so.'

'He's only on a pitiful wage. We shall have to tip him well. Off you go, Kevin. You may use the bathroom to change in. You're off the hotel's time and you're in my time now.'

'Yes, Ms Sorenson.' He hefted the bag and went eagerly to change. Effie watched the door click shut behind him, listened to the hiss of the shower as it started up. She was amazed at Karla's capacity to make people do things.

'What are you thinking?' Karla said, smiling at her.

Effie's voice surprised her by coming out in a croak. 'He seems like a pleasant young man.'

'Because he does what I tell him?' Karla laughed. 'And, as yet, I haven't paid him a penny. He's just happy to do for me, bless him. He's under my spell.'

Effie coughed. 'I think that's marvellous.'

'Do you?'

She nodded. 'I never got the knack of getting what I want.'

'Oh, you should try it some time.'

Effie wondered where her sense of scandal had gone. Here was Karla with a man young enough to be her grandson showering himself and singing in the en suite and she was saying he was under her power. And here was Effie, sitting and listening and, yes - if she was honest - trying to picture the dark young man in the next room. She couldn't deny it. She didn't think she had thoughts like that anymore. Why should the bodies of boorish, clattering younger men attract her notice at all? Let alone her imagination. They might as well be of a different species to her.

But something about Karla's rakish ease and her talk of will power and spells had sent Effie's thoughts straying. Well, everything was unaccustomed this evening. Her outfit was making her conscious of the shape of her own body is a way that clothes were never often permitted to do. She felt she had completely different boundaries tonight. So she couldn't help thinking about the warmth of the dark, young body in the next room, soapy, wet, alive under the showerhead. This was all Karla's doing. She brought about an atmosphere that made you - it certainly made Effie - capable of anything. She managed to make you feel more present in the world. And that meant all of Effie's senses.

Karla was eyeing her. 'I'll give him to you, if you like.'

'You what?'

'I mean it. He'll do anything I tell him. You could do with a toyboy, Effie. You should give him a go.'

'Don't be ridiculous! I'm ancient!'

'I don't believe you've completely dried out and healed up yet, have you?'

'I've never heard such awful talk. Besides, you can't just ... give people away like that.'

'Why not? He's keen as anything. He'd do it to please me.'

'But...' Effie was staggered. 'That's because of who you are. I'm no one. And anyway, what you're suggesting is grotesque and horrible. I'm sure you'd see the last of him if you go round making suggestions like that...'

'You don't understand. I really do control him. He's given up his will. If I want him to see and appreciate the beauty in you, then he'll happily do so.'

'The beauty in me...' Effie laughed mockingly.

'Don't knock it,' Karla warned.

'I think you over-estimate your so-called spells.'

'No. They really are spells.'

'Like magic? Like a witch?'

'Exactly.'

'I don't believe that for a second,' said Effie primly. 'That's what Sally said about you. But it's fake, isn't it? It's just publicity for your acting. It's ridiculous. No one does magic. Not even you.'

Karla smiled. Then she clicked her fingers and said, in a quiet voice: 'Kevin?'

A moment later Kevin reappeared in the bathroom doorway, soaked and wearing a white bathrobe. He looked a little dazed. 'Yes, Ms Sorenson?'

Karla sat back in her tall chair. 'You think Effie here is beautiful, don't you? You find her attractive, don't you? Even a mature woman like her..?'

Effie flinched as Kevin turned, dripping, to inspect her. She felt that Karla was being cruel, to both of them.

'Do you want me to, Ms Sorenson?' he asked.

'I do.'

He nodded and Effie watched his blue eyes staring down at her. He nodded slowly, as if a tune was running through his head.

'See?' said Karla. 'I told you. Now you can tell him to do just what you want.'

'I don't believe it,' Effie burst out. 'It's hypnosis. It's per-

241

verted.'

Karla's warbling laugh came again as she hunted for her shoes under the dressing table. Effie felt very disconcerted. 'Oh, go and get dressed, Kevin.'

'Sally was right about me, whatever she told you,' Karla said. 'I'm up to no good. I'm not to be trusted. Do you still want to be friends with me, Effie? Really?'

The bathroom door was open and a bank of pearly steam shifted into the room. Effie looked away from the dark young man as he dried himself mechanically and she turned back to Karla. 'Yes. I do want to be friends with you. That's why I'm here, isn't it?'

'He can grease in all he likes. I've had it with him, though. This is the end. I've been good to him. A proper pal. The only reason I'm going along tonight is because I want to tell him to his face. Our friendship is over. That's his lot.'

Vicki thought Raf would have been in a better temper. She was surprised to hear him raging at Colin again. She kept looking sideways at him as they walked through the town centre and he seemed dead set. Colin wasn't forgiven. Even though he had phoned them at the shop and even though this invite to dinner seemed like the perfect way for Colin to make amends, there was no mollifying Raf. He had taken the phone call very coolly, accepted the invitation, rang off and told Vicki all about it. All very calmly. She had screamed. Then they shut the shop early (there would be trouble about that) and dashed off to their respective homes to prepare.

Now they were both in the very best clobber, marching towards the restaurant. 'Clobber' was a Vicki word, she realised. She wore clobber, Raf didn't. She had on a green fluffy jacket, leggings and boots and Raf had greeted her by saying that she looked like Orville the duck. Well. She wasn't elegant, she knew that. 'Clobber' would just have to be good enough for her. Her whole look, she thought, was somewhat punky, sexually ambivalent and with just a touch of humour about it. It suited her. Vicki didn't like to think she took herself too seriously. Irony would do for her. Still, she wasn't sure about looking like a duck. Especially when meeting stars.

Inside she was a jangling, quavering mass of nerves. It felt like all her organs were going into spasm at once. She was bound to keep going to the toilet and she would have to refrain from eating anything at all. She had the most obnoxious irritable bowel. She was just the kind of sensitive person to be afflicted with a bowel like that. It was how she was made. And she was imagining that the bowel was turning her usual gait into an unfortunate waddle.

She struggled hard to keep pace with Raf.

He was forging ahead through the streets in a very tight new denim two-piece. It was all ripped and bleached, with the lining hacked out and hanging in careful tatters. He had explained the whole look to her. The idea was to look as if you'd been attacked, molested, ravished and left for dead in an alley. He adored this whole thing, even though it was quite expensive to achieve. He called it fucked-in-the-gutter chic. He must have got that out of some magazine. He'd even applied some false bruising and grazes to his face with blusher, mascara and lip gloss.

'He's right in with that Lance,' Raf said as they went skirting around the great, pale, circular bulk of the Central Library. 'He said 'We'd' like to invite you. 'We'd' love it if you both came along. To 'our' little dinner tonight. He was really putting on airs.'

'Maybe he was just being nice. To make up for ditching us.'

'He's had his head turned,' Raf snapped. Vicki smiled. She knew that by taking Colin's part she'd set Raf against him even more. 'He's rubbing our noses in it. Thinking he's just excellent.'

It was curious, thought Vicki. Neither of us have mentioned the obvious. Neither of us have said a word about Karla. Hardly once. That's who this is all about. That's what's driven us home and made us come straight back out again. The thought of seeing her. That's why we're walking so fast and talking so rapidly. And I know that even Raf is excited and nervous inside. I just know it. There's an inverse ratio at work on him. The cooler and more vituperative he becomes, the bigger mess he is inside. I know him, Vicki thought, with some satisfaction. I know that boy inside out. And that's because I love him.

Raf had stopped at the crossing in front of the town hall. 'Fuck me,' he said softly.

Vicki, about to brave the gap in the traffic, stopped herself and looked up in shock. Raf was rigid at her side. He grabbed her arm, pinching her skin through the fun fur fabric.

'What is it?'

'Look at the fucking thing,' he gasped. 'The City Council must have gone mad. Jesus.'

Vicki stared and did some swearing, too. She always swore more when she was with Raf, though she didn't like to really.

There was a vast inflatable balloon woman surmounting the slate tile roof of the town hall. She was clinging to one of the venerable towers and her tree trunk legs were straddling the very apex of the roof. She was the same size, and had the same absurd grandeur of the colossal inflated Santa Claus the council erected on their rooftop every December.

It was Karla Sorenson and she was thirty feet tall. It was unmistakably her. All the trademark signifiers of vampire ladyhood were on her, at least, as defined by Karla. The shapely fishnetted legs; the black cape that could have covered a tram; the manic lilac eyes and the flashing fangs (poised as if to rip into the clock tower) and her zeppelin-like breasts which bobbed and boggled on the gentle evening breeze, far above the pavements of Central Manchester.

'She's even more famous than we ever thought,' Vicki said. 'We thought she just belonged to us. But even the council has put out a welcome.'

'It's ...' Raf looked close to tears. 'It's magnificent!'

NINE

The bar they were perching at was heavy, solid zinc. It had a warm, somewhat dull silver sheen to it, and it felt as if you could scratch into it with a fingernail and leave an impression. It was like resting your elbows on something almost alive.

Their drinks arrived on little placemats, which the barman slid in front of them as they sat down. He was as quick as anything, flipping the leather menu of cocktails under their noses. He and all the others here behaved as if pleasure was a very serious, weighty business. You had to be ushered in, you had to be seated comfortably, you had to devote all your attention to what you most wanted in all the world. And you had to be attended to.

Lance, Colin and Sally sat along one stretch of the softly gleaming bar with tall champagne cocktails and they admired everything going on around them.

There was a great deal of activity. The waiters called to each other in Italian and swerved and swirled about expertly, managing a huge number of diners on the two levels of the restaurant.

They were having to wait a little while for their table, but were made to feel that the extra time, savouring these aperitifs and watching everyone else, was a natural beginning to their evening. Sally had already said something to the effect that they were living the high life, that she wasn't used to places like this. She had made Lance laugh, telling him about her last night out, to a singsong fish and chip supper on the ring road. She hoped her best black dress didn't smell of chips still.

Here the music was jazz standards with some kind of dance beat behind them, making everything seem like one endless, ongoing song that throbbed and undulated over the chatter and clashing and the scraping of chairs.

They had seen the vast and inflated Karla over the town hall on their way past. It had taken their collective breath away and it made them nervous about what reaction Karla might receive upon arrival at the restaurant. It could be a circus.

Colin was glad his gran was here. He was sitting between her and his new fella and, if he stopped to think about it at all, he was amazed at his good fortune. Everything had moved so fast. Really, as far as he was concerned, in the moment the three of them toasted each other with their peach-pink cocktails, the story could well be over. The credits could run, the title theme could swell and drown out their voices forever and they could live in some hypothetical happy ever after. He would be content.

But then, of course, the evening continued. Time was running on. They were wondering whether to order another drink. The others were a little late. Lance called out to the barman again.

'I think I'll try something else this time.' Sally was flipping the drinks menu. Colin watched her purse her seamed face in concentration. 'These cost eight pounds each!' she gasped.

'Never you mind about that,' Lance said. 'I'm rich, remember? Nothing is too good for us.'

At these words a shudder ran through Colin. He didn't know if it was happiness or foreboding. Something in him became alert then and he started to worry.

He was trying to put that fretfulness to the back of his mind when Raf and Vicki turned up. They squeezed themselves through the mass of people waiting for tables and Colin couldn't help thinking they were both dressed bizarrely.

'Have you been in a fight?' He stared up at Raf's false bruises and scrapes.

'It's a LOOK,' Raf said heavily.

'Oh.'

They nodded at Lance, and at Colin's gran and thanked them politely for the invite. There was a stiffness in the air. Raf's expression was set and serene, his eyes flicking around the surging room. Vicki's face was squinched up with the effort of trying to seem pleasant, Colin thought. It must take a lot of effort to conceal her usual scowl. It made him sad that Vicki was always so peeved. It seemed like such hard work for her and it only put everyone off.

'You're the one who chewed my ear off on the phone on Saturday,' Sally said accusingly. 'You're that Rafiq, aren't you?' She took hold of her new cocktail, some sort of coconut concoction.

Raf looked as awkward as Colin had ever seen him. 'Yes. I'm sorry about that.'

Sally grunted and sucked at her straw, dismissing him from her mind. Colin wished he had her talents. Somehow he could never emulate his gran. She was never in thrall to people, or sucked in by them, or dangerously over-impressed. She'd never make a fool of herself over anyone and never had. She wouldn't go running around after them. He loved the way she waved her hand under Raf's nose and dismissed him from her thoughts, the matter of the phone call closed. If only I could have done that with Raf, Colin thought. I've been scared of him. That's what it is. I've been too scared to tell him he's not much of a friend. I've not had the strength of mind to tell him, I don't want to knock about with you any more, mate. I don't even enjoy your company.

Wow. Some clarity there. Where was all this clear-headed thinking coming from? It felt like he was looking at things properly for the first time. He was seeing what made him happy, and what didn't. Colin caught Lance's eye as Lance sipped his drink and there was a bright, amused spark there. He just knew Lance was laughing at Colin's friends. He could almost hear him saying, 'What's Raf meant to be wearing?' And Colin didn't mind. He didn't care what Lance said about Raf. In a way he wanted to show Raf up. To knock him off his pedestal.

The barman was telling them that their table was almost ready.

'We're still waiting for some people...'

'She's bound to be ages late,' Sally said. 'She exists in her own universe. That's if she turns up at all.'

'Oh, don't say that,' Vicki burst out. 'We have to see her now!'

Sally gave the girl a curious look. 'Who are you again?'

'Vicki. I'm a friend of Colin's, too.'

'He's never mentioned you, love.'

'Oh,' said Vicki. 'I was with him on Friday. When he ... met Mr Randall.'

Vicki wouldn't even look Lance in the eye. She couldn't. She felt she'd cry if she did. He was like a burning, blinding presence at the end of the banquette. He made her eyes prickle as if she was sitting too close to the TV screen.

'I have to go to the toilet,' she announced, not looking at anyone. 'I've got an irritable bowel.' Then she was up and stumbling through the crowd.

'Is she autistic?' Sally asked Raf.

'She's nervous,' Raf said. 'She gets like this.' He put down his drink, finished all in one gulp. 'I'll go and check on her. She doesn't really have irritable bowel, you know. It's all inside her head.'

Sally cracked out laughing at this unfortunate remark.

'Colin?' Raf said severely. 'Would you mind coming with me? I want to have a quick word.'

Colin was surprised. He shrugged and squeezed through as Raf led the way to the basement stairs.

Lance watched them go through the well-dressed crowd. 'I don't trust that boy one bit,' he told Sally.

She nodded. 'I think he's depressing, don't you? All that posing, squeezing his cheeks in. And what does he think he's wearing? I can't see why Colin pals around with him at all.'

'He won't need to now,' Lance smiled. Then he saw that Colin's gran was frowning at him.

'I do hope, Mr Randall, that you're not going to smother our Colin, and keep him away from everyone. I can see he means a lot to you. But I think it's all happened a bit quickly. I've never known the like. I've watched you all today and I believe you're sincere...'

'Well, thanks!' Lance laughed.

'He's a special boy,' Sally said. 'Not just some rich man's plaything. And he's all I've got.'

'I know.' Lance swallowed. 'I'll look after him.'

Sally smiled. 'Because if you upset him, I'll come round your flat and cut your balls off. You know that, of course.'

Lance nodded. He thought about Colin, going downstairs after Raf for their little chat. It was funny. Colin running around everywhere, thinking himself in charge of his own life. Sometimes, even, thinking he was so alone and no one was bothered what he got up to - whether he was happy or miserable or in danger or lost. That's how he assumed the world worked for him. He'd told Lance that. He felt alone, neutralised, under everybody's radar. But now Lance could see how they all hinged upon Colin. He had all these people looking out for him.

Then Sally was breaking into his thoughts. She had been open with him, she had warned him, and now they could allow themselves to be thick as thieves. She nudged him bonily in the ribs. Lance suddenly felt approved of, and that they were bonded together against the world.

'Here comes the Queen of Sheba,' she told him.

There was a bustle of activity in the glass lobby. Karla Sorenson had arrived with her guests and the whole restaurant was turning to see.

***

Downstairs in the dim red light, penned in by green walls and rubber plants, Colin and Raf were standing outside of Vicki's locked cubicle.

'Are you sure?' Raf was calling.

'I'm fine...'

Colin leaned back against the blue glass cube of the wash basin. 'It sounds like she's giving birth.'

Raf grinned, then remembered to look stern. 'She has

problems. You should be more sympathetic.'

Colin sighed and then winced as Vicki made a squeak of discomfort behind the plywood door. 'She's just too excited about meeting Karla.' He coughed. 'But she'll miss her altogether if she sits on the bog all night.'

'I won't be long,' Vicki whimpered. 'I do want to see her. I really do. But...' She wailed mournfully. 'Oh, I'm spoiling it for you, Raf. You go back upstairs.'

Raf was staring at Colin. 'I want a word first.'

'With me? Owww-ww.'

'No. With him.'

Ah. Colin tried to look pleasant. This was the 'Listen, lady,' moment they occasionally had in all the best soap operas. Where you get barrelled into a corner and told some home truths. 'What about?'

Someone appeared on the stairs. Raf ushered Colin quickly into another cubicle. They disappeared inside, cramped together and Raf locked the door, barring the way back out. He let Vicki's noises cover up his whispering. 'I suppose you're really pleased with yourself. Nabbing Lance like that.'

Colin felt his face flush. 'What's wrong with you, Raf? I knew you were pissed off. What's it got to do with you?'

Raf was looking furious. At first he didn't say anything.

'Come on, Raf. Tell me. You went so weird on Friday night. What's wrong with me seeing Lance? I thought you'd be glad. What - should we all not start seeing anyone? Just stay single so we can run around and commiserate with each other all the time?' This was a bold statement for Colin. When he was out with Raf and Vicki this was exactly how he felt. That they were acting like losers together. They were deliberately acting superior because they stood themselves apart.

Vicki was wailing more loudly now.

'Talk to me, Raf. You're resenting me. I don't think that's fair.'

Raf lashed out: 'I deserve to be happy before you do!'

Colin laughed. 'What?'

'Look at you! You're nowt special!'

'I never said I was!'

'Yes, you do. You think you're so great now.'

Colin tried to get past him, to get out. Then Raf was grabbing hold of his arms. 'What about me?' He sounded desperate, keeping his voice quiet as he could. Vicki had gone quiet too, and Colin knew she was listening in.

'I can't make you happy, Raf. I can't sort your life out. I can hardly manage my own.'

Raf's beautiful, angular face looked very strange in the murky light. Bruised and intent. He lunged forward suddenly. 'You idiot, Colin. You fucking idiot.'

At first Colin thought he was going to get slapped. He stepped back against the toilet but Raf was pulling at him, trying to get him to hold him. Now he was sobbing and forcing Colin to lift him up.

'What the fuck are you doing?'

Raf was smothering him, pressing his face into his chest. His voice came out raggedly. 'I thought it would be us. I thought in the end, we'd...'

Next door Vicki started making a great deal of unpleasant noise. Colin was shocked.

'I thought we would get together... I really did. And now you're with him and it's serious and...'

He was a dead weight in Colin's arms. Colin was trying to brace him up. Raf had made himself heavy somehow, and helpless and he was sinking fast.

'Raf, you've never said. This is ridiculous. We've been through all that. We're mates. Just mates.'

'Fuck-buddies,' Raf snarled, twisting hold of Colin's shirt and his jeans. 'That's all. You fucked me a couple of times ages ago. Cause there was no one else around.'

'Raf... I...'

'You never once saw. You never once felt anything...'

Colin was desperate to keep him quiet, to stop him crying and to stop him from dropping onto the tiled floor. His thoughts were all over the place, but first among them was wanting to make Raf feel better. To tell him he was wrong. He had got it all wrong.

He put one hand on Raf's head, ruffling his thick black hair gently. He thought: that's how bad Raf really must be. He hates anyone touching his hair.

'That's just not true, Raf,' he hissed. 'I love you, mate. I always have. I thought you'd just laugh at me. I was too ordinary. I was never good enough for you. You really hated it when we shagged. We weren't compatible. It was embarrassing to both of us...'

'No,' Raf moaned. 'That's not how it was. You just used me when you wanted to.' He pressed his face right into Colin's stomach and the vibration of his voice felt weird. 'And I wanted you, Colin. Really, properly wanted you.'

Colin kept quiet at this. The two of them were still for a moment and he could feel genuine shudders going through his friend's body. There was no more noise from Vicki.

Colin breathed deeply and wondered how they could back out of this scene. It seemed like they would be trapped here forever. No one would back down. Lance, his gran, everyone upstairs in the gleaming restaurant was forgotten.

There was a different, tingling vibration then. Colin blinked and realised what it was. One of Raf's slender hands was at his fly zip and was coaxing it gently down, struggling a little over the tight, belligerent obstacle of Colin's erection.

'Raf...' he said softly.

Raf glanced up briefly and their eyes locked. Colin couldn't describe what he saw in Raf's expression. There was supplication there and maybe love. Triumph, too, perhaps, but then Raf looked down again, at his own careful, cool fingers as they hooked Colin's cock out into the air. To Colin's shame it sort of sprang free, the end of it startlingly red. Raf made sure Colin was watching as he darted forward to lick it tenderly. Colin had only a moment to gasp, to think about protesting, before Raf swallowed him up, greedily, ardently, and Colin realised that there was no going back.

TEN

'What do you suppose they're all looking at, when they look at me? I've thought about this a lot. I've had years to mull it over. Decades to ponder this phenomenon. They stare at me when I arrive in places like this. They stand and goggle in the street. It's not just being famous. That's a different quality of attention. That's what I imagine Lance gets. A few autographs, a few snaps with gurning punters. But I get looked at differently. As if I represent something to them. Shall I tell you what that is?'

Karla was holding forth at the head of their table. They had been given a private alcove, away from the rest of the diners. The table was sparkling and everything was so perfect no one wanted to touch it yet. Only Karla rested both elbows on the snowy cloth as she held court and gazed into each of their faces in turn.

'I think it is evil,' she said. 'I think that when they look at me, that's what they think they are seeing. Essential and glamorous evil, actually in their midst. And naturally they are fascinated by that. Amazed and appalled and they want to draw closer to the unnatural woman. Just to touch that presence. Just once. Just briefly. Then they can return to their normal lives of goodness.'

A pause then. Sally broke it by picking up her glass and taking a swig. 'Crap,' she said. 'It's because you're always showing your knockers off.'

There was a ripple of laughter round the table, mostly from Lance. Even Karla smiled a little.

'Oh, come on, Sally. You can't tell me you've never thought I was wicked through and through. Isn't it you that goes round telling everyone I'm possessed by the devil?'

Sally raised an eyebrow. 'What have you being saying to her, Effie?'

'I don't know.' Effie didn't look at all herself. She was sitting inbetween Karla and Kevin the porter and she was very formal and stiff. She looked across the table at her oldest friend and didn't seem to know what to say to her.

'She probably told her what you're always saying,' Lance said smoothly. 'That Karla really is a malign old bag and she should watch her step.'

There was another burst of laughter from the table. Everyone laughed except Raf and Vicki, who sat dumbly, drinking in every word. Colin tried to focus on the conversation and to work out what his gran and Lance were doing. It seemed to him like a very clever double- or triple-bluff: jokingly accusing Karla of being evil and up to no good and covering the fact that that was exactly what they thought about her. Karla wasn't at all perturbed by the conversation. She was enjoying herself. When the waiter came to dance attendance she ordered for herself and her two companions. There was something very strange and half-asleep about Gran's friend, Effie. He could see that his gran was provoked by that, her expression when she looked in Effie's direction seemed strange, but she didn't say anything about it.

The wine arrived in sparkling carafes, black-red, pink and pale green, dry and frosty, fruity and deep. Then came large silver platters of antipasti, in a promiscuous jumble of leaves, beans, folds of meat, slivers of cheese. They were encouraged to pitch in, to tussle over mouthfuls. The waiters egged them on, responding to the curiously stilted, bristling atmosphere. They wanted to bring their table together by pressing on them wine, food, chatter, camaraderie.

It was difficult. Karla's guests had that weird, trancelike quiet on them. Vicki and Raf had been awed into silence, though Colin had caught Raf doing something very like winking at Karla down the table. Lance was oddly removed and thoughtful, and that made Colin frightened. He hardly dared turn his head sideways to watch him.

But Lance couldn't know what had gone on downstairs. He had no way of knowing. Even so, Colin felt shifty and weird and wanted to run out into the streets, hail a cab and get as far away as he could. He was scalding over with shame and annoyance and maybe Lance had picked up on that. But we played it cool, Colin thought. We came back up here only when we had calmed down. We waited until Vicki had gone at last, and then we silently got our breath back, we cleaned up, rearranged ourselves. Me and Raf didn't say anything to each other. We couldn't. I certainly didn't want to.

In the seconds after coming, thickly, desperately, noisily, into Raf's mouth, a wave of awful dismay had crashed over Colin's head. He felt a cold surge of horror, as if he'd done something terrifically violent. Raf kept sucking at him, harder and harder, and he'd started to hurt him. Just then Colin didn't feel a thing for Raf. He had even started to feel tricked. That feeling steadily increased as Raf straightened up and he was calm now, almost cold. All that begging, all that vulnerability had gone out of him. And they didn't say anything else. Just attended to practical things. Made it seem that nothing had happened between them. Staved off the post mortem till afterwards. First they had their table to return to, a famous lady to meet.

Trogging up the stairs to the restaurant, Colin knew there would be no post mortem. Raf wouldn't talk about it again. He would pretend he had never said those things. It was all a sham. It was his revenge. In a crash of light and logic as they re-entered the silver, white, boisterous room, Colin saw how Raf had taken his revenge. He'd knocked Colin off his stroke. He'd held up Colin's supposed loyalty and sudden link with Lance and he'd destroyed it. Easily. He'd proved he was better, he thought, irresistible.

Colin watched Raf as he ate a few leaves of rocket. He was moving very fastidiously and it made Colin blush, thinking about how eager he'd been, how stupidly eager he'd been to shove his cock in that mouth again. It horrified him now. Beside Raf, Vicki had forgotten all about her nervous, fractious intestine, and she was eating as much as she could, heedless of the fact that others were meant to share from the cold dish before her. And she was listening to us, too, Colin thought miserably. She listened to most of what went on. They planned all of this. But what was the point? Just to make me feel shit? Then he thought, well, yes. That might be exactly what they wanted to do. He sighed and reached for his glass and hated the way his cock felt wrung out and wet inside his jeans. He was wretched and struck by the thought: this is Karla's influence. It's her evil spreading out amongst us all. She brings out the worst in everyone. She's flaunting her vile presence over all of us like her huge effigy is doing over the town hall.

But he kept quiet, and the pasta course arrived, steaming and scented with tarragon and garlic. The perplexed waiters couldn't understand why the special table wasn't happier. Why there was no celebratory air. Why no one seemed glad they were together.

Then Colin said to Karla, raising his voice so that everyone could hear: 'Did you know Raf writes stories about you?'

Karla blinked, twining spaghetti onto her fork. 'What was that, my dear?'

'That's what he does. As a kind of tribute to you. He writes what they call Fan Fiction. And it's all about you. Sometimes he pretends he is you.'

'Oh,' said Karla blankly.

Colin glanced at Raf and pressed on. 'Do you remember, there was a convention in Birmingham last year and you were the judge of a competition? They were all dressing up and writing these stories.'

'Oh, goodness, yes,' Karla chuckled. 'I remember. Some of them were downright filthy.'

'Well, he went in for that. He was horrified when he didn't win.'

Raf was looking at him daggers. 'Yes, all right, Colin. That's enough.'

'I think I just picked one at random from the pile,' Karla shrugged. 'I only cast a quick eye over them when the convention organisers gave them to me. Christ, I wasn't going to read all that stuff.'

'WHAT?' This was Vicki, through a mouth stuffed with ravioli. No one had heard her speak so loudly. 'You didn't READ them?'

'Of course not,' said Karla. 'It was weird stuff. It gave me the creeps, actually. And to be staying in the same hotel as all those people...! Some of those stories were very, very filthy.'

'But Raf spent ages on his story! He still does! He's written hundreds! He writes them all the time!' Vicki was rasping. She stopped abruptly. Raf must have kicked her under the table.

'Do you, Raf?' Karla smiled, gliding over the awkwardness. 'And what do you write about me?'

Suddenly all eyes were on Raf. All of his poise had fled as he stared down at his tangled dinner. For the first time ever Colin heard him mumble. He didn't look up and he just said: 'I write, like, vampire adventures.'

'Sexy ones?'

'Lesbian stuff.'

'How lovely,' smiled Karla. She was talking to him as if he was simple.

'Isn't that a bit sad and pathetic?" said Colin's gran loudly. 'I'd have thought a young man like you would have better things to do with your time.'

Raf didn't reply. Karla shouted Sally down, 'Leave the boy alone, Sally. He's obviously very happy in his own little way. What do you want him to do, write sexy stories about you?'

Sally laughed uproariously. 'I think my days of sexy stories are over, thank you very much!'

'What a pity,' Karla smiled nastily.

Then Effie spoke up, her voice croaking. 'I want to have sexy adventures.'

They all looked at her. She had picked up her wine glass and was staring into it. She looked up at them all. 'It's true.

You needn't look so shocked, the lot of you. It's about time I did. I've had precious little fun in my life.'

Colin stared at the faces around him. This is all down to Karla, he thought. She's making them act like this.

His gran was looking shocked. 'Effie! You don't talk like that!'

'Yes I do, Sally,' Effie said sadly. 'You'd be surprised if you knew half the things I said. Inside my head.'

'Sexy adventures!' Sally exclaimed. 'At your age!'

'You do what you want, love,' Lance said firmly.

'I intend to,' said Effie. She picked up and then set down her cutlery. 'I believe in the magic. I believe in Karla.'

Karla looked very pleased by this as Effie struggled into her coat. They all watched as Effie put a possessive hand on Kevin the porter's sleeve.

'Karla's been a real friend to me, Sally, just this past couple of days. And she's used her magic to put a spell on this nice young man for me. Now he can see the true beauty inside of me. Deep down. She's made it so he can appreciate the woman I truly am. Isn't that right, Kevin?'

She was standing up.

'Um,' said Kevin, blinking.

'You never made me feel as good, or as wanted as that, Sally. And you call yourself my oldest friend.'

Sally sat back flabbergasted. Colin saw that Karla was watching all of this shrewdly, a delighted smile spreading across her face.

'Well, now I intend to start living my life to the fullest,' Effie announced. 'And I'm leaving here now. I've had sufficient to eat and drink, thank you ever so much, and I'm tired of your sniping at each other. I'm going out now and taking a cab home, so hang the expense. And I'm taking this pretty young porter home with me, whereupon I shall allow him to ravish me to his heart's content on my new living room carpet because...' She straightened up inside her smartest outfit. 'Because I am a beautiful human being and Karla's dark arts have allowed me to see that for the first time ever. What is more, I have had the most clumsy, bloody awful sex precisely twice in my long and boring life and, to be honest, what I could do with now is a damned good rogering.' She scraped back her chair with finality. 'Are you coming, Kevin?'

'Um,' he said again and, for one awful second, Colin thought he was going to say no. But he stood up obediently and gazed into Effie's blazing eyes.

'Well,' she said. 'Good night, everybody.'

As she left, with the porter at her heels, there was a scattering of applause from the other tables.

'Blimey,' said Lance.

Sally was glaring at Karla. 'You evil woman. You're messing about with her mind.'

Karla smirked. 'I don't think it's her mind you should be worrying about.' She wafted a hand. 'Effie's lived too narrow a life. You know that. You've been responsible for holding her back. You and all the people around her.'

'How can you know what people want?' Sally burst out. 'You're like a ... Satanic agony aunt.'

'I like that,' said Karla. 'That's good.'

'Buggering about with people's lives...'

'She looked happy, didn't she?'

'How do you know? What do you know about happiness?'

'More than you, you wizened up old sow.'

'Really? How happy are you, really, Katy?'

Karla shrugged. 'Happy to see Effie get laid for once. That Kevin really isn't bad, you know. I've brought him on by hand.'

'Pah,' Sally snapped. 'Why is it all about sex, Karla? Why is that the only way you can make Effie happy? She's never been bothered about it. She told me that herself. You've managed to twist her mind so she's parroting you. Why should sex be the only thing? The only answer? Why is it important at all?'

'But it is important,' Karla said. 'It is vital. It's vital to magic and it's vital to me. It's all I know. It's the only way you can know someone wants you or knows anything about you. Trust you, Sally, not to see the point. You've never understood.'

'No,' Sally said. 'I don't see the point of you, I'm afraid. I came here tonight thinking I'd give you a chance. I thought you might have mellowed and changed. Stupidly. But you're the same selfish, twisted, angry little girl you always were. Scrimping by on sex. Selling your dirty arse and anyone else's just to get your own way. And then having the gall - the absolute bloody gall - to think that puts you above all of us! That that makes you anyone at all!' Sally was up and out of her chair.

'Gran?' Colin got up to help her.

'It's all right, lovey,' she said tersely. 'I'm only going to the lav.' She scowled at Karla again and shuffled off.

Lance grasped the nearest bottle of wine. 'Well, you've managed to piss off nearly everyone, Karla. I can see that working with you is going to be a lot of fun.'

Her lilac eyes flashed out at him. Then: 'By the way, did you see the outline for my first show, Lance, darling? It was appended to next week's scripts.'

'No,' he said. 'Too busy too look at them. Why? Should I have looked?'

She grinned broadly. 'Don't you know? We're having an affair. I'm to be your love interest, it turns out. I'm the one who turns your character's head at last.'

Lance was choking on his Montepulciano D'Abruzzo. 'You what?'

She nodded slowly. 'Oh, yes. You see, the great viewing public have gone off you being gay. I can't say I blame them. So you're getting a chance to taste real woman flesh.' She laughed throatily. 'Mine,' she added.

He groaned. 'I knew it,' he said. 'I knew they'd do this to me.'

'I must say, you've never really convinced me as a gay man,' Karla said lightly. 'I mean, look at the one you're with. That doesn't look right at all. He's just some scrawny little boy off Canal Street. He's not even all that young. What are you doing being seen with that?'

Colin was feeling weirdly removed from the scene.

Raf was laughing. 'I don't believe it, either, Karla. I've told Colin. Everyone will laugh at the two of them.'

'And you're obviously a man of great perspicacity,' Karla told him and Raf glowed. He glinted back at her, expertly.

Lance's voice went steely as he leaned across the table. 'I'm with Colin because I love him. Remember that, Karla? Remember what love is?'

She considered. 'No,' she said crisply. 'And if I did, I'd try to forget. What a waste of time.'

'Hear, hear,' said Raf.

'Raf,' Colin shouted. 'Just fuck off, would you? You've caused enough damage. Stop chiming in with her.'

'I'll ask for the bill,' said Lance. 'I think we should all calm down.'

'Oh, the lovers are dashing off into the night,' said Raf. 'Tell us, Colin. What do you know about love?'

'More than you. I know who matters. You're just smarming around Karla. She doesn't give a shit about you.'

Then, startlingly, Raf started to cry. He trembled and shook and his great big eyes were welling with tears. 'How can you talk to me like that? It's you who's turned nasty, Colin. After everything we said downstairs...'

Lance looked sharply at Colin. 'What were you saying downstairs?'

'I...'

Vicki spoke up. Her voice was loud again and vehement. 'I was there. I heard everything. Colin told Raf he loved him. And then, if I'm not mistaken, Raf sucked him off.'

There was a rigid silence that stretched out until the waiter appeared. 'Who wants the bill?'

Karla took it swiftly and looked at Lance. 'I think you're

wrong, Lance. Quite wrong about love. I have loved. I loved your mother, you know. And I loved you. And you'll never give me credit for that, will you? You'll never believe me.'

Sally returned from downstairs. 'What lovely toilets they've got. Oh - are we leaving? What about coffee?'

Lance tried to take the bill from Karla, but she snatched it back. 'Coffee at my place,' he said tersely. 'We've all got things to talk about.'

ELEVEN

'Walking across town at this time of night could be a big mistake,' Colin told his gran.

She gripped onto her handbag. 'I can protect myself. I'm armed, you know.'

'I didn't mean that. I meant, to get to Lance's flat we'll have to go right through the Village. When they see Lance with Karla it'll turn into a Mardi Gras parade.'

'That's a thought. Should we warn them?'

But Karla and Lance were walking too far ahead. They were turning the corner into the gaudy hullabaloo of Chinatown, with Vicki and Raf clicking along at their heels. Colin was lagging back with his gran, who was out of puff. Already it had been a long night. Colin wished Lance hadn't demanded that everyone come back to his flat. He wanted some time with Lance alone. But to say what? He couldn't claim that Vicki was lying about Raf sucking him off. The silence following her revelation had been too long and dreadful. Yet he would have to do something to patch it up. Explain how Raf had tricked him and begged him. And he knew that would never wash. Lance had thrown in his hand, so winningly and whole-heartedly with Colin. He had talked about love and that meant Colin should have tried to behave himself. But what have I promised? What have I pledged myself to? I haven't said anything yet.

He could tell how hurt Lance was, underneath all his quiet and cool.

At least Gran hadn't been there to hear the news. She'd be really ashamed of me. Especially after what she said about Karla, and how she assumes everyone uses sex like she does. Like Karla thinks everyone is as big a slag as she is. And, God, I am, thought Colin. I fell for it. I fall for it every time. Being needed. Being flattered.

He watched Lance and Karla striding past the crowds in the middle of Chinatown, strolling by the pagodas in the garden square. He wondered what they were talking about, whether they were arguing. He was just starting to enjoy the cloying, spiced aromas from the restaurants when another thought struck him.

'What did you mean, you're 'armed'?'

His gran winked at him. She opened her handbag and carefully produced a decorative curved blade, worked in silver.

'Fucking hell, Gran. Put it away! What the hell's that?'

'Something I usually keep tucked away in my knitting bag for safety's sake. You could do someone a mischief with this.'

'Where did you get it?'

'Ah,' she smiled. 'Fox Soames gave it to me. Donkey's years ago. When I was a kid and staying at his house in the Ribble Valley. He knew how things stood. I never thought I'd need it, but he thought I'd want protection from the dark powers he could see clustered all around me. He knew they were in Karla. And he knew she would bring them to my door one day...'

Colin was staggered. 'Jesus. You brought a lethal weapon out to dinner with you?'

'Oh, I carry it around quite often. If I'm going somewhere rough, at any rate. I'm always on my guard.'

As they caught up with Raf and Vicki by the main road Colin was wondering if his gran hadn't gone a little crazy. It was possible. He didn't like the way she took all this dark arts business so seriously.

'You'll have to watch out for your Lance,' Gran told him softly.

'What?' He was having some difficulty hearing her over the noise of the traffic. Lance and Karla were already across, slipping quickly past Yates' wine lodge, down the street towards the Village. They were keeping their heads discreetly bent, tucked in close as they talked, evidently hoping no one would notice them. They were twinned in their furtive celebrity.

'Lance is right, you know,' Gran told him. 'He is the reason she's come back to Manchester. He was right to assume that. She's been sent to get him.'

'Sent?'

'Looking at her, I'd say she's still possessed. By someone or something. The devil himself, I bet.'

'Gran,' Colin shook his head. 'You make this sound like something out of one of Raf's rubbishy stories.'

The traffic slowed for them, and he helped her to cross.

'He's the one you should be wary of, Colin,' his Gran told him. 'That Raf. He doesn't want you to be happy. He's one of those mad, destructive people. They can seize hold of you and at first it's lovely because they're determined to be your friend. You can get swept along in that. You don't know why you've been chosen and you're glad. But then they soon go on the turn. They get fixated on you. Then their madness comes out. All their badness. And you can't get away from them. They leach onto you and suck and suck and suck...'

Colin was feeling very uncomfortable. Raf and Vicki were only a few feet ahead of them, in a hissed conference of their own. He knew they were talking about what Raf had done with Colin, and Vicki didn't sound very happy at all.

Colin's gran patted his arm. 'I'm telling you all of this to protect you, lovey. That's always been my job. Since your poor parents died and you came to me. I won't be here forever, you know.'

'Don't say that, Gran.'

'Well, you know. That's just how life is. Unless you've made a pact with Satan, of course. I have to tell you what I know about the dangerous people, the sad and crazy and obsessive people. I mean, I call it the devil, but that's because I'm a silly, superstitious old woman who grew up in a different age to you. When I talk about evil, I might as well call it sadness, despair. Lonely obsession. People trying to fill their own emptiness by seizing on to other people. Trying to take over their lives. That's what it is when the devil gets into you. Sometimes it looks like love. It's the very opposite.'

Colin knew she was right. As they shuffled past the heaving, late night crowds round the canal, surging out of Clone Zone, queuing at McTucky's, dodging the taxis on the bridge, he was thinking about how people latched onto other people. He watched Vicki's green furry arm and how she'd hooked it around Raf's slim waist. They were all moving together under the pink and orange lights of near-midnight and the tarmac was glistening underfoot. Colin watched drunk people, all dolled up on a weekday night, striding and jostling and catching up with each other. Teased and primped, tousled and shorn, some buffed up and some letting it all hang out. Everyone trying to look their best, agleam from the bars and sparkling with wit or despondency or elated on booze and pills and company. A frothing, pulsing crowd, all glancing round at each other and all of them thinking: Recognise me. See me. Look at me in my best clothes. This is me at my very best. Me at my prime. You've got to latch onto me now, before it's too late. Catch my eye. Watch me. Wander into my orbit. Talk to me, someone. Some stranger. Come and talk to me now. Lift me out of my life and into your own.

'Oh, look,' Gran said mildly. 'Your two friends are having a scrap, Colin.'

'Hm?'

Up ahead, Vicki had turned feral. She was spitting and screaming at Raf, punching and pummelling at his chest. He was trying to push her away. She yelled something that none of them could make out. The passing, promenading crowd slowed a bit to watch her and the cars had to squeal their brakes as she turned and dashed over the road, and plunged into the small civic park beyond.

Raf turned to Colin and his gran as they hurried over.

'Has she gone doolally?' Sally asked.

'Too right,' said Raf. 'She reckons I've broken her heart. You'll have to help me. She's going to chuck herself into the canal.'

He pointed at the slender, silver monument at the edge of the park. It was poised on the very brink of the canal.

'There she is, look. The silly cow's going to throw herself off the Beacon of Hope.'

TWELVE

Lance and Karla hadn't even noticed that the others weren't behind them. They were so keen on not being recognised, and slipping like shadows through the crowds. They needn't have bothered. Everyone was focused on their own pleasure, their own ongoing dramas.

Lance led them to the door hidden in the alley where he usually did his therapeutic bottle-smashing. The glass crunched underfoot and the air was laced with wine and piss and, strangely, lemongrass and ginger, too. 'Charming spot,' Karla purred.

'The back entrance,' Lance said curtly, unlocking the door.

'That figures.'

They were, he realised, behaving like secret lovers, the way they were stealing determinedly back to his rooftop pad. The very thought made him come over queasy and he remembered again what Karla had told him about the upcoming plotline on Menswear. That fucking Adrian had forced them into a romance. He would have to pretend to make love to this beast of a woman on the studio floor under bright lights, for the crowing delight of millions. And, the show being Menswear, they would have to go further than they would in any other show. She had managed to ensnare him. To humiliate him. He would have to be naked. She'd take hold of him, take possession of him at last.

He held the back door open for her. 'Where are the others?' he suddenly asked.

She shrugged, impeccable in her sharp, black, mannish suit. 'They'll catch up. I presume your Colin knows the way.'

'You shouldn't have said what you did about him,' Lance told her. 'He isn't anything like what you think. There's more to him than that.'

'Is there?'

'Yes. I've never felt like this about anyone.'

270

'I wonder what your mother would have thought of him. Not much, I bet.'

'Don't you even talk about her, Karla. I'm warning you.'

She didn't reply. She slipped up the heavily carpeted staircase and Lance pursued her, to the top floor and home again.

***

There wasn't that many people about in the small, dark city park. Just a few pub-goers and dossers drinking on the damp grass. Colin took hold of his gran's arm and she put on a surprising turn of speed as they hurried after Raf. He was yelling at Vicki's determined silhouette as she clambered onto the concrete base and clung to the shiplike mast of the Beacon of Hope.

Across the other side of the canal, punters at tables outside of Via Fossa were starting to take notice of her. They turned round in their aluminium chairs under the newly-blossomed trees and gave a cheer at the sight of her in her green furry coat, preparing to leap into the unknown.

'Vicki!' Raf shrieked. 'Don't you fucking dare, lady! If you do this to me I'll never forgive you!'

'I don't care!' she rasped. 'You hate me! You only ever tolerated me! I'm nothing to you! Not really!'

'Of course you're not, you silly cunt!' Raf yelled and then he amended it to: 'I mean, of course you're not nothing to me, Vicki. You're not nothing! You are something! You are someone!'

She was peering down into the turgid sheen of the slow and mucky canal. 'Thanks a fucking bunch! But you still don't love me! You don't!'

'Oh, don't give me that one!' he cursed, exhausted with shouting. 'Why does everything have to be about love?'

Vicki turned round to face them all and she looked suddenly savage and startling in the full glare of the monument's lights. 'Because that's all there is, Raf. There's only love. And I was a frigging mong for ever wanting it from

271

you. You haven't got any to give anyone.'

'Just get down from there!' Raf urged her. He knew he could never dash across and grab her in time. Not in these shoes. 'Get down before you slip!'

Vicki snarled at them all. 'Look at you lot! You're all in love with each other! All running around after each other! What have I got, eh? What -- Oh, fuck.'

She slipped then.

***

'Arse over tit into the stinking canal,' was how Raf put it, later, whenever the story came up, and he had to tell it, again and again, blow by ridiculous blow. He always relished the telling of it, though. How the three of them watched, hugging each other, horrified, on one side of the canal, and how on the other, a great wail of dismay and applause went up outside the Rembrandt and Via Fossa. Everyone dashed to see Vicki splash-land and vanish and bob up screaming and sink again and disappear from sight, sucked under the hellish recesses of the bridge.

It was a story Raf became expert in and he eventually grew to love recounting. How Vicki careened downstream, swallowing gallons of black water as she went, helter skelter the length of the Village, with a whole cheering crowd dogging her progress as she went, pointing out her sleek, black head when it popped up now and then.

And how, eventually, she twatted herself on the lock gates and was fished out by gruff and leather-clad bouncers. How she was dredged out and she was coated in poisonous weed and she was coughing her guts up. It was a story he got to tell at her wedding, when he gave her away and she went and married one of the bouncers responsible for saving her life. The bouncer was called Mandy and, in his own wedding reception speech, he touchingly explained that to him, Vicki was his very own Ophelia and as soon as he clapped eyes on her shivering, retching, greeny-black body he had known he was destined to spend

272

the rest of his life with her. He was a dreadful-looking pig of a man who drank far too much, as Raf was fond of pointing out, but he made Vicki happy. Which was not only incredible, but exactly the kind of outcome her ludicrously melodramatic gesture had intended to net for her after all.

THIRTEEN

'Some kind of fuss about nothing,' Karla Sorenson said, peering over the balcony. 'Someone jumped into the canal. They're alive, I think. The ambulance has just turned up.'

Lance had poured them a gin and slimline each and he brought it out to her and they watched the confusing fuss below them with interest, shivering in Lance's meditation garden.

'Cheers then, my dear,' she said solemnly, and they clinked their chunky tumblers. 'Here's to working together.'

He grimaced. 'I don't know where Colin and everyone else has got to.' Lance wasn't keen on being stuck alone with Karla.

'Oh, he'll be off having a row with his strange little Asian friend,' she sighed. 'Doesn't that bother you? That he let him gobble him off in the lavvy?'

Lance shrugged. 'Boys. Sometimes that's just how it is.'

'My, my,' she said. 'Quite the libertine.'

He didn't rise to this. 'If Colin wants to stick with me, he'll let me know. I've told him where I stand. I'm here if he wants me. The thing with him is, he lets people wrap him around their little finger. He's good-hearted. But that tends to bring trouble.'

'Don't I know it,' Karla grunted, and fished in her pocket for her black Sobranies.

'You? You aren't good-hearted.'

'I know,' she said, sparking up. 'That's what I mean. I'm the one who causes trouble for all the good-hearted people.' She leaned over the railing again and the two of them stared at the tall, dusky, orange-bricked buildings and towers of the Village.

'That's true enough,' he agreed.

'I don't want to cause trouble for you, Lance. Really I don't.'

'I think you already have, lovey.'

'Sometimes...' She hissed out her smoke and it dwindled

away lazily. 'Sometimes I could believe, really believe in this legendary curse that's supposed to be on my head. The curse that's fucked up every relationship and movie I've been in. The curse that's killed people and made all my films shit. I really could believe I'm a kind of Jonah.'

'I think we make our own luck.'

'You're talking 'dialogue' to me, Lance. You don't believe in what you're saying. You've bumbled along the same as everyone else we know, bumping into the furniture and prey to everything.'

He hated her predatory metaphors. He looked down into the drifting crowds as they started going home and felt like he lived above a shark pool.

'Tell me,' she said. 'Why do you think everything and everyone around me goes to hell? I make people fall for me and fall under my influence until they wreck their lives. I cause chaos. All I've wanted is an ordinary life, a smaller life. Like all of you lot there, tonight. Even you, Lance, famous as you are - you've managed to be ordinary and small. Why haven't I got that?'

He crunched on an ice cube and hurt his teeth. 'Do you really want that?'

She frowned, suddenly looking her age. 'I don't know. I can't imagine what it feels like. You know, I loved walking in the streets tonight and no one seeing us. No one calling out my name.'

'Sharing my obscurity.'

'No. They knew you were there. They respected your privacy. That's nice.'

Lance was surprised by this more thoughtful, gentle Karla. 'You tell me, then, Karla. Why do you think everything goes to hell around you? What is it about you?'

She smiled and threw back her head, laughing sadly. The length of her slender white throat was like a blade against the meagre light. 'Well,' she said at last. 'That's easy. I really did sell my soul to the devil. When I was about ten, in a forest outside Kendal. Big ritual, lots of booze and flames and chanting and then he appeared in a crack of lightning to take away my immortal soul in exchange for stardom.'

'Oh, yes? And what did he look like?'

'Between you and me? He looked just like Adrian the producer.'

'I can believe it. Give me a drag on that ciggie.' She passed him the last inch of fag. 'So,' he said, through a plume of indigo. 'The devil really exists. Everything you've ever said about black magic is true?'

Karla nodded. 'Oh yes. Every word. I'm still connected to a coven that sends me instructions to go about their evil work. It's a bit like temping. Or having a very aggressive agent. I couldn't get out of it if I tried. I mean, I've stopped going to the black masses so regularly, but I'm there for major festivals like Beltane. Keep my hand in at sacrificing goats and pledging my allegiance to Beelzebub. All that. A girl's got to look after herself.'

'I believe you,' Lance said mildly. 'You know ... you make it sound ridiculous. But I think I really believe you.'

'Good,' she said, watching him stub out the golden filter of her cigarette. 'That's very important to me, you see, my dear, because...'

'Because you've been sent to enlist me? To make me sign the same blood pact?'

'Why, yes...' She nodded, grinning at his cleverness. 'Yes, you've...'

'Just like you made the same offer to my mother. All those years ago.'

Karla's mouth fell open as if she had been slapped. She stared at him and quickly regained her composure.

'And she refused,' he went on. 'She wouldn't have anything to do with you. Fox Soames had warned her off you. That's what you fought about. You tried to take her over and she was strong enough to tell you where to get off.'

Karla's expression was hardening, her lilac eyes going narrow.

Lance's hands flashed out, grabbing both of her wrists. Their gin glasses smashed to the floor and she jumped, but didn't resist him.

'You killed her, didn't you? You evil fucking bitch. You destroyed her. You put that tumour in her head. You sat by her bedside right till the end, willing it to grow...' His words were lost in a roar of fury that erupted out of him and he pushed Karla right back against the terrace wall. He was shaking her hard so that she was winded and gasping. She howled and bit her own tongue so hard her mouth filled with blood and her wig slipped sideways, freed of its clips. She started to scream and Lance slammed one palm over her mouth.

'One more sound and I'll break your neck,' he said.

She nodded, eyes wild.

He pressed himself against her, shoving her back and back until she was sitting on the ledge. And Karla knew, just from the air at her back, on her neck and the unwigged bit of her head that the drop behind her was sheer. Five storeys down to Canal Street, where revellers were starting to look up to the noise.

Her eyes were pleading at him. Close up.

'She said no to you,' Lance snarled. 'And then you killed her. And then you wanted me. You still want me. To join you in your filthy world.'

Behind them, a voice called out inside the flat. 'Lance...?'

Colin and his gran had toiled up the back stairs. They were hunting through the flat for him and Karla.

Something shifted in Karla's eyes. She realised that help might be at hand.

'Lance?' Colin called again. 'You'll never guess. That daft mare Vicki chucked herself in the canal! Raf's gone off in the ambulance with her! Lance!'

Lance held his face very close to Karla's. He shouted: 'We're out here.'

He heard Colin and Sally talking. Then the french windows shushed open and he knew they would see him in the full glare of the living room lights. Lance Randall, star of the famous porno soap, dangling Karla Sorenson, ageing lesbian vampire queen, over the very edge of the terrace wall of his meditation garden.

Karla was trying to shout through his hand. She made mmmpphing noises and she still had some fight in her. He imagined her fangs ripping through the tender flesh of his palm. But no, she didn't have fangs. Not really. She was just a pathetic old woman who happened to be possessed.

'Lance!' Colin shouted, shocked to see them locked together against the wall.

'What's going on?' Sally was asking and they came stumbling warily across the concrete and pebbles of the rooftop garden.

'She's admitted it,' Lance said thickly. He was struggling not to let his emotions take over. 'She's admitted that she's in league with Satan. And that she always has been.'

Colin froze, staring in horror at Karla, perched on the wall, feebly struggling, and at Lance, tall and implacable, holding her tight with one fist and gagging her with the other.

He had gone bonkers, Colin knew it. Oh, great, he thought.

'Lance,' he said. 'Let her go. Put her down. She isn't worth it.'

Sally was inching forward. 'Don't do it, Lance,' she said coaxingly. 'If you do, they'll bang you away for good. You've got your whole life to live. You're young. You've only just found Colin. Don't chuck it away on the likes of her.'

Lance's whole body was shuddering as the tumult of his feelings started to overwhelm him. 'But she told me. She told me what I always thought was true. I knew it. She told me I was right.'

'What?' Sally asked. 'What's she said now?'

'She killed her!' Lance moaned. 'She cursed Sammi. Sammi Randall died because of her.' He sobbed bitterly and Karla almost went over the edge then. But he took the lapels of her suit jacket in both hands and yelled into her face: 'She murdered my mother!'

Colin and his gran stared and found they couldn't move.

Lance was crying hard and they were scared he would lose his grip on Karla.

But, weirdly, Karla didn't look at all concerned any more. She balanced there easily on the precarious ledge and now that Lance's hand was away from her face they could see that she was smiling. It was a horrible smile.

'I murdered your mother?' she said gently. 'Oh, Lance. You've got it wrong. You see, dear, I am your mother.'

And that came as a shock to all of them.

It was too much for Lance. He tried to push her over the edge right then and there. Colin darted forward and there was a flailing, struggling mass of limbs for a moment as he found himself wrestling with his new boyfriend to save Karla's life. For a split second she was a goner, but he managed to wrench them all back. All three of them clattered to the ground, panting and tangled and, luckily, on the safer side of the terrace wall.

Karla was on top, screeching still. 'It's true! You weren't hers! You never were! She stole you from me! You are mine, Lance! You've always belonged to me! You've always been a mother-fucker!'

Then she gave a terrible scream. It was right in Colin's ears, because he was trapped where he'd fallen, underneath Lance and Karla's thrashing bodies. So Colin was deaf for a minute or so and he was confused as to why Karla had stopped using human language. It was like she was speaking in tongues. Or screaming.

Colin looked up to see his gran, silhouetted against the glossy night sky and the soft french windows. She was holding the silver ceremonial dagger aloft and it was dripping and gleaming in front of her face. Colin whipped his head back round and only then could he see that his gran had stabbed the bitch, right through the heart.

FOURTEEN

'Jesus,' said Dennis the milkman, who was watching a gaggle of over-excited queens. They'd watched the ambulance come and go and now they were speculating about all the noise from one of the rooftop gardens.' You always see something different down here, don't you?'

Dennis the milkman had turned to say this to his neighbour, at the next aluminium table under the trees, outside Eden. Of course, the milkman wasn't dressed as a milkman tonight. He'd come out dressed as a lesbian vampire.

His neighbour was nodding in agreement. They had watched the various Canal Street palavers: the half-drowned duck woman, her skinny friend and the bouncers climbing aboard the ambulance and then they had tried to figure out what was going on above their heads. For a while they had thought someone was going to jump. Now Dennis the milkman's neighbour at the next table was gazing appreciatively at Dennis's stocking tops. I should be home by now, the milkman thought. Early start tomorrow. I shouldn't be out at all on a Monday night. But something grabbed hold of me and made me want to be out tonight. Something turned me into a lesbian vampire and that's always worth doing. And at least I saw someone nearly drown in the canal. That was worth seeing and it's something I can tell my regulars when I take them their milk tomorrow. Lance will laugh at the story when I bring him his gold top. And then I can find out what all the noise was from his terrace tonight.

The milkman glanced up at the top studio flat by Slag! It was quiet now. No one had flung themselves off the terrace. The lights were on and the blinds were drawn. Well, I'll see him tomorrow and hear the tale and tell mine. And I should be going soon but, in the meantime, the bloke at the next table is still staring at me as the blood-hungry crowd disperses and there's nothing more to see here, everyone go home, it's all over now.

'Hi,' said the bloke at the next table. Slick-looking bloke

in an Armani suit. Public school accent, pointy little teeth. Not bad. 'It's funny,' he went on. 'The way you're dressed tonight...'

'Oh, yes?' smiled Dennis the milkman who, to be truthful, looked quite burly and bizarre in his vampire lady costume.

'You look exactly like the new star of my TV show. I work in TV. I'm Adrian.'

'Oh,' said Dennis. 'I'm a milkman.'

Adrian was still looking him up and down, slightly disappointed that Dennis wasn't more impressed by his working in TV. 'Do you fancy a shag, mate?'

Dennis the milkman shrugged. 'I've got an early shift. Delivering everything they need up and down these streets, first thing tomorrow. All my regulars. But, yeah, go on.' He finished the last of his alcopop. And Adrian the producer stood up and took his hand and shook it, and was pleased at the firmness of the milkman's grip. Must be strong and dextrous from carrying all those bottles, he thought.

They walked off purposefully through the Village.

'So you work on Menswear, then?' the milkman asked. 'I know Lance Randall in real life, as it happens.'

Adrian grinned. 'I'm his producer.'

'Great,' said Dennis. They were dodging past the late crowd at the New Union. 'So,' he said. 'This Karla Sorenson. Is she really as big a cunt as they say she is?'

Adrian laughed out loud over the noise of the buses, the squabbles, the laughter, the karaoke. He looked back at the softly glowing windows of Lance's studio flat. 'Oh, no,' he said. 'She's lovely. It's all an act. That's just showbiz. You ask Lance.'

'I don't think Lance is keen on working with her.'

'Really? I'm surprised. You should have seen them at the photo shoot this morning. They were delighted to be together. I think it'll all work out just fine. You'll see the pictures in tomorrow's papers.' Adrian stood in the road, hailing a taxi, watching it veer gently towards them.

'I usually take Lance his paper in the morning,' Dennis the milkman said. 'That's when I hear all his news as well.'

'Sounds cosy.' They climbed in, and Adrian gave the driver his address, somewhere in Castlefield. Another studio flat.

'I suppose I'll hear all about it in the morning,' Dennis said. 'All the dramas.'

'I guess you will,' the producer said as they drove off and he reached across the seat to Dennis. He laughed. 'That Lance. There's always dramas with him. Sometimes he's murder to work with. Bit of a diva, don't you think?'

EPILOGUE

One of those Travel Lodges
Somewhere near the Lake District
On the motorway,
Friday

My Dear Effie,

You'll never guess.

Actually, that's very true. You never WOULD guess what's been going on, and why I've ran away and disappeared. I expect you might be quite shocked. But didn't we say our lives had gone too small and quiet? Didn't we say we lacked excitement?

I know you won't approve. In fact, if I told you everything I'm quite certain you wouldn't. You always WERE a bit more proper than me. So I won't tell you the whole story. Just in case you're tempted to take this letter to the police. I know they'll be after us. We've seen the front of the tabloids. How Karla and Lance are supposed to have vanished, and everyone thought at first they'd done a moonlight flit together. Well, as if!

But then the police found the signs of struggle in Lance's flat and the blood-stained knife and all that shocking, Agatha Christie-style stuff.

And, I admit, Effie, all of that IS a bit melodramatic, and I'm sorry for any upset that's caused you since the weekend. But there wasn't time to warn you. We all had to vanish, pronto.

We had to get rid of the body. Karla's body.

See? You've got me confessing allsorts – in writing! – and this was only meant to be a note to ask you to forward some clean underwear, my passport and some Steradent in a Jiffy envelope.

You see, I think we're going to be on the run for a little while yet. All hell has broken loose.

You wouldn't believe half of it, Effie, because it involves

black magic and what Lance calls the necromantic powers of the Brethren who had Karla under their wicked spell ... all her life!

What we are doing is attempting to find a way back. A way back from those dark and magical woods that me and Karla strayed into, all those many years ago.

It's why we're up in the wilds again. Me and Lance and Colin. Oh, if you could only see the two of them together, Effie. They seem so suited. It seems that adventures and adversity have really brought them together. Lance seems like part of our little family now.

Anyway – we've got Karla with us.

In powder form.

This is the really shocking bit, Effie – so just hang onto your hat.

You remember how evil she was becoming on Monday night. Well, after you'd gone she got worse and worse and I was getting more and more worked up. And we were all convinced – quite correctly, it turns out – that she was under Satan or somebody's influence.

And when I stabbed her (All right! There's my confession! It's true! But don't condemn me out of hand! No one condemns Van Helsing, do they? He stabs Dracula and the evil's over and the credits roll up dead quick – and we never see Van Helsing dealing with the consequences do we? No, the story's finished. Good has triumphed, hasn't it?)

So ... when I stabbed her, up in Lance's patio garden – well, blow me down if she doesn't go and explode in a great big puff of black coal dust!

We stood staring for a moment and then, quick-thinking Lance ran off for a dust pan and shovel and Colin found some Tupperware under the kitchen sink.

Only her handbag was left of her. Inside we found her mobile phone. Lit up with a message in old Gothic letters:

Daughter? Are U there? Have U succeeded with Randall?

Lance texted them back.

He is with us now, masters.

And, almost immediately, the phone went bleep-bleep and:

Then bring him 2 Kendal. 4 the ceremony. Bring him 2 the dark, dark woods.

Lance had gone right pale by then. 'I'm going,' he said. 'And I'm taking Karla to them.'

'I'm coming with you,' Colin said. Lovely moment then – when they smiled at each other. Bonded in unholy peril!

Well, I was buggered if I was going to be left out.

So off we went.

And last night we bore Karla's remains into the dark, dark woods. Into the heart of my own private darkness. And we found the Brethren up to their daemonic malarkey and we took the granulated Karla to them ...

It all got a bit confusing from them on – but rest assured, Effie, the three of us managed to get away safely in the end. There was quite a lot of noise and shouting, and a bit of a punch-up, but we're safe. For now. We delivered Karla to them and then we pelted for it.

So we're hiding out in this motel thing. Now I think on, you probably can't send me my pants and sundries in the post, because I don't think we're going to be in one place long enough to have an address. We're fugitives! As Lance says, the Brethren can be quite nasty and we've gone and poked a very pointy stick straight in Beelzebub's eye.

And there's the other thing, as well. The fact that they took those ashes in the Tupperware container and the way that the robed grand master with the golden peacock mask tossed them into the sacrificial pyre...

Well, Lance and Colin and me – we stood there staring for a second or two – along with all the other revelling Brethren. And, just before we high-tailed it out of there – we saw her again! In the flames, Effie! All young once more and vigorous! Shrieking out for revenge!

They have brought her back to life!

Don't fret too much, though. These things have a habit of sorting themselves out. And, with Colin and Lance to look after me, I don't even feel all that scared. Not even with all the screaming hordes of hell and the resurrected Karla Sorenson at my back. I'd better sign off now, Effie, because we're off to have a bite to eat in the Little Chef now, and then it'll be time to get on the road again.

So … don't expect to see us any time soon.

With much love from your old friend,

Sally.